Dream Café

R J Gould has been published by Headline Accent and
Lume Books. He is the author of five previous novels,
*The Engagement Party, Jack and Jill Went Downhill,
Mid-life follies, The bench by Cromer beach* and
Nothing Man. He is a (rare male) member of the
Romantic Novelists' Association. Having been
selected for the organisation's New Writers
Programme, his first novel was short-listed for the
Joan Hessayon Award. Ahead of writing full time, R J
Gould led a national educational charity. He has
published in a wide range of educational journals,
national newspapers and magazines and is the co-
author of a major work on educating able young
people. He lives in Cambridge, England.

www.rjgould.info

Dream Café

R J Gould

R J Gould
(Richard)

This novel was previously published as *A Street Café
Named Desire* by Accent Press in 2014. This 2021 revised,
edited and updated version is published by
FeedARead.com Publications [2021]

Acknowledgements

There are several people who merit a huge thank you for helping me to publish this novel. Joss Alexander, Thure Etzold and Angela Wray, fellow members of the Cambridge Writers Commercial Editing Group, for immensely valuable support ranging from proof reading to detailed consideration of plot and characterisation. My reader launch team – Alex, Helen, Jan and Mary – for providing feedback on my final draft and for being so positive about my writing. Terry Chance for her encouragement and perceptively tough judgement of my wilder ideas. Ken Dawson at Creative Covers for the cover design.

I dedicate this novel to all who are brave enough to follow their dreams.

1

He was forty-three. Autumn shouldn't be such a surprise anymore but the annual explosion of colour never ceased to amaze him.

Here they were at their twenty-five year school reunion, crowded around the bar area of the upmarket Hotel Marlborough in Henley. Huge sash windows provided a magnificent view of a fast-flowing, grey River Thames. Rowers were flying downstream. Beyond the river was a steep bank with a stunning display of autumn trees.

'David. You're David!'

Turning, he was clamped in a bear hug by a woman whose strong grip took his breath away. A face with two scarlet lips came hurtling towards him. His desperate attempt to avoid impact failed and their lips collided.

'Well, well. David. Incredible – just incredible.'

He considered what she meant by "incredible". That he'd hardly changed? That he'd transformed

1

beyond imagination? She stepped back and her vice-like grip transferred to his shoulders.

'David. David.'

How long would this continue – wasn't she going to advance the conversation? He knew he was David. Obviously she did, too. Unfortunately he couldn't assist because his natural response – Hello Alice, Hello Barbara, Clare, Diane, Elizabeth, Fiona, or whatever – was impossible. He had no idea who she was.

'You do remember me, don't you?'

'Yes, of course I do.'

'That field trip!' She had released her grip, but the physical assault continued with a punch on his upper left arm. It was no more than a prod really, but right on the spot where the flu vaccine had been applied.

David winced. She noticed.

'You're too strong to worry about a little tap like that. Well you certainly were back then,' she continued with a cross between a conspiratorial smile and a grotesque smirk. She gave him a slightly harder punch in the same place.

'Helen, darling!' The boxer turned to acknowledge the greeting as another unrecognisable ex-schoolmate approached. Now that he had her name, a distant memory of teenage groping with a lithe blonde girl during the field trip to the French Alps came to mind. There had been a substantial change in size and shape since those schooldays.

'It's, let me see now, don't tell me. It's … it's Sharon!' Helen screamed. The two women jumped up and down before regressing into adolescent reminiscences about poor behaviour in various lessons at school. If he closed his eyes he could be listening to his own teenage children. But he didn't close his eyes because a shaft of late afternoon sun had burst through the voluminous clouds and now the trees beyond the bank were ablaze in their full glory.

A few weeks ago the leaves would have been green. Now they were dazzling reds, yellows, oranges and browns.

'Are you listening, David? You agree with me, don't you?' Sharon asked.

'Yes, I do. Absolutely.'

Of course green wasn't one colour, he reflected. There were shades – light to dark with nuances like sage and jade.

'That's not true. It wasn't like that, was it, David?' This was Helen.

'No it wasn't. Absolutely not.'

'But a minute ago you said it was,' Sharon complained.

'It's all to do with perception,' David mumbled, reluctant to disrupt his train of thought. Without doubt there was a wider choice of colour when it came to identifying the reds, oranges, yellows and browns. Bronze, sienna, ochre and sand for starters. Chocolate. Copper. Mahogany. Rust.

'Are you with us, David?' Helen delivered a punch to precisely the same spot. Her accuracy was uncanny.

'He always was a dreamer, drifting into his own little world,' Sharon added, her voice high-pitched and piercing. The women's giggling was making it difficult to focus on colour. He was ill at ease because there was a frustrating gap, a missing colour on the tip of his tongue. Then it came to him, the dominant shade out there across the river.

'Russet,' he announced.

'David, what on earth are you going on about?'

He turned away from the autumn beauty; both women were frowning at him.

'Rush it, you said. Rush what?' David remained silent as Helen continued. 'We were remembering how Mr Strickland used to take the piss out of you in Geography.'

'Highlight of the week, that was.' Helen laughed coarsely as Sharon took over, speaking with a deep voice in an attempt to impersonate their teacher.

'And where are we now, David? I hope in the Australian outback with the rest of us.'

'Toss-er' Helen added in teenagespeak.

'I rather liked him,' David announced to the gap between the two women. 'Excuse me ladies, must circulate.'

He turned and headed towards the bar.

'Well, look who's here.' Twenty-five years on and the approaching Bill Thatcher's mocking tone had persisted.

'It's our little David,' came another unchanged voice. This was Ben Carpenter.

An overzealous slap landed on David's back. 'You buying the drinks, mate?' Ben asked.

David realised he was no longer scared of them.

How could you be, looking at the two pot-bellied, balding, greying men with sallow puffy faces? They had lost their menacing edge. Also, he was prepared to admit later having had time to reflect, he wasn't scared because he didn't care what ensued, not after the events of recent weeks.

He eyed Ben. 'Why don't you get *me* one?'

Ben looked aghast. 'What?'

'I'll have a bottle of Bud, thank you.'

'Is little David acting cocky?' Bill enquired.

'I believe he is,' Ben contributed.

'It's not a case of acting cocky, it's about growing up. And I seem to be making a better job of it than you two.'

David gave Ben a firm tap on his pot belly. 'I suppose keeping fit helps me. The judo.'

'You do judo?' sneered Bill.

'Yes. And not drinking as much beer as you will have helped,' this statement followed by a generous whack onto Bill's pot belly.

On analysing his actions afterwards, readily admitting it was a step too far, David wondered whether the catalyst for his minor assault had been the annoying physical maltreatment from Helen. But probably it all came down to his profound unhappiness – he couldn't care less about the outcome of his actions. Not at that instant at any rate. But he did care a few nanoseconds later when Bill floored him with a right hook to the chin.

Bill was looking down with contempt. 'You gonna try your judo on me, little David?'

Of course there never had been any judo, only badminton, which had kept him in reasonable shape but clearly hadn't prepared him for a fight. David gazed up at the gathering of his ex-classmates in a circle around him, some with a look of concern, but most smiling. Helen and Sharon were in the smiling group but at least Helen did have the decency to tell Bill and Ben to lay off him as it was a festive occasion.

The crowd dispersed and David stood gingerly, making his way to a chair by the window. In the short interval between boredom and humiliation, dusk had enveloped the trees. Now they stood as forlorn grey silhouettes. Despite there no longer being anything of interest to see, he chose to stare out the window rather than look towards the room hosting the alcohol-fuelled gathering.

'One Bud coming up.'

He turned. The woman handed over the bottle and sat down next to him, a glass of white wine in her hand. 'You OK?'

'Just my pride hurt a bit. Well my chin, too.'

'Poor you. Those two were appalling twenty-five years ago and they haven't improved by the look of things.'

David recognised the voice, the engaging Scottish lilt from all those years ago.

'I'm Titless,' the woman added.

He glanced from her face to her upper body and saw shapely curves. When he looked up she was smiling and he reddened.

'Not anymore, but I was then. I took a while to develop. Too long for Bill and Ben so that was their nickname for me.'

'I remember you. Bridget.'

'Congratulations. You're the first to know my name this evening, not that I've spoken to many.'

'Well, you've changed beyond all recognition,' he declared, intent on focusing on her face and not her breasts.

Like every parent, David had told his children the story of the ugly duckling that turned into a beautiful white swan. While he appreciated the moral symbolism, he had never seen such a transformation in real life until now. Bridget had been a plain, awkward girl, liable to blush the instant someone addressed her. She had appeared friendless and was known as "Spotty Swot" amongst his circle of friends. He hadn't been aware of the "Titless" nickname, not surprising as he kept away from The Crew, as Bill and Ben's gang called themselves. Her legs, he remembered, had looked too spindly to support her. He'd felt sorry for Bridget, a sad-looking loner, but he'd been too shy to do anything about it.

The woman by his side was divine – a goddess. Not in a garishly sexy way, just naturally beautiful. Each facial feature was of textbook perfection, her narrow face with high cheekbones, the upturned button nose, slender lips, soft powder-blue eyes. Eyes that were now smiling at him.

'I feel like I'm being inspected. Do you approve?'

'Yes, yes. You're lovely if you don't mind me

saying.'

'Thank you, I never say no to a compliment. I was wondering though – what on earth made you come along to this awful reunion?'

'It's a long story.'

'It's a long evening.'

2

Two weeks ago. That's when David made the decision to attend the reunion. And that was just two weeks after Jane had told him she was leaving. Not only Jane, Jim was there too. His best friend Jim.

It was a sunny Saturday and David was sitting in the garden with a mug of tea, flicking through the Daily Mail. He had never been able to understand why this was Jane's newspaper of choice and he was addicted to mocking the content.

One article covered a new drama about vampires which was, claimed the journalist: *Sucking the innocence out of our children with a shocking tale of depravity that has become the norm on television*. His daughter Rachel loved the programme. David couldn't detect any sucking out of innocence; she was probably no different to any other sixteen-year-old.

Overleaf, readers were informed that a woman's life of drink and one-night stands had left her feeling hollow. Then she found the answer: *I decided to become a nun*. Two photographs showed the before and after. The first, a smiling woman with a rather low cut top, holding up a glass of red wine. The second, a dour woman, her mane of jet black hair shorn and her head covered by a nun's customary habit. David smiled self-righteously, the writer's implied preference for the nun at odds with the saucy underwear display: *To capture your man* on the opposite page.

What a contrast between the women featured on these pages and sensible, practical, lovable Jane – he was lucky to have such a wonderful wife.

All in all it had been a satisfying afternoon. He'd pruned the roses, taken the dead heads off the geraniums and swept up the first wave of fallen leaves. The garden waste was in the green recycling bin ready for the Monday collection. It was his turn to cook tonight. The lamb was out the freezer and a bottle of Pinot Grigio blush, Jane's favourite, was chilling in the fridge.

His wife was out shopping, of late her regular Saturday pastime. She went to Brent Cross rather than the local precinct despite its distance and the inevitable queues of drivers who would be battling to get into the inadequate car park. There were two walkways inside the mall, as vast as athletics tracks. At least in a race everybody went the same way, but at Brent Cross a stream of determined shoppers would be pushing past those going in the opposite direction. David knew this from past experience when he had selflessly accompanied Jane on her expeditions. A while back she had volunteered to go shopping alone which a grateful David welcomed. He had no idea why she continued to go there because she never returned with any purchases, but she seemed happy enough to do so.

He didn't hear the back door open and only looked up when Jane called his name.

There was an urgency to her tone. 'David,' she repeated.

Smiling, he turned to face her. 'Hello. Had a good afternoon? Oh, Jim. Everything OK with you?'

Jim stood by Jane's side, his face serious. The pair were holding hands. On seeing this David's heart began pounding, his skin itching with prickly heat, his mouth dry. He couldn't speak. His mind raced, searching for an explanation beyond the single obvious one. As he awaited the inevitability of what was to come, the few seconds' interval stretched on endlessly.

It was Jane who spoke first, getting straight to the point. 'Jim and I are in love, David, we've been seeing each other for some time and know what we need to do. We can't live apart. I'm sorry, but I'm moving in with him.'

There was a pause, perhaps inviting a reaction from David, but he remained speechless. Unexpected tears welled up, blurring his vision, trickling down his cheeks. He trapped some of the salty moisture with his tongue.

Now Jim was speaking in a this-is-the-sensible-way-forward-for-mature-adults manner. David caught phrases like: 'I'm sure we can do this amicably', 'We hope a divorce can go through as smoothly as possible', and worst of all, 'We must remain friends after a healing period.'

It was Jane's turn to add some unemotional soundbites. 'It's not as if we have shared interests anymore,' she declared, followed by 'All the children hear is us arguing.'

Did they argue? Admittedly they didn't chat or laugh as much as they used to but he couldn't remember there ever being conflict.

His thoughts turned to the children. How on earth would they cope with this news? And where would they live, did Jane expect them to move in with the person they knew as Uncle Jim? Would lawyers determine that?

'What about the kids?' David blurted out though "What about me" was equally on his mind.

Lawyers would not be needed because Jane had already decided. 'The children can stay here. After all, this is their family home. But of course I want to see them as much as possible. I've explained everything in this letter.' She handed an envelope over to David. 'Please pass it on to them and I'll be back tomorrow morning to chat once they know what's what.'

David's self-pity and concern for the children were replaced by anger. 'So you expect me to let them know? "Rachel. Sam. Come here a minute. Just to say that mum has left us, she's gone to live with Jim." Is that what you want me to say?'

'There's no need for sarcasm, David. I can't face them today, it's too difficult for me,' Jane said in an actually-I-feel-tough-enough-to-face-anything voice.

'Surely you understand how poor Jane feels,

David,' Jim added. 'Show some compassion, for God's sake.'

Jane took over. 'I need to pop upstairs to pick up my suitcase then I think we should go. But as I've said, I'll be back tomorrow to speak to the kids.'

She turned to leave. Jim remained facing him. 'You take care of yourself now, David.' He extended his arm for a handshake which sent David into such a state of shock that he sat down, his mouth agape.

And with that Jim turned and followed Jane into the house. The goings on during his wife's Saturday afternoon so-called shopping trips were now apparent to David. He should have realised things didn't add up. How could she deliver the news in such a cold and detached manner after all their years together? Perhaps it had come across like that because she was nervous, but even so.

He was still sitting on the white plastic chair with the mildew-covered orange and brown striped cushion when Sam came into the garden; he wouldn't have missed Jane by more than a few minutes. How could David explain the situation? Sam was a mummy's boy and he would be distraught. He allowed his son to talk about how he and his friend had tested Adrian's radio controlled car in the local park, about the cool design and speed of the Lamborghini model, about how he would love to own one so that he could race against his friend.

'It's only £69.99 at Argos, Dad.'

This pause for his dad to consider the proposition was the opportunity David needed.

'Sam, listen, something terrible has happened. It's your mother.'

'She's not had an accident, has she?' asked Sam, his tone suggesting surprisingly little concern.

'No, not an accident,' replied David, for an instant wishing she had.

'Good, that's alright then. What about an advance Christmas present? If I had to wait until December I wouldn't be able to use it straight away because of mud and snow and stuff. It would be brilliant if I could have it now. What do you reckon?'

'Maybe, but listen. Your mother.'

'Yes?' Sam enquired impatiently.

'She's leaving us. Well, me to be more precise, although I suppose also you because she doesn't intend to live here. She's going to live with Jim.'

'Uncle Jim?'

'Yes, Uncle Jim.' As he spoke there was a sudden gust of wind and a medley of early falling leaves swirled down from the cherry tree.

'Mum's always going on about how helpless he is since his wife died. She goes over to check he's OK. They're friends, Dad. She isn't going to live there.'

'I'm afraid she is, Sam.'

'You must have misheard.'

There was a pause as David weighed up the value of convincing Sam that he was wrong.

'Who's going to cook dinner then?' said the boy, whose calm, practical outlook on life had always been in sharp contrast to his sister Rachel's emotional outbursts.

'What?'

'If Mum leaves, who's going to cook dinner?'

'Well tonight's my turn, it's Saturday,' David mumbled, struggling to adapt to the change of topic.

'But what about other days?'

'I haven't given it a lot of thought. Me again, I suppose.'

'Oh. It's just that Mum's a better cook than you. It's OK to say that, isn't it?'

'Yes, it's fine,' said David reassuringly, wondering whether food was Sam's way of dealing with the traumatic news.

'What are we eating tonight?' Sam persevered.

'Lamb.'

'I like the taste, but when you see lambs jumping about outside in the fresh air it does make you think.'

'We live in the middle of London. When did you last see a frolicking lamb?'

'Last week. Not live, on TV.' Sam returned to the big issue. 'I'm sure everything will turn out OK, about Mum, I mean. She'll stay with us, just you see.'

David wasn't convinced; it had seemed pretty final to him.

'Dad, will you have a good think about the car?'

'Yes, I will,' David replied. Although he was pleased the news hadn't made Sam panic-stricken, there was a degree of despondency that his son was more focused on a meal and a radio controlled car than on his father's plight. Perhaps it was too much to expect a thirteen-year-old to have sympathy for an adult.

'See you later,' Sam said as he turned and headed indoors. His once white trainers were caked in mud though the luminous green Nike ticks were as prominent as ever. He was wearing faded jeans and a black T-shirt with an appropriate skeleton cartoon over his painfully thin frame. A good boy, David reflected.

'Take your trainers off before you go upstairs,' he called out.

David went into the kitchen, opened the wine and poured himself a generous glass. He rarely drank before dinner but this was no ordinary day. During the conversation with Sam his distress, mixed with anger, had subsided. Sitting down at the kitchen table the shock resurfaced but there was no time to think things through.

'Hello, I'm back.' It was Rachel.

'In the kitchen,' David called out.

There was the sound of the light brisk walk that he loved.

'Hi.'

When Rachel kissed him on the cheek he could smell the stale tobacco on her clothes. He'd confronted her about the dangers of smoking several times over the past months but to no avail. Jane hadn't helped. 'She's sixteen, David, she needs to experiment. You can't expect her to listen to an old fart like you,' she had said. At the time, David took the "old fart" description as a jest, but now he was less sure.

'You OK, Dad? Lost in thought?'

'It's your mother.' Rachel stepped back with a look of concern. At least this was a better start than the conversation with Sam. 'She visited this afternoon.'

His daughter gave him an impatient teenager look implying a questioning of sanity. 'What do you mean "visited"?' She has such an expressive face, David reflected as she continued. 'She lives here.'

'Jim was with her.'

'I love Uncle Jim. It's like we're friends, he's so easy to talk to.'

This made David contemplate the danger of continuing. Maybe she would be pleased her mother was moving on from an old fart to such a nice man. But there was no option other than to persevere. 'She, well actually they … look, straight to the point because you're old enough to understand,' he blurted out. 'They're having a relationship and now Mum is leaving me and going to live with him.'

Rachel was stunned into silence, a rare occurrence. Her face reddened with anger.

David pressed on. 'They came round this afternoon together, hand in hand, and told me.'

'God, I'm an idiot. That explains things.'

'What do you mean?'

'Lately if you call to tell us you'll be late home from work she's off as quick as a flash to see him. Says he needs support since his wife died. I bet she gives him support all right.'

'Obviously things were going on that I had no idea about. She'll be back tomorrow morning to talk to both of you. Meanwhile she's written –'

'Great. She's pissing off and didn't even have the guts to tell us herself. You're left to do her dirty work.'

Rachel was by the fridge. She'd taken out the orange juice and was drinking straight from the carton.

'I'm sure it's not easy for her. Anyway, here's a letter for you.' David lifted up the envelope that he'd put down on the kitchen table and handed it to her.

'Not easy! Are you mad? How can you defend her? What about us?'

She was right and David was ready to agree.

'Fucking bitch!' Rachel continued as she ripped up the unopened letter. The little squares tumbled to the floor like confetti. 'Well I won't be seeing her.' She was holding back tears. 'I'm going round to Hannah's.'

She strode out the kitchen then immediately came back. 'Are you OK, Dad?'

'Yes, don't worry about me. You go.'

A few seconds later there was the slam of the front door.

David finished his first glass of wine and poured a second. He switched on the oven and began to prepare the lamb, potatoes and carrots for the dinner for either two or three of them, depending on when Rachel decided to return.

3

David's account of how he'd ended up at the reunion was interrupted by an ex-classmate's announcement.

'Eating time,' screeched the woman insecurely balanced on a chair, dressed in adult school uniform – short skirt, fishnet stockings, tight white shirt and a kipper tie. Like everyone else at the reunion she was in her mid-forties and she looked ridiculous.

She appeared unable to speak like a normal grown up. 'It's bad, bad news, you'll need to leave the bar. Sorreee. I know that's gonna be hard, but it is yummy yum yum buffet food. Just take the first door on the right.'

Like an air hostess demonstrating emergency procedures she waved her arm in the appropriate direction, the clumsy motion sending her plunging into the arms of the man standing by her side. They both ended up sprawled across the floor, the brave man cushioning her fall to prevent injury to anything beyond pride.

'I'm glad I'm a grown-up,' Bridget said. 'Let's eat.'

'Yes, good idea,' David agreed.

They entered a grand room with dark wood panelling, rich golden velvet drapes and ornate chandeliers. There was a glass vase with a single white rose on each of the round tables. The tablecloths were the maroon of their old school blazer with matching serviettes neatly folded into the wine glasses. They made their way towards food laid out on trestle tables at the far end.

'I love roast lamb, don't you?' David exclaimed as he looked at what was on offer. 'What a wonderful smell.'

'Actually I'm a vegetarian.'

'Oh, I am sorry.'

'I'm not.'

They joined the short queue with Helen and Sharon standing behind them.

'Hello again, David. Recovered?' It was Helen.

'Yes, thank you.'

'And who are you?' Helen asked, looking at his companion.

'Bridget.'

'Were you in our year?'

'Yes.'

'Bridget who?'

'Bridget Wilkinson.'

'Well I don't remember you. Sharon, do you remember Bridget?'

'No, I don't.' With that, Helen and Sharon lost interest and turned to chat with those behind them in the queue.

David handed Bridget a plate. She walked past the

large silver platter of meat garnished with strong smelling rosemary, past the roast potatoes and the broccoli too, stopping at a small bowl. There was an untidily written note on a folded piece of grey-brown cardboard behind it. *For vegetarians only*. She took a spoonful of the pasta dish, added salad, and then turned to wait for David who had paused by the lamb.

'I don't think I'll have this,' he said as much to himself as to Bridget.

'No need to do that for me,' she said cheerfully.

'It's not that. I haven't had lamb since the night Jane left and it's brought back unpleasant memories.' He moved on to the pasta and was about to put some on his plate when he saw the notice banning consumption by meat eaters. He placed the serving spoon back in the bowl.

'Don't be silly, David. Take some. I've hardly had any so you'd be sharing my portion.'

He dropped a small pile of the sticky, cheese-saturated offering onto his plate. 'Mm, looks lovely,' he said unconvincingly. He lifted it up towards his nose. 'Smells good too.'

They sat at a table in the far corner of the room, Bridget eating while David stirred his food with a fork. Other tables filled with their groups of six but no one joined them until the queue had diminished. Finally, a man and woman approached, each holding a plate of food piled high.

'Aren't you David Willoughby?' asked the man, smartly dressed in suit and tie. 'I'm George, George Pickford.' He extended his arm and David shook his hand. 'And this is my wife, Patricia. Patricia Thwaites she was then, weren't you darling? We married soon after leaving school.'

'Hello, David. Nice to see you after all this time. You're looking well.'

Patricia, dressed in a long emerald green gown, bent down and pecked him on the cheek. 'Is this your wife?' she asked, looking across to Bridget.

'No, it's Bridget. She was in our year. Bridget Wilkinson.'

Patricia looked down at her with curiosity. 'That's odd, I don't remember that name and I'm known for my memory. Do you recall her, George?'

'No, I don't.' George peered down and examined her face intently. 'Are you sure you were in our year?'

'Well, I think I was,' Bridget replied, the sarcasm missed by the questioners.

'Anyway,' George continued, 'do you mind if we take a couple of chairs and some cutlery? We want to join Samantha's table, rather a lot of catching up to do.'

The move was already commencing as he spoke, George and Patricia edging backwards, each with a chair in one hand and a plate with cutlery in the other.

'Go ahead, you won't find any interesting conversation here,' Bridget muttered.

She smiled at David. 'I made a lasting impression, didn't I? Actually I'm glad we aren't being bothered. I'm dying to find out more about what happened. Only if you don't mind though. In fact, I'm being absurdly nosy, aren't I?'

'No, you're not and I don't mind. Where was I up to?'

'Your daughter had gone to a friend.'

'Yes, that's right. Well, after she left I carried on cooking while drinking rather too much wine. Sam came racing downstairs.'

~

'Dad, Adrian's invited me over. He's got *Blasters of the Universe,* it's the newest game. Can I go? He said I could stay over.'

'Well, I suppose so. Have your dinner then I'll drive you there. No, actually, it's best I don't drive. I'll call a taxi.'

'No need, he said I can eat with them and his dad will pick me up. He's on his way back from somewhere and has to pass this way.' As if on cue there was a ring at the doorbell. 'That'll be him now. Bye Dad, see you in the morning.'

And Sam was gone. As the front door closed the phone rang and David lifted the receiver.

'Dad, I'm staying at Hannah's tonight. Will you call me tomorrow? But only when Mum's gone. I don't want to see her.' There was a pause. 'Are you OK?'

'Yes, I am. Thanks.'

'Good, see you tomorrow then. Must go, bye.'

David served up a third of the food he'd prepared and sat in uncomfortable silence in the kitchen picking at the lamb, potatoes and carrots.

On the fridge was a photo of the four of them – mother, father and two children – smiling on their half-term holiday in Brittany. It rained for much of the week but that day the sun had burst through. They'd rushed down to the beach and the kids had splashed around in the sea. David enjoyed watching them play, for once without the inhibiting need to be cool that teenagehood seemed to require. Jane sat reading a novel. It was only a few months ago and she seemed perfectly happy; now he knew that wasn't the case. Why hadn't she talked things through rather than deceive him?

A young English couple staying at their hotel were walking by just as David was about to take a photo of the two dripping children, one each side of their mother. All smiles.

'Join the others,' the man said, so David handed over his phone and there was the result on the fridge. Four beaming faces, the backdrop of the sea and to the left the edge of a craggy low cliff. A bright blue sky. Others running around on the sand behind them. A multi-coloured ball on its way down into a bikini clad woman's outstretched hands. And a seagull, top corner right. Funny what you can see when you look closely. Until that lonely dinner he had only been aware of the four of them. Smiling.

David poured out the last dregs from the wine bottle and lifted the glass to his lips. Dizzily, he tilted his head back to drink. Now the wine tasted rough and acidic. He stumbled upstairs and still clothed, dropped down onto his double bed for one.

He slept intermittently, dreaming of being in a hurry and having to do something with great urgency.

He was unclear what that something was. He knew action was required but he couldn't engage in it. He struggled to get the unknown task accomplished as the ringing and knocking persisted and grew louder. Now awake he sat up unsteadily to the sound of continued banging coming from below. It wasn't a dream. He stood, made his way downstairs and opened the front door.

It was Jane. 'I've been standing here for more than five minutes ringing the sodding bell. I left the bloody keys at Jim's.'

'Come in. Fancy a coffee?'

'No, not now thank you. To be truthful I'm nervous about talking to the kids, but I appreciate I have to do it. Are they upstairs?'

'No, they're out.'

'What do you mean by "out"?'

'Rachel's at Hannah's and Sam is with Adrian.'

'But you knew I was coming over to speak to them this morning. How could you do this, David?'

'They decided last night and just went. I was …'

'You were what? Spiteful? Vindictive? I suppose you're going to tell me you tried to stop them but they pushed past you.'

'I was ... I was a little drunk, I wasn't thinking properly.'

'I can't believe how selfish you are, getting drunk when this is so important. When are they due back?'

'No idea. Actually, Rachel said she didn't want to see you.'

'And I suppose you were happy for her to get away

with that.' Jane strode into the kitchen. 'Actually I will have a coffee.'

Noticing the uneven squares of paper scattered across the floor, she stopped abruptly and peered down. 'My letter. How dare you! You tore up my letter!'

'It wasn't me, it …' David began as Jane swivelled round to face him. He had second thoughts. Why should he betray Rachel? A rare surge of anger sent his heart racing as he shouted, 'Perhaps if you'd waited yesterday to have a conversation with them there and then it would have been nicer than a letter!'

'I refuse to listen to this.' Jane headed into the hall and opened the front door. She turned and pointed an index finger at him. 'How dare you tell me what I should be doing! You can't imagine what I'm going through, you inconsiderate bastard.'

David had known Jane for twenty years. Now it struck him for the first time that she had never been able to admit she was the one in the wrong. And it was happening again. According to Jane he was the one who was selfish, inconsiderate and spiteful, when it was she who was walking out on him.

'And now you're smiling!' she shrieked.

'You have their mobile numbers; I suggest you phone them. Oh, and Jane …'

'What?'

'I hope things don't work out for you.'

He saw surprise and perhaps a little fear in her eyes before she slammed the door shut.

4

'You said that. Good for you,' Bridget declared.

'Well, I did feel rather guilty afterwards, but at the time it was like a release of tension.'

'I can understand that.'

The woman dressed in adult school gear was making another announcement. She had climbed onto one of the table tops and was swaying perilously, stiletto heels and alcohol not combining well to help her maintain balance. 'It's time for the music! A back to the 90s disco in the bar. Non-stop hits so let's rock, rock, rock.' She started to dance on the table and sent the vase with its solitary rose crashing to the floor. 'Roger, where's Roger? Help me down will you, it's not safe up here.'

Bridget stood. 'I suppose we'd better mingle. Let's dance.' She took hold of David's hand and pulled him towards the music. *Ice Ice Baby* was blaring out and those already dancing were chanting the words at approximately appropriate times.

'Not this one, I can't stand it,' David pleaded.

'OK, let's see what's next.'

'This is better,' David said as Mariah Carey's

Vision of Love began. They moved to the centre of the room and leapt about in similar fashion to the other partygoers. The dance floor was crowded and every so often there was a "Sorry. Oh, hello David" as they bumped into another couple.

Aerosmith and B-52s hits followed Mariah.

'Now let's slow it down for all you young or not so young lovers out there,' the DJ announced. 'It's from 1990, it's Sinead O'Connor. *Nothing Compares 2 U*.' There were sighs and screams of "I love this!" as the first sad chords were struck. Bridget put her arms round David's neck and he responded by placing his hands on her waist, lightheaded with the warmth of her body against his.

He wanted the closeness to linger but she pulled away at the end of the song. 'I'm desperate for a drink.'

Together they went to the bar. David ordered another Bud and a glass of house white which he was handing to Bridget as Bill Thatcher approached them.

'Well, if it isn't me old mate David again. And who's this? A neat looking bit of skirt for you to be hanging around with.'

'I'd rather not be called a bit of skirt; people with brains gave up saying that about twenty years ago. My name's Bridget. Get out of the way so we can get past.'

'You what?'

'Just piss off out of the way, will you, or else I might accidentally spill my wine all over your ugly face.'

'You what?' he repeated, standing his ground.

'Or does your repertoire extend to hitting females?'

Bill had a bemused look on his face; David feared it turning to an aggressive one.

Bridget seemed unconcerned about potential danger. 'You look confused, Bill. Oh, it must be because "repertoire" is rather a difficult word for you to understand. It comes from the Latin, *repertorium*, but of course you were far too thick to be in the Latin class at school. Well let me put it another way. Either hit me now or fuck off out of it.'

With that, she turned and walked past Bill with David following her.

'Bloody hell, Bridget. There I was thinking you were an exceptionally delicate and polite woman, but then you manage to intimidate the school bully. Rather high-risk, but well done.'

'I've had years of practice.'

'What do you mean?'

'It's a long story.'

'As you told me a while back, it's a long evening.'

'Not now, maybe another time. But I'd love to hear more about what happened to you. Let's go somewhere quieter.' Led by Bridget they left the bar and reached the reception area. 'We could sit there,' she suggested, pointing towards two vast red leather armchairs. They sank into them and placed their drinks on a smoked glass coffee table littered with back copies of *Country Life*.

'You still haven't answered my original question. How come you ended up here tonight?' Bridget asked.

David glanced back towards the room they had come from, expecting Bill, Ben and a lynching party of their associates to arrive at any moment. But the other guests remained at the bar or on the dance floor. A Faith No More song was playing, he couldn't remember the title. 'Good idea us sitting here,' he joked, looking across to the muscular night porter with shaved head and beefy arms covered in tattoos. 'He'll protect us when Bill arrives.'

Bridget smiled, one of those smiles that encourage you to smile back. 'You were up to when you told Jane you hoped she ended up unhappy, or something like that.'

David paused. He took a gulp of beer to give himself time to consider what to tell Bridget. She seemed genuinely interested, even concerned, but he had only just met her, well since childhood anyway. How much should he be relating about painful personal affairs?

'It was a distressing time for me and the children with Sam convinced everything would end up fine and Rachel threatening to murder her mother. I was sure Jane wasn't going to change her mind. She'd already started taking whatever she felt like from the house without even asking which I thought was outrageous. It was a mess and to a large extent it still is – if you don't mind I'd like to leave it at that for now.'

Bill, Ben, and five other men came into the reception area. David tensed in anticipation of a confrontation but the group walked past without making eye contact, cigarettes at the ready to be lit as soon as they stepped outside.

'Jane still hadn't sat down with the kids to explain what was going on,' David continued despite his resolution to stop. 'She should have tried harder even though Rachel was rejecting her approaches.'

Bridget nodded, her sympathetic face as beautiful as her smiling one. David had succumbed to teenagesque infatuation together with the angst that inevitably goes with it. He was an adolescent again, the twenty-five years since school washed away by this chance meeting.

'I'll tell you what's odd though. I was devastated when Jane first told me, but only a few weeks on and I'm not nearly as unhappy as I thought I would or even should be. It's made me realise that our relationship had become stale so I share the responsibility for what happened.'

Bridget interrupted. 'Hang on a minute, you weren't the one who ran off with someone else without any discussion.'

'I suppose you're right – the shock was huge.'

'I bet it was. You must have struggled to come to terms with it.'

'Yes, the fear of loneliness was the worst. Friends have been brilliant though, suggesting all sorts of things to help me cope: cinema, bowling, concerts, dinner parties, even clubbing to find a new partner! That's the last thing on my mind. In fact I've yet to take up any of their offers because I feel the pressure of the responsibility to support the kids. But I do appreciate their concern.'

'So how come you came here tonight?' Bridget persevered as David was thinking that finding a partner, this partner, was no longer the last thing on his mind.

David wanted to impress her with light and witty patter. Instead it was like being in a counselling session. 'Another drink?' he asked.

'No, I'm fine thanks. Carry on.'

With reluctance he did so. 'Well, one evening I was watching some TV drama and there was a young girl who looked the spitting image of Marianne Dunnell. Do you remember her?'

'I certainly do.'

'We used to call her Marianne Faithfull. She looked just like the singer – all the boys thought she was an absolute stunner.'

'Us girls called her Marianne Unfaithful. She hopped from boyfriend to boyfriend and her girlfriends didn't last long either.'

'Oh, I never knew that. Anyway, I had a sudden impulse to contact her even though she'd had little to do with me at school. I searched on Facebook and the first Marianne Dunnell to come up was her. Her profile was public, she's living in Oxford, Boars Hill to be exact. I messaged and got a quick response. Facebook's so good for finding people, isn't it?'

'I wouldn't know, I hardly use it. I can't be bothered. My kids tell me they've got about three thousand friends. Or is it three million? But they only recognise about five of them.'

Bill, Ben and their entourage had come back into

reception, their laughter raucous.

'You fuckin' didn't?' one of them enquired.

'I fuckin' did,' another responded.

'Fuckin' hell,' a third piped in, their voices so similar it was impossible to tell who was doing the talking.

Bill, who was leading the group, stopped and looked down at Bridget. The other men formed a row behind him, facing her.

'Bitch,' he declared and the others thought this was highly amusing.

'Yeah, bitch,' another of the faceless nobodies muttered as he followed Bill back into the bar.

'Those ...' David began.

'Never mind them, they aren't worth thinking about. What happened with Marianne?'

'Her first message wasn't much more than a *Yes, I do remember you*. I wasn't going to let her get away with that so I wrote back, rather a long message that I later discovered could be read by all her friends and their friends. Possibly the three million you mentioned. It was highly embarrassing as I'd written about all the boys at school fancying her and I asked if she wanted to meet up for old times' sake.'

'Did she reply?'

'Yes, beginning with instruction on how to send a direct message on Facebook. Apparently she'd been teased about this long-lost admirer. Then she provided an update. Not long after leaving school she married a man training to be a cleric. She has five teenage children, two dogs and a hamster and she works as a librarian.'

'Marianne a librarian! Hard to believe. In fact, being married to a vicar and with loads of kids presumably from the same father is also a revelation.'

'Well, in our short flurry of messaging she mentioned the reunion and gave me the email address of the organiser, that woman who stood on the table. Marianne intended to come along herself but messaged me a couple of days ago. Her husband had organised a surprise weekend away so she was cancelling. Since I'd signed up and booked the hotel by then I thought I might as well come along.'

Bridget glanced at her watch then across to the night porter who was leaning over the reception counter reading a newspaper. He yawned, she yawned too. The 1990s hits were still blasting out.

'Well, I'm pleased you made it but I'm afraid I'm done for the night if you don't mind.'

'No, I've had enough too. I don't mean enough of talking to you, just that if you're heading off then I don't feel like mingling with anyone else.'

Taking the wide staircase with its plush red carpet and ivory and gold striped wallpaper, they reached the first floor landing.

'I'm this way,' Bridget announced.

'Me too.'

They walked along the corridor in silence, glancing at the prints of hunting scenes. Bridget stopped outside Room 134. 'This is mine.'

'I'm next door. 136.'

'Coincidence. Hey, it's been nice chatting, David,

I've enjoyed this evening loads. Maybe see you at breakfast.'

David didn't reply. He was too busy thinking of what to say to delay their parting, the closeness of their bedrooms a nagging contributory factor. Possibilities crossed his mind.

Fancy a coffee before bed?

Would you like to see if the décor in my bedroom is the same as in yours?

What about sharing a bed tonight?

Before he could come up with something appropriate, Bridget had taken hold of his shoulder and was planting a kiss on his cheek.

'Goodnight,' she said, key in hand.

David was left standing alone in the corridor to mull over the elusive one-liner that might have prolonged their time together.

5

The days after that dreadful weekend when Jane walked out, the days he hadn't wanted to tell Bridget about, had been hell. The disastrous Sunday morning meeting with his wife left David fluctuating between guilt and a questioning of sanity that he should even be considering an apology for his unkind words. Three times he lifted the phone and three times he replaced it before guilt triumphed and at 12.07 p.m. he called her.

Jim answered her mobile. 'What do you want, David?' he snapped.

'To speak with Jane if you don't mind.'

'I'm not letting you.'

'I want to speak to my wife.'

'Not after what you said to her. She wants nothing more to do with you.' Before David could gather his thoughts Jim was launching into a severe tirade covering decency, loyalty, compassion, morality and quite possibly much more, but David had hung up before the end of the monologue.

He walked round to the newsagent to buy the Sunday Times. Everything on the short journey was the same as ever – Isobel pushing the pram in a vain attempt to stop her baby crying, Lawrence washing his BMW, Mrs Grant nurturing her flowers and plants with care beyond the call of duty. Was his the only life that had changed?

'Good morning, Mr Willoughby, and how are you today?' asked Stanley Entwhistle, the newsagent who had run the shop since David first moved to the area. The man had a wild mop of white hair with matching strands leaping up from his eyebrows and poking out of his ears. Stanley had watched David's children grow from infancy to adolescence. Now he would be seeing his marriage go from ceremony to cessation.

'I'm fine thank you.'

David dropped the newspaper onto the counter and took out his card.

'What about your Mail on Sunday?'

'I won't today.' He held back from explaining the reason behind the abandonment of a long-standing purchase.

Back at home David half-heartedly read the newspaper, vaguely acknowledging that severe economic decline, an acceleration of glacier-melting and a major motorway pile up were more traumatic than his own crisis.

He dashed into the hall on hearing the return of one of his children. Rachel had opened the front door, cigarette in hand.

'Put that thing out,' David ordered.

'OK,' she said, throwing the stub behind her onto the small tidy front lawn, 'but I smoke. I won't inside the house, but that's all I'm agreeing to.'

David didn't have the energy to argue.

'And have I missed my fucking bitch of a mother?' Rachel continued.

The previous day's fury might have excused the swearing but David was not prepared to tolerate the habitual use of that word from his sixteen-year-old daughter. 'There's no need for that.'

'Fucking bitch, fucking bitch, fucking bitch,' Rachel chanted as she brushed past him and headed up to her room. A minute later Ariana Grande was belting out of her music system.

David stood in the hall trying to remember what he had been doing ahead of Rachel's return.

The phone rang; it was Sam.

'Dad, could you pick me up? Now, please. Adrian and I have had a bit of a bust-up. He's blaming me for ramming his car into a skirting board, but he didn't tell me it was turbo charged. It's only the bumper that's broken and his dad says a bit of glue will sort it so I don't know why he's so angry.'

David agreed to set off immediately and called up to Rachel to let her know. Having exited without keys he rang the doorbell to get back in to pick them up, ringing again when the Ariana Grande track had ended and Rachel could hear.

'I've never forgotten my keys, I can't think clearly anymore,' he informed his daughter.

'Fucking bitch,' she muttered as she headed back upstairs.

He drove through the comfortable suburban streets of Mill Hill feeling sorry for himself, jealous that for those in the immaculately ordered houses he was passing, life would be as secure as the day before. Well maybe not, he reconsidered, his mind now racing with what ifs. Perhaps the loss of a job or a death in the family. Or conceivably like him, a wife leaving, leaving to live with a so-called best friend. On wishing that others were facing similar grief, a surge of self-disgust was added to his concoction of emotions.

He turned into the gravelled drive of Adrian's impressive Totteridge house, an ornate structure with classical pillars by the front door. Armless marble Romanesque statues stood on each side, a semi-naked man and woman facing each other. The doorbell chimed *La Marseillaise* – Adrian's mother was French. David knew the father dealt in property sales in Europe and had heard that he was struggling to cope with the post-Brexit laws about British ownership. Clearly he wasn't struggling sufficiently to have to vacate this palace or trade in the Porsche and Daimler on the drive.

Mrs Grainger came to the door. 'I am so sorry to hear your news.' She took hold of David. 'You poor, poor, poor thing,' each "poor" accompanied by a consoling pat on the back. He hardly knew the woman but if there was anything she could do to help he was told, all he had to do was ask.

She stepped back and looked him in the eye. 'I know exactly how you feel,' she uttered. Was she indicating that all was not right between her and Mr Grainger?

Sam, a few paces behind her, mouthed 'Can we go,

Dad?'

Just as David felt there was an opportunity to exit with Mrs Grainger finally silent, Mr Grainger came racing downstairs. The conversation was pretty well repeated though Mr Grainger was far cheerier than his wife had been and there was no reference to "I know exactly how you feel."

'I want to leave,' Sam uttered when there was a pause in the conversation.

Declining Mrs Grainger's offer of a cup of tea or coffee and Mr Grainger's additional option of something a little stiffer, David and his son edged out of the door with a promise that if help were needed they would ask.

Back at home, Sunday stretched on endlessly for all three of them. Rachel listened to music while wading through French and Science revision for school tests on Monday. Sam played computer games in between racing through Maths and History homework that he found insultingly easy. David resumed reading the newspaper without taking much in. He shuddered at the thought of Jane and Jim together, reading a paper the last thing on their minds.

Intermittently throughout the day he heard the children's phones ring, Rachel cutting out her Coldplay theme without answering and Sam engaging in whispered dialogue after a brief *Star Wars* burst.

'Was it Mum you were speaking to?' David asked Sam as they were eating the leftover lamb later that evening.

'Yes,' Sam admitted.

'Well you're an idiot then,' Rachel attacked.

Sam didn't rise to the bait nor indicate what had been said.

Monday, the first day back at work and school for the decimated family, brought new concerns. As usual David needed to leave home ahead of Rachel and Sam, but now there was no Jane to get the children on their way. She'd been the one on hand for last-minute panics like signing school letters and searching for PE kit. Rachel assured him that she could take care of things and he was prepared to trust his daughter, this somewhat countered when he spotted a packet of Marlboro Lights resting against the packed lunch container inside her school bag.

With little enthusiasm, David drove into the underground car park of the concrete block that accommodated the complex web of local authority services. He was an accountant in the social welfare department, responsible for allocating funds to family members who had power of attorney over relatives residing in care homes. It didn't take Jane's words for him to acknowledge that doing this work for too long had turned him into a boring old fart. Recently he'd applied for more stimulating and higher-paid positions within the county council – Hospital Capital Projects Manager; Policing in the Community Supervisor; and top of the list, Parks, Open Spaces and Countryside Director. In each case he'd been short-listed and interviewed to be followed by a rejection letter. Frustrated, he had considered a move into the private sector, but the seemingly endless recession made such a step risky. He'd lose the generous local authority final salary pension, too.

A career change daydream was to open an arts café, but the likelihood of that was more remote than Jane returning. So he was stuck in a rut, tied to the local authority with little chance of promotion. He worked hard, by nature conscientious, but it was ever more difficult to please the public what with diminished government funding available to support the aged.

David took the concrete staircase up to the ground floor and purchased a so-called cappuccino at the café. He sipped the powdery synthetic liquid in the polystyrene container as he made his way to the lift, nodding to fellow employees as he travelled in silence to his fourth floor office.

He hoped for an easy day on that first Monday but it wasn't to be. One of the junior staff had offered more care home places than there was funding for. It was left to David to deal with irate callers who had been granted assistance during a telephone conversation only to see their application rejected by letter. And it was David who was confronted by the head of service accusing him of reckless decision-making. When he explained that it wasn't his mistake, her criticism switched to his poor management of the team.

Mary Dyer was his boss. On her appointment six months previously, the staff newsletter profiled her as a high-flyer with a first class honours degree in Accounting and Finance from the London School of Economics. She had thrived working at one of the global management consultancies but now wanted "to give something back to the community." What the article failed to mention was that she believed the local authority to be rife with inefficiency and full of lazy staff; she saw her task as shaking things up.

'I'm at meetings most of the day, David,' Mary said during their brief telephone conversation. 'I should be back by four o'clock. We'll sort out your over-generous promises then.'

'I've already told you, Mary, they weren't my promises.'

'And I've already told you to better control your reckless staff.'

Four o'clock turned out to be well gone five. Mary came into his office with a pile of case note folders which she dropped onto his desk before sitting down to face him.

There was an ongoing departmental joke about what Mary wore. Female colleagues claimed she never had on the same outfit twice and some of the males, though not David, emailed suggestions of titles for her attire. Today's label doing the rounds was *Eastern European Peasant*. Looking at her flowing skirt and brightly coloured layers of T-shirt, blouse, cardigan and jacket, David could appreciate the choice.

His friendly welcome was instantly quashed as she attacked him for wasting her valuable time. She then proceeded to waste *his* valuable time by plodding through each case at pedestrian pace.

'Mrs Thornton next. I can't find the date when she

was moved from the hospital ward to the convalescence unit. Do you have that information?'

'No, it wasn't my case.'

'And who advised that she should go into residential care rather than return home?'

'I don't know. I've already said, this wasn't my case.'

'Were we included in that discussion?'

'I'm not sure.'

'Do we have access to her financial records?'

'I expect so.'

And so it went on for over an hour until David apologised for having to terminate the meeting as he had to pick up his daughter. Mary gave him a look rather like the one men have been giving working mothers for generations when they're faced with the need to juggle work and family. With reluctance she agreed to delay further castigation until the next morning. Picking up the pile of folders, she left him to fume.

A disgruntled David shut down his computer. When he came out his office Jabulani was waiting for him. 'What's going on? She's been on the warpath all day.'

'Mary thinks we're wasting money because we're supporting old people on low incomes.'

Although he'd only been working at the local authority for a few months, Jabulani had a sound grasp of the office politics. 'She wants a department with no deficit and she's found a way of achieving it. Zero income and zero expenditure.'

David appreciated his sense of humour and would have shared a light-hearted moan about his meeting with Mary if he'd had the time. 'More tomorrow, Jabulani. I've got to dash to collect Rachel.'

Rachel had a good voice and loved drama; she'd performed in the annual play since her first year at secondary school. This year's choice was the musical *Fiddler on the Roof*, giving her the opportunity to both sing and act. Rehearsals were after school on Mondays and as usual on that Monday, David arranged to collect her on the way back from work. He was late following the ordeal with Mary and by the time he arrived Rachel was sitting alone on a low brick wall in front of the school gates. When she saw him approach she dropped her cigarette butt, stamped on it, and walked towards the car.

David hoped that her smoking was an angry reaction to her mother's behaviour and would soon cease. He wouldn't be reprimanding her; instead his demeanour was light and cheery as he greeted her. 'Hi Rachel, sorry I'm a bit late. Had a good day?'

'No. I'm fed up with this bloody musical.'

'Rehearsals don't always go well. That's why you have them, to iron things out.'

'It's nothing to do with that. I'm only in the chorus and I'm better than some of the so-called stars who are acting like prima donnas.'

'Well maybe …'

'Maybe nothing.'

They sat in silence, progressing slowly through the rush hour traffic.

Rachel broke into song.

'If I were a fucking bitch,
Yubby dibby dibby dibby dibby dibby dibby dum,
All day long I'd biddy biddy bum,
If I were a fucking bitch.'

'Stop that! Now!' David ordered and Rachel reverted to humming the *Fiddler on the Roof* melody. On arriving home she got out the car without speaking, opened the front door, walked past Sam and marched upstairs.

'What's up with her?' Sam asked.

'Just upset about Mum,' David replied. 'How was school?'

'Fine. Me and Adrian have made up. Dad, you know that car I told you about, I would really like it soon. Have you had time to decide? I promise if I get it I won't ask for anything else for Christmas.'

'There's over three months to go before Christmas.'

'I know. Or what about lending me the money then giving me money for Christmas and I can pay you back?'

'Let me think it over, Sam. I'm going to make dinner now. Have you got homework to do?'

'Yeah, some. What are we eating?'

'Pasta. Is that OK?'

'I suppose so. Your cooking isn't bad, it's just that Mum's is much better.'

'Yes, you've already told me that. Several times. I'm doing my best.'

'Sorry.' And with that Sam turned and headed

upstairs.

David was left to make Spaghetti Bolognese with little chance of it being a popular choice since Rachel wasn't keen on cooked tomatoes and Sam had already given his verdict.

An hour later, as they sat eating in silence, David was wondering how he would be able to cope with the day-to-day necessities. There was so much that needed doing – fitting in grocery shopping around work, extending the range of what he could cook, helping the two of them with their homework, being a chauffeur, handling discipline – generally all the things associated with a single parent bringing up two teenage children.

His understanding of the plight of single mums soared.

6

The traumatic days after Jane had left weren't what was on his mind as he sat alone in his bedroom at the Hotel Marlborough having parted from Bridget.

Having relieved his erection while thinking rather obsessively about that slow dance with her, he lay in bed scheming how to set up a further meeting. Infatuation had kicked in big time after only one short encounter. Lust, love, friendship, acquaintance, any of these would do, but lust was top of his wish list. Unable to sleep, he wondered whether he had ever had such an intense feeling for Jane. Surely he had during their first years together.

One thing was clear, he had to see Bridget again. He mulled over the fact that she had acquired all sorts of information about him but he knew little about her beyond her name. Why had she come to the reunion? She'd mentioned children, but how many and how old were they? Since she had children did that mean she was married – he had noted the absence of a wedding ring? Where did she live? And work?

The scenario he created filled him with despondency. A husband she was devoted to, as he was to her. Five adorable children. Blissfully dwelling in a dreamy, thatched cottage which Bridget took great delight in returning to at the end of the day having toiled selflessly in a job she was passionate about. Probably working for a charity supporting the world's needy.

The belief that he might never see Bridget again filled him with despair. Surely she'd still be around in the morning he reasoned. His angst waned, only to immediately resurface with the thought of her desperate to set off at the crack of dawn to get back to that blissful life with husband and five children in their dream home.

Sleep was impossible. He put on the bedside light and made himself a cup of tea which he drank with the pack of complimentary biscuits.

For a foolhardy instant he contemplated knocking on Bridget's bedroom door there and then. But then what?

I'm making tea, care for a cup?

I was making tea but there aren't any milk cartons. Do you have one I could borrow?

I know we've only just met, well as adults, but I've fallen hopelessly in love and want to spend the night with you.

No, not a sensible idea to barge in at 2.49 a.m. however good an excuse he could think up. A counter plan had emerged, rigorous in its simplicity. He'd get up ridiculously early the next morning just in case she was an early riser and the first to have breakfast. He'd hover outside the dining room until she appeared then pretend it was a coincidence they had arrived together. With the plan established he returned to bed, setting his mobile for a seven o'clock alarm call. Still unable to unwind, besotted with thoughts of Bridget, he rehearsed the conversation.

What a coincidence coming down at the same time for breakfast.

Shall we sit together?

Let's not wait another twenty-five years before we meet up again.

Do you by any chance live in a thatched cottage?

Sensible thought was being clouded by exhaustion.

He tossed and turned throughout the night, sleeping intermittently until the alarm sounded. Stretching across to the bedside cabinet he switched it off. The dream that followed was of he and Bridget lying on a sun soaked tropical beach engaged in conversation that was generating much laughter. Then a dark cloud rolled in from the sea and deafening cracks of thunder disturbed their peace. Bang! Bang! Bang! Then again. Bang! Bang! Bang! But it wasn't a dream – someone was knocking at the door.

'Coming!' he shouted as he glanced at his phone. He'd gone back to sleep and it was now half past nine. Rushing to the door he pulled it open.

'Bridget! Thank God it's you.'

She looked startled. 'David, perhaps … erm'

'Yes?'

'Perhaps you should put on trousers or something.'

David had taken off his pyjama bottoms during the night (for reasons linked to obsessively thinking about

Bridget).

'Oh no!' he exclaimed having looked down to check the validity of Bridget's observation. 'Just a minute,' he stammered before slamming the door shut. He immediately re-opened it a fraction and edged his head around the small gap. 'Sorry, didn't mean to slam it in your face, I'll leave it ajar.'

He gently pushed the door to then raced to the side of the bed and pulled on his jeans.

'Just another minute,' he called out as he darted into the bathroom to clean his teeth on the off-chance that Bridget would be prepared to kiss a lunatic answering the door naked from the waist down. He had never been so embarrassed in his life, although getting drunk at the Christmas lunch the first time he met Jane's parents was a close call. On reflection, even worse was fainting in the delivery room when Jane was giving birth to Rachel.

He opened the door. 'I'm ever so sorry, Bridget.'

She seemed unperturbed. 'That's OK, at least you were partly dressed. I don't wear anything when I sleep.'

This created a stirring between David's legs and he was grateful he now had something on to cover the movement.

'Did you sleep well?' she enquired.

'Why are you asking?'

Bridget frowned. 'Well, I was being polite I suppose. I slept like a log.'

'Me too.'

'Anyway, I wanted to say goodbye and thank you

for a fun evening,' she continued. 'Without you it would have been an absolute nightmare.'

Bridget's comment left room for interpretation. What she said didn't necessarily imply she had enjoyed their time together, merely that it prevented a nightmare. 'I had a wonderful time,' he countered.

'Your chin's come up with a massive bruise, Bill must have hit you pretty hard. Does it hurt?'

'It was great to see you after all these years.'

'Poor you, what a terrible few weeks you've had.'

'I loved the dancing.'

'I still can't believe what you told me about Marianne Dunnell.'

'Bridget!'

'Yes?'

'Are you married?'

'What?'

'Are you married?'

'No, why?'

'I just wondered. You have children though, don't you?'

'Yes, two. Kay's twelve and Andy's sixteen.'

'Where do you live?'

'Lots of questions, David.'

'Well, I was thinking in the night that I didn't ask anything about you, we only talked about me.'

'That's not your fault. If you remember I was keen to hear about you. There was no time to discover anything about my boring existence.'

'Maybe we can meet again, then I can be the judge.'

'Yes, I'd like that.'

David walked across to the table and took a sheet of the hotel's headed paper. He tore it in half, wrote down his name and number, and handed it to Bridget along with the pen and the other half of the sheet. He watched as she jotted down her number and email address. She added a smiley face.

'I left my name off, I'm assuming you'll remember who I am,' she said as she handed it over. 'We're daft, we should have kissed phones.'

'What?'

'To capture our contact details. Never mind, this is fine,' Bridget said, holding up the piece of paper. 'Anyway, I'd best be heading home.'

'Where is home?'

'London. I live in Muswell Hill.'

'I'm London, too. Mill Hill.'

'Almost neighbours. OK, take care and I look forward to hearing from you.' She kissed him on each cheek French style then took a step back and lifted her hand for a small wave. Having picked up the lime green canvas bag on the floor beside her, Bridget headed off down the corridor. David watched, hoping she would look back for a final acknowledgment, but she didn't.

It was gone 9.45 am and downstairs the dining room was near deserted. There was one reunion member there, the loud woman who had made the announcements the night before. Her school uniform had been replaced by a more fitting jeans and blouse. She gave him a watery smile of acknowledgement.

'One of the few,' she commented as he sat down by her side.

'What do you mean?'

'I think most people gave up on breakfast, too hungover. I'm also in the hungover category but since I was awake I thought I might as well get down. How come you made it?'

'I probably didn't drink as much as most.'

'You were with Bridget, weren't you? She still upstairs?'

'No, she's headed off home.'

'Us over-age teenagers. You getting off with Bridget, me with Roger. I wouldn't have touched him with a bargepole back then but now I get so pissed I end up in bed with the man. It was his snoring that woke me up. Panic and guilt too, my husband would kill me if he found out. Hopefully Roger'll be gone by the time I get back upstairs.' She sliced a piece of bacon, lifted it to her mouth, and rather ungraciously chewed. 'You or Bridget married?' she asked, her mouth still full.

'I am, though separated. I don't know much about Bridget. But before any rumours start to fly, we didn't spend the night together.'

The woman took a slurp of coffee. 'Why not?'

'That's a daft question. Why should we, we were chatting?'

'Oh,' she replied, looking at David in puzzlement. 'You seemed to be getting on well enough.'

'But that doesn't mean we should end up sleeping together,' David retorted with a degree of admiration for this woman's black and white decision making process. No principles, just doing what you fancy at that moment. And of course he would have loved to have spent the night with Bridget. 'There is such a thing as morality,' he stated with false conviction.

'Sor-ree,' she replied.

'No, I'm sorry, I didn't mean to lecture. And I'm afraid I don't even know your name.'

'Penny Tratton. I know you're David because I handled the bookings. We were in different classes in school, I don't think our paths crossed much.'

'Penny Tratton? No, I can't say I remember your name.'

'The boys changed it, of course. Penny Tration they called me.'

'Penny Tration. Why?'

'Penny Tration, penetration. I lived up to the nickname a bit, I'm afraid. And I did again last night so that's going to do my reputation a power of good.'

She burst into tears. David stood, walked to the other side of the table, and put an arm around her shoulders. 'Come on, don't be upset. You can walk away from today and forget all about it. And you did organise a great reunion.'

'Thank you, you're very kind,' she said, the tears disappearing as quickly as they had arrived. 'I'm going to wake Roger up and tell him to get to his own room if he still wants to sleep, then I'll pack and head off to my lovely family.' She stood, sobbing again as she melodramatically strode out the room.

David went across to the buffet table where a

waitress was clearing away the plates.

'Sorry sir, it's gone ten, we're closed for breakfast.'

'Can I at least have a coffee?'

''Fraid not, but there is a Starbucks round the corner.'

7

David decided against a Starbucks coffee and set off immediately after the Sunday morning conversation with Penny Tratton. Tired and irritable, he had little enthusiasm to return home. The very word "home" had a cosy ring to it but any link with cosiness had been shattered.

~

The Tuesday after Jane had left was even worse than the Monday. Rachel came downstairs for breakfast with a new song based on the Queen hit *We Are the Champions*.

She is a fucking bitch
She is a fucking bitch
No time for losers
'Cos she is the biggest bitch – in the world

It was a track David quite liked and he had to admit Rachel sang the updated version perfectly – what a lovely voice. Half-heartedly he acted out the enraged parent but for the rest of the day he couldn't get the tune or words out of his head.

He was humming it as he entered the local authority underground car park. It had been constructed for tiny vehicles alone, the concrete columns demanding preposterously tight turns. David failed to negotiate carefully enough and the front passenger side of his car donated a Flame Red streak to the multi-coloured assortment of scraped paints on the pillar. The parking bays were so small it was difficult to open a door without knocking against a neighbour's car. His door no more than tapped against a Toyota, but it was enough to set off the alarm. He made a run for it.

Work began with a continuation of the meeting with Mary Dyer to discuss overspend on residential care home support. Today the office gossips had described her attire as *Ms Footsie 100 CEO*. She was wearing a tailored navy pinstripe suit with a crisp white blouse buttoned to the neck.

There had been no welcoming smile, not even a greeting, as he entered her office. He was on time but she made a point of looking at her watch before gesturing for him to sit down opposite her.

'I'm pushed for time this morning, David, but we need to get this done. We're already £350,000 over budget and that's with half the financial year to go. Before we discuss details I want to make it clear that you're the one who should be addressing this, it's within your remit.'

David was prepared. The previous evening he had constructed a watertight explanation for the deficit. 'A couple of points before you continue, Mary. Did you know that –'

'I'd rather you didn't interrupt. Let me finish.' She

made steely eye contact before continuing. 'Some questions. Are you double-checking how many assets these old people have before we start dishing out money? Do we ask if their children can contribute? And are we encouraging them to consider having their parents move in with them?'

'Yes to all those things. Applicants have to complete Form F43-H27/B and attach evidence and then ...' He looked up. Mary was sifting through files and it was evident she wasn't listening. She didn't even notice that he'd stopped speaking mid-sentence.

'I've been doing some checking and I believe this department is out of control.' She pulled out an invoice. 'Even the stationery budget is way over. You spent £286 on Post-its last month. Why on earth would you want £286-worth of Post-its?'

'That was a mistake. Diane was asked to get 400 but she mistook the instruction and ordered 400 packs and there are ten sets of Post-its in each pack.'

'So now we have 4,000 booklets. How many pieces of paper in each? A hundred? That's 400,000 Post-its.'

'I don't think there are a hundred in each booklet, I could get Diane to check.'

'Hardly the point, David. David? Are you listening?'

No time for losers, 'cos she is the biggest bitch – in the world he was thinking, dividing his anger between Jane and Mary.

'Well, that's an aside, I think we should get back to the main issue, don't you?' Mary continued, her implication being that it was he who had raised the

Post-its controversy.

There was a timid knock on the door. It was Diane. 'There's a phone call for you, David.'

'Not now, I'll call whoever it is after this meeting.'

'I think you should take this one.' Diane was frowning and nodding intently.

'Excuse me, Mary, I'll be back soon.'

David returned a couple of minutes later. 'I'm ever so sorry, I'm going to have to pop out. Something's cropped up with one of my children at school. I'm sure it won't take long. Could we continue this afternoon?'

Mary looked at him in disbelief. 'I appreciate family concerns can be important, but you can't constantly put them ahead of work matters.'

*She is a fucking bitch...*played inside his head. What a cheek, twice hardly constituted constantly. Over his many years of service at the local authority he had rarely missed a day's work. 'Yes, I suppose you're right. Apologies,' he said as he edged out the door.

When he arrived at Rachel's school the receptionist escorted him to the Head's office. It was a nice room with a relaxed and welcoming feel to it. The walls were filled with children's art work. Oriental and African artefacts were strewn across a cabinet top and two low tables, one in the middle of the room and one by a window overlooking a neat quadrangle with sturdy wooden benches and tables. A white dish on the nearest table caught David's eye. Across its centre was a brightly coloured dragon, the tail extending beyond the edge of the plate and running on underneath. He recognised this from a photograph in the most recent school newsletter. During the exchange visit to an English-speaking college in China the staff had been presented with this gift.

David rather liked the Head. John Edwards was a tall, lean man with a sweep of sandy brown hair across his brow. He wore horn-rimmed spectacles that made him look full of wisdom. He was tapping his fingers on a large desk covered with papers. As David approached Mr Edwards sprang up and strode across the room to greet his visitor with a firm handshake.

'Do sit down,' he said, directing David to a drab beige armchair that had seen better days. Mr Edwards sat opposite him on a matching seat. On the coffee table between them were three delicate enamelled boxes colourfully painted with pagodas and trees with twisted branches.

David looked up and Mr Edwards began. 'We have a problem with Rachel. She was caught smoking this morning when she should have been in class and that was the second time this week. When Miss Franks told her off she called her an f – ing bitch. It's unacceptable and I have no option but to suspend her.'

'I agree that such behaviour is improper, Mr Edwards, but there are extenuating circumstances. My wife walked out on us, me, last Saturday and Rachel has reacted with considerable anger. That's no excuse for her smoking or her rudeness but I hope you accept that at least to some extent it explains things.'

'I'm sorry to hear your news, Mr Willoughby, and

yes, of course something like that is going to affect behaviour.' He looked down at a sheet of paper with handwritten notes. 'However, the first smoking incidents took place well before the weekend and my staff have been complaining about her insolence for quite a while. Apparently today she announced she's quitting the musical, too.'

'Well, she hasn't told me that. Look, I accept your dissatisfaction, but I'm worried about the effect a suspension might have on Rachel. The situation with my wife is particularly awkward, she's in a relationship with a family friend, someone we've known for years. Rachel was fond of this man, Jim Wainwright, she trusted him implicitly.' David noticed the headmaster reddening, obviously a sensitive soul. He pressed on, sensing the chance of a rethink. 'Surely you appreciate my point, Mr Edwards?'

'I won't pass comment on your personal circumstances, Mr Willoughby. However I should mention that Jim Wainwright is one of our governors, a highly valued member of the team. It would have been better not to have mentioned a name. I suggest we focus on Rachel's behaviour.'

'It's a tough time for her. Would you be prepared to put the suspension on hold?'

Mr Edwards paused and took off his glasses, placing them on the table. He looked across at David who felt like a miscreant pupil himself.

Finally the headmaster responded. 'Yes, I'll agree to probation instead of suspension, though with conditions. Rachel must apologise to Miss Franks and show me an action plan setting out how she intends to improve her behaviour and performance. She's an able girl and she's in danger of substantial underachievement.'

'Thank you, I appreciate your decision. I'll make sure she does both things you've asked for.'

'One other point though. She needs to know that if she steps out of line, however slightly, that will be it and she will face suspension.'

'Fair enough, I'll make sure she behaves properly.'

The headmaster stood and David did likewise. 'You might want to help her put together her plan of action,' Edwards suggested. 'I want to see something that demonstrates a sustained effort to improve.'

'Agreed.'

The pair shook hands. 'Rachel is in reception, I'll take you there. She can't go back into classes today but we'll see her and her plan tomorrow.'

David glanced at his watch on their way out. It was 11.56. He'd told Mary he'd be back by one o'clock at the latest and he might still make it. Mr Edwards led him to a tiny windowless room, as near as a school could get to having a cell. There were two plastic bucket seats, one occupied by Rachel and the other by a teacher who was marking exercise books on his lap.

'You can go home now, Rachel,' the Head said before David had a chance to speak. 'If you do what your father and I have discussed we'll see you tomorrow.' He turned and left without waiting for a reply.

'Shall we go?'

Rachel nodded and raced out the room, out the school, and towards the car.

There was silence on the journey home until David turned into their street. Then Rachel spoke. 'I'm sorry, Dad. Things must be hard for you and it's not fair for me to make them worse.' David glanced to his side and saw tears rolling down his daughter's cheeks. He pulled into the drive and switched off.

'We need each other to get through this, but please know that I'm always here to support you.' They leant across the handbrake to cuddle and Rachel shook as she sobbed. He couldn't leave her at home alone in this state. Mary would have to wait.

He made ham sandwiches for lunch and while they were eating, outlined his conversation with Mr Edwards. The key messages were the need for an apology and an action plan. As soon as she'd finished eating Rachel opened her bag, took out a pen and pad and got going.

'This is easy,' she said as she wrote.

1. *No smoking in school or nearby*
2. *Polite attitude towards all teachers*
3. *Work as hard as possible*
4. *Give in homework on time*

She tore out the piece of paper and handed it to David. 'Done it.'

'Well, if you stick with these that would be great, but they're a bit open-ended.' He'd attended countless meetings to set SMART objectives but decided not to burden his daughter with a process that she would probably encounter far too often in the future. He chose an intermediate path. 'Perhaps you could give an indication of how you intend to reach these actions.'

'What do you mean?' Rachel replied, a glimmer of outraged teenager re-emerging. 'I've said I won't smoke, will be polite and work hard. What more do they want?'

'Break them up a bit. For instance, which subject will you have to work hardest in to be successful? Who exactly do you need to be more polite to? Maybe the one you swore at today?'

'Yeah, the fucking bitch.'

'Rachel!'

'Only joking. OK, back to the drawing board. I'll take it upstairs if that's all right.' She stood and planted a kiss on David's forehead.

It was gone three and he hadn't called work to apologise to Mary. A difficult conversation was now needed. Luckily a friendly voice answered the phone. 'Hello, Diane. Would you track down Mary and apologise for me? I'm not going to make it back in this afternoon ... Yes, everything's fine, just a spot of bother at Rachel's school ... Tell her I'm in all day tomorrow so we can meet whenever is convenient ... No, I don't need to speak to her now ... Oh, and Diane, out of interest could you let me know how many Post-its there are in one of those little packs?'

8

David had arrived back from the reunion, his journey having comprised of upbeat thoughts about his evening with Bridget interspersed with dark ones about events since Jane had left. His emotions were all over the place, a melange of anticipation, concern, rage, animosity, confusion and indecisiveness. Having parked his car, with the children still at friends, he decided on a walk to clear his head.

Everything around him was the same as ever – Isobel pushing the pram in a vain attempt to stop her baby crying, Lawrence washing his BMW, Mrs Grant nurturing her flowers and plants with care beyond the call of duty.

'Good morning, Mr Willoughby. All good today?' asked Stanley Entwhistle at the newsagents.

'Yes. Wonderful.'

David put the Sunday Times on the counter and took out his card.

'No Mail on Sunday?'

Was Stanley digging for gossip? Surely the Jane and Jim news had got around by now.

'I won't be buying it anymore,' David announced

as he scanned his card, leaving the newsagent to consider the implications.

Plunged into lethargy, David abandoned the idea of an invigorating walk and headed home.

This Sunday turned out to be identical to previous post-Jane ones with the remaining three family members doing little more than hanging around waiting for the new week to begin.

Back at work on the Monday, David was pleased to be tackling departmental finances without interruption. The uncomfortable sessions with Mary had come to an end; she had left him to get on with it. He instructed his team to devise new rules, codes of conduct, terms and conditions, information booklets and application forms. At the regular Monday morning meeting a committed colleague expressed concern that the complexity of applying for financial support would result in people giving up.

'While this might address the problem of over-budgeted expenditure,' the woman declared, 'the outcome is going to be hardship for many families.'

She was right and David was struggling to fight a hopefully temporary lack of interest.

Lunchtimes were always enjoyable in Jabulani's company. Having pointed out yet another gloomy and overcast day from the office window, his friend read out an extract from Bill Bryson's *Notes from a Small Island*, the part where the author describes being in England feeling like life inside a Tupperware box.

'When I first read this I thought it was funny. Now I know it's true.'

Jabulani spoke of the sunshine and heat in Zimbabwe with such passion that David could feel the warmth and the energy it instilled. The conversation gave him renewed enthusiasm to tackle the challenging afternoon tasks.

Rachel had rejoined *Fiddler on the Roof* so David collected her after the rehearsal. 'Go well today?' he asked.

'Rubbish.'

'Why?'

'The director's making the musical into a comedy. A whole community is being persecuted and that idiot is going for cheap laughs. It's like a pantomime.'

'He's your drama teacher, isn't he?'

'Yes.'

'Well, he does have experience of what works. Maybe you should go with the flow.'

'He's wrong. I'm right.'

The journey was completed in sullen silence. Rachel announced she was going for a walk and David watched her extract a cigarette from her school bag as soon as she was a short distance away from the house.

Indoors, David picked up the post from the hall floor and tore open the letter from Rachel's headteacher with trepidation. Since the meeting at her school David had been unable to get Rachel to talk about progress beyond a perfunctory statement that everything was fine.

> *Dear Mr Willoughby*
> *I am pleased to report that there has*

been a substantial improvement in Rachel's attitude and performance over recent weeks. The action plan she presented to me was realistic and well thought out and she has tackled the points listed with gusto.

In particular she has worked hard in those subjects that in the past she has shown little interest in. Grades for Biology and French have risen significantly. Teachers are now able to report on the Rachel of old, a polite and well-mannered girl. Having returned to the cast of the school play, much to my staff's amusement she is heard humming 'If I Were a Rich Man' with an engaging smile as she walks along the corridors. Another song too by all accounts, the pop group Queen's hit 'We are the Champions'.

Thank you for your involvement. Let us hope that she maintains this progress. Do tell her that we are delighted to note the upturn.

Yours sincerely
John Edwards
Headmaster

David breathed a sigh of relief – one worry was out of the way though perhaps it was time for the humming to cease. Behaviour at home had improved, too. Jane's name could now be spoken without the associated swearing and according to Sam, daughter and mother had spoken a couple of times.

Over dinner David announced the arrival of the letter and congratulated Rachel for the improvement. There was the teenage dismissive response to the praise.

Mealtime wasn't a success though, starting with Sam's reaction to what he saw as another culinary failure.

'Eat up, Sam, you like fish and chips,' David urged on seeing his son looking down at the plate, his knife and fork stationary on the table.

'But what is this?' Sam asked.

'What do you mean what is it?'

'It's fish, you idiot.' This from Rachel.

'I mean what type of fish?'

'Sea bass.' This from David.

'But I only like fish with breadcrumbs. Cod, I like cod.'

'Stop being so bloody fussy.' This from Rachel.

'I thought it would be nice to try something different.' This from David.

'OK, I'll try it.'

'Thank you. I'll get cod next time. What about you, Rachel? You've hardly touched yours either.'

'I don't want everyone to think I'm fat on stage.'

'They won't have to think it, they'll see it.' This from Sam.

'Shut your face.'

'Of course you aren't fat.' This from David.

'Yes she is.' Sam again.

'Get lost, you fucker.'

'Rachel, please! Could we be nice to each other?'

The pair of them picked at their food, the moving of chairs as they got up breaking the silence.

'Wait a sec, Rachel,' David said.

'Why?'

'Because I want to say something.'

Rachel sat with her arms folded, impatient, in anticipation of a telling off.

'You know in the car you said that you were right and the drama teacher was wrong ...'

'Yes?'

'I've been thinking about that. Sometimes in life you have to do what you're told even if you don't agree.'

'Why?'

'Because that's the way it works, the world is what it is, not what you'd like it to be.'

'That's pathetic. What about people like Nelson Mandela and Martin Luther King? Or Bill Gates and Mark Zuckerberg. They challenged, they changed things.'

'So did Hitler and Attila the Hun,' David added, regretting the foolish put down as he spoke.

Rather than ridiculing his choices, Rachel was prepared to out-debate her father. 'Of course there have been evil people but the world is a better place now than ever before. On balance the people who have set out to change things have done more good than bad.'

Checkmate.

It was evident Rachel knew she had won hands down. 'Good discussion, Dad. Thanks,' she said with the tone of the victor. She stood up. 'I'd like to carry on, but I must do homework so I can earn another letter from the head.'

With both children upstairs, David disposed of the high volume of leftovers, cleared the table and loaded the dishwasher. Bridget had been on his mind and now he was imagining her in the kitchen with him, sharing a bottle of wine, chatting as he tidied up. All good clean fun until the fantasy about removing each other's clothes and making love on the kitchen table.

Apart from going to the reunion he'd done nothing to kickstart life without Jane. There were reasons for inactivity – the shopping, the cooking, the planning of meals, the cleaning, the chauffeuring, the disciplining of the children, the supporting of the children – but how much were these self-imposed barriers? There were times when both Rachel and Sam were out, including at sleepovers with friends, when he could have been doing something for himself.

Bridget. Was it too soon to call her?

As he carried the saucepans from the draining board to the cupboard he glanced at the letter from Rachel's headteacher, now smeared with a line of tomato ketchup. Her improvement had been guided by an action plan so perhaps that was what *he* needed.

A plan to change his world! A silly idea but with time to kill and nothing better to do he would develop something for the fun of it. A plan with SMART objectives. Ready to go with paper and pen he decided that while the S, M, A and R were of value, he had doubts about being precise with the T for Time. Rather than be exact he would subdivide actions into short term, to be accomplished within the next month or so, and long term for everything else.

He put on a Clannad CD.

Short-term objective number one was easy. He had yet to tell his mother about the separation from Jane. He wanted to inform her face-to-face rather than over the phone. Rachel and Sam had stuck to their promise not to mention it and when he was speaking to her, in answer to her customary "How are things with you?", he responded with the bland "Everything's absolutely fine." He would visit her one Saturday soon to break the news.

Number two was about Jabulani. David's work colleague had come to the UK from Zimbabwe approaching a year ago. Although a qualified accountant he couldn't get employment to match his experience – his job at the local authority was low-level and poorly paid. They had developed a strong bond and met regularly for lunchtime chats. Jabulani knew more about English history and culture than David did, right down to the names and locations of the major London stores. He had a particular obsession with Harrods. With Jabulani's birthday approaching, David would take him for tea at the Ladurée Café one Saturday afternoon within the next month or so.

Jane had made it clear that she wanted a quick divorce. She intended to marry Jim as soon as possible which did make David wonder how long their clandestine relationship had been going on. In an email arriving one evening the previous week she had stated her target of a divorce by the end of the year. The following day he had received a letter from her solicitor suggesting that as a first step a financial settlement could be tackled henceforth. David decided to go along with Jane's wish – what would be the point of stalling? Getting started was made a short term objective even though completion might take some while.

Next he turned his attention to Bridget. He really should be concentrating on her – she should be right at the top of the list. He knew what was needed, a call to ask if she'd like to meet again. It was impossible to predict the outcome, perhaps a no thanks, perhaps the start of a wonderful new relationship. A no was the more likely, David reckoned. Or in some ways even worse: "I do like you but only as a friend".

The Clannad CD had ended and it was approaching ten o'clock. David considered this a good time to stop with the short-term objectives completed.

1. *Inform mother about separation*
2. *Take Jabulani to Harrods for tea*
3. *Start process to obtain an amicable divorce from Jane*
4. *Call Bridget to arrange a meet up*

Self-mockery surfaced as David read over what he had written. It had taken an hour to put down a mere twenty-six words. In terms of priority, number four should have come first but he'd listed it last. Why?

Cowardice probably, fear of rejection. Was it too late in the evening to call Bridget? Possibly yes, and anyway he needed time to prepare what to say. But it wasn't too late to phone a long established night owl.

He dialled. 'Hello, Mother.'

'Who is it?'

This infuriating reply was the norm. She would have seen his name on the display, she would have recognised his voice, and no one other than her only son would be calling her "Mother".

'It's me. David.'

He knew more or less what would follow. 'David?' she said in a tone implying amazement. 'I was wondering when I'd be hearing from you again. I suppose you're much too busy to call an old lady. Mind you, I'm not complaining. How are things with you?'

He ignored the implicit accusation of neglect. 'Everything's absolutely fine. And you?' this the cue for another standard response.

'I suppose I mustn't complain. My bones are creaking but what can I expect now that it's getting so cold?'

She hardly ever left the house which she heated to oven temperature. He let the comment pass. 'I'd like to visit on Saturday if it's convenient.'

'Convenient? You know it is, it's not as if I have a social life. Are the children coming with you?'

'No, only me. Rachel's got a *Fiddler on the Roof* rehearsal and Sam's playing football.'

'I hardly ever get to see them now they're grown

up. No time for their old grandmother, more important things to do.'

'Mother, you saw them five weeks ago and they phoned last week.'

David was surprised but pleased that his mother hadn't asked whether Jane would be joining him; she'd soon be finding out why not. 'It's better without the kids because I need to talk to you about a couple of things.'

'Well, I'll see you when I see you then,' she said in the dour Brummie accent that David had tried hard to lose.

9

He set off early that Saturday, a pleasant morning with a golden autumn sun making the M1 a little less unattractive than usual. Almost the whole of the journey from home to his mother's house on the outskirts of Birmingham was along motorways, the M1 then the M6. It had always been a taxing drive owing to the high volume of traffic whatever time of day or night he travelled, but that day it didn't bother him in the least because he was happy, more than happy, ecstatic, following his Friday evening conversation with Bridget.

He'd been nervous dialling, but Bridget's greeting immediately made the conversation easy. She joked about the reunion before accepting his invitation to meet the following Wednesday evening after work for a drink. He was a teenager again, his heart racing as he asked her, then mumbling incoherently after she had accepted.

About halfway to his mother's house and so far so good as he sped past the Junction 14 Milton Keynes turnoff. Having listened to *From Our Own Correspondent* on Radio 4 he switched off, needing time to consider how best to tell his mother about the disintegration of his marriage. Being from the generation of female stay-at-homes whose lives were devoted to supporting their husbands and children, she would be furious that Jane had shattered the closely knit family.

David recollected the past enthusiastic greetings on their return from school. "Tea, dears?" were her first words.

His "Yes please, Mum" was swiftly followed by her bringing a pot of tea and plate of biscuits into the lounge. Charlotte rarely joined them, instead going straight up to her bedroom to blast out post-punk music. His sister thought he was the favoured child and resented it.

Mother and son would sit on the same two armchairs, she intent on extracting every detail about his school day, even the most minor of achievements. "You must tell your father, he'll be so proud of you," she would declare.

He could visualise the ashen-faced, swollen-eyed mother who met him at the front door on the day his father died. A policewoman was supporting her. As he stepped in she rushed up and squeezed him with extraordinary force.

'Daddy's dead,' she wailed. 'Daddy's dead,' over and over again. 'My poor Cyril.'

A heart attack at work. No warning and no second chance. Dead on arrival at hospital. David was seventeen and Charlotte two years older.

His mother struggled to cope and considerable

responsibility was placed on Charlotte's and his own young shoulders. Between tears she would reminisce about family times together. The same stories over and over again. Journeys to the seaside in their Ford Escort. Who would be the first to spot the sea as they reached the summit of the South Downs? Breaking into a refrain of *Oh I do like to be beside the seaside*. Striped windbreakers as protection from the harsh breeze. Thick, grey clouds filling the sky, obliterating the blue. A rapid gathering of possessions and a dash back to the car. Then the slow journey home, stretched out and exhausted, the two children asleep in the back seat. He was unsure which stories were genuine memories and which were family mythologies.

It was a strain supporting his mother and thirty years on, he remained guilty about how he had abdicated his responsibility when she was in need of his support. A matter of months after his father's death he left for university in faraway Exeter. "The Great Escape" Charlotte called it, bitterly resenting David for having dumped her with additional duties. She was still living at home, doing secretarial work at a local estate agent. From there she plotted her own getaway, achieved three years after their father's death when she married one of the managers.

It was many years later before the children found out that the official account of their father's death was untrue. One Christmas, an intoxicated uncle blurted out the lurid details to the full extended family. Their father was having an affair with a work colleague and had died astride her in her bedroom. His mother knew the truth all along of course because the emergency team had been called to the distraught woman's flat, but she had protected them from the facts. "I'll be home late, I'm rushed off my feet," their father had told his family on that ill-fated morning. On discovering the truth, upstairs in Charlotte's old bedroom, drunk and far removed from the tragedy of it all, they had laughed. "He was rushed off his feet well enough, but he didn't expect to be off his feet forever."

David had reached the Junction 18 exit to Daventry, only minutes from the M6 turnoff. He was making excellent progress.

His mother had been embroiled with bitterness after the death of her husband and once David had found out the truth he could understand why – family was everything and her husband had betrayed her. Bearing this in mind how would she react to Jane's infidelity? He would need to choose his words carefully.

David joined the M6. Even this horrendous motorway merging point was devoid of congestion.

He'd decided long ago that he didn't much like his mother, at least not the one who had emerged after his father's death. Since leaving home for university there had always been admonishment in her tone when he visited, the accusation of insufficient interest in her wellbeing. And the truth was that the more she behaved like that, the more he backed off.

Having reached Junction 4 at Lichfield he was met by the flashing lights of an overhead sign alerting drivers of a 50 mph speed restriction. This was superfluous because ahead there was a complete standstill. He braked sharply. He was ten miles from his destination and it was anybody's guess how long it would take.

Jane had known how to handle his mother, refusing to tolerate her behaviour.

'Are you sure it's not too much bother visiting me? Surely you haven't got the time,' his mother would ask Jane during a telephone call to suggest a visit.

'Come to think of it, we are busy this weekend. That's very understanding, Glenda. Let's postpone until sometime next month.'

The tactic worked, his mother wary of a negative end result when speaking to Jane.

The traffic was moving again and David edged past a stationary lorry on the middle lane with its warning lights flashing. At university there had been a lecture explaining why there could be severe traffic congestion even without any accident. It was something to do with declining rates of acceleration he recalled, partial differentiation was needed for the calculation. He cast his mind back to the manic lecturer with wild ginger hair and thick black glasses writing formulae at great speed on a wide blackboard. In the uni bar students had imitated his high-pitched, squeaky voice. David tried to remember how to partially differentiate but the maths was way beyond him now.

Once past the lorry the congestion ceased and he was turning off the motorway for the final short stretch of the journey. A flutter of nervousness rose in his stomach as he pulled into the street with its two rows of solid Edwardian houses. Stepping out of the car he picked up the bunch of dusty pink roses he'd bought at the garage.

There was an audible shuffling towards the front door before it was opened. 'Hello, Mother, some flowers,' David said with an encouraging smile as he held them out in front of him.

She frowned as she took hold of them. 'Flowers, what am I going to do with them? You needn't have bothered.'

Here we go again, David thought. He contemplated snatching them back but instead maintained his attempt at warmth. 'They're to cheer you up. Let's get a vase.'

'No need to cheer me up, I'm not miserable,' she snapped grumpily. Together they walked into the kitchen and then descended into a time warp from his school days.

'Tea, dear?'

'Yes please, Mum.'

'Well, you go into the lounge and I'll bring it in.'

The two armchairs of thirty years ago were gone, replaced by near-clones – high, wing-backed sage green Dralon monstrosities with little squares of matching fabric over the arms. He peered round the room. The sideboard was crammed with pictures of him and Charlotte as children and as adults with their families. Unframed and leaning against an empty cut glass vase was a copy of the photo from his holiday in

Brittany, the one pinned to his fridge. Jane, Rachel and Sam with him – all smiles. His mother entered carrying a tray with matching Royal Albert china teapot, milk jug, two cups and saucers and a plate of biscuits.

She noticed him looking at the photograph. 'Lovely photo that.'

'Mother, I have to tell you something.'

'If it's about Jane leaving you, David, I already know.'

'How do you know?'

'Jane telephoned to tell me. The poor dear, she's finding it all rather difficult to cope with.'

'She's finding it difficult! What about me? Don't forget it was she who –'

'I know what you're going to say, but it takes two to tango. She's a lovely girl and I can understand how she feels.'

'You what!'

'No doubt she has her reasons. Let's face it, you aren't the easiest person to live with.'

David was flabbergasted, speechless. After how her own husband had betrayed her she should be furious with Jane. Snatching a digestive biscuit he shovelled it in, his mouth so dry he was unable to swallow the fragments.

He stood up. 'Wug a munnet.'

'What?'

'Wat-a-minnet'

'Don't speak with your mouth full. I've been telling you that since you were a little boy. Why don't you listen?'

'Wait a minute!' he managed to enunciate, crumbs showering out in front of him.

In the bathroom he spat out the remains into the sink, cupped his hand to collect some water and washed down the residue. With both hands he gathered more water and threw it against his face. He looked in the mirror. His face was red from choking and with rage. He took deep breaths before returning to the lounge where his mother was calmly pouring tea.

Looking up, she smiled. Why? She never smiled! 'Perhaps Jane leaving will give you the opportunity to make something of your life. You can start afresh.'

Thoughts about how to respond raced through his mind.

Do you realise that raising the children has been left to me?

Actually, Mother, I do have an action plan – I'm seeing a wonderful woman on Wednesday.

You're a fine one to talk, you've had years and years to make a fresh start since the death of your two-timing husband and you've done bugger all.

But he said none of these things and the conversation turned to small talk about Rachel and Sam, Charlotte and her family, Mr and Mrs Andrews, her next door neighbours to the left, and Mr and Mrs Gupta, the new neighbours to her right.

Forty-two minutes on, with a lull in the conversation, he stood and announced his departure.

'That's a short visit. No doubt you've got more

important things to do than sit and chat with your mother.'

He was close to saying "Yes, much more important" but instead reverted to one of his old faithfuls.

'I need to get back to collect Sam.'

On the long, lonely journey home he calmed down listening to Freya Ridings, Oh Wonder and London Grammar.

10

It took ages for Wednesday – the first day of his new life – to arrive.

Before setting off for the rendezvous with Bridget, David scrutinised his twenty-six word short-term objectives list, unnecessarily so because he now knew it off by heart.

1. *Inform mother about separation*
2. *Take Jabulani to Harrods for tea*
3. *Start process to obtain an amicable divorce from Jane*
4. *Call Bridget to arrange a meet up*

He had made a promising start. APSTO1 (action plan short-term objective one) achieved and APSTO4 exceeding all expectations, Bridget having accepted his invitation.

Arriving early, David sat at a scuffed table near the entrance inside The Greyhound, anxiously running his hand over the initials crudely carved into the dark wooden surface. The pub appeared to be a popular after-work venue, packed with predominantly male youngsters talking loudly, laughing and swigging from bottles of lager. Music videos blared out from two giant wall-mounted TV screens. Whispering sweet nothings to Bridget would not be easy.

Despite the excitement of the imminent meeting, he was struggling to dismiss the negativity brought on by another awful day at work. Mary wasn't giving him time to implement the strategies to cut costs agreed during their recent sessions. She was blaming him for insufficient control of his subordinates having previously instructed David to give them more responsibility. He'd arrived that morning all set to push on, but as soon as he'd settled down with a mug of coffee and a chocolate biscuit she'd stormed in demanding that the matter be resolved immediately.

'What matter?' he'd asked.

'You don't even know, do you?'

'Know what?'

'The Head of Finance has published a league table and our department is bottom in terms of deviance from budget.'

She let him know that she was free all evening and expected him to stay on with her to develop a cost-cutting strategy. However long it took.

There was no way he was going to cancel Bridget. 'Sorry, not possible. A family commitment.'

'Perhaps it's time for you to set your priorities.'

(That's what I've done. Get lost, Mary.)

He'd left work on the dot of five, rushing home to prepare for this life-changing liaison, and now, sitting in the pub with minutes to go before the time set to meet Bridget, David was practising his greeting smile. Abruptly he stopped on noticing a group at the bar pointing and laughing at him. He transformed his smile into an expression of deep thought, resting his elbow on the table and placing his clenched fist against his forehead in a Socratic pose. He let out a long, audible sigh.

'David, are you all right?'

Bugger, it was Bridget standing by his side staring down at him with a look of concern.

'Hello. I'm fine, just a hard day at work,' he said as he reversed the facial contortions back towards the awkward welcoming smile.

She remained standing with David all too aware that he had missed providing any customary civil greeting like standing up, shaking hands, hugging, cheek-kissing or whatever.

'What would you like to drink?' he blurted out.

'I'll have a –'

'No, not here though!'

'Oh.'

'It's too loud. Not that I have a problem with loudness, but if we want to talk it won't be possible.'

'Well, I imagine we would want to talk so somewhere else is fine. Any ideas where?'

David reddened with embarrassment. He had planned to start their meeting with easy-going charm. He'd failed.

'There's a coffee bar a couple of doors away. Unless you're desperate for alcohol.'

This was intended as a joke; it wasn't received as such. 'I'm not desperate, coffee's fine.'

'I wasn't implying you had an alcohol problem,

I…I…'

'Shall we go then?'

The café was quiet with a winding-down-at-the-end-of-the-day feel.

'Here we are,' he declared, setting down a latte and a double espresso. 'I hope you don't mind this place. Actually, their coffee isn't bad even though the ambiance isn't up to much.'

'What makes a place feel right?'

'Not being one of a chain for starters. I like individually owned quirky cafes, interesting places with things to see or listen to.'

'I agree. At any rate, this coffee's fine.'

The conversation turned to the drama of raising teenagers. David opened up about how things had changed now that Jane had left. Bridget admitted that having to set off to work before hers departed for school was something she worried about.

'What work do you do?'

'Sales in a gallery for mid-priced contemporary art.'

'How much is mid-priced?'

'Usually between £20,000 and £50,000.'

David's gasp was audible and Bridget smiled her beautiful smile. 'And all I get is a measly salary of not much more than the cheapest painting I sell. Actually, a bonus too, so I shouldn't grumble.'

Bridget outlined how she'd ended up at the gallery. At college while studying History of Art she met her husband, Roland, a sculptor who even as a student was acquiring a considerable reputation. His work was taken on by a dealer in Old Bond Street who at the time was recruiting an additional member of staff. With no career plan in place Bridget took the job, useful because she was able to work flexible hours when the children were young.

'And when my husband died I stayed on.'

'Died! I'm so sorry to hear that; how awful.'

'I suppose it was.'

David was unsure what Bridget meant by that comment. Perhaps the passage of time had diminished the pain. 'How long ago did he die?'

'About five years.'

'May I ask what happened?'

'An accident, but I'd rather not talk about it. Perhaps another time.'

'Of course, I understand,' David said with a degree of sincerity but with the hope that she wasn't in a sorrowful state of permanent mourning like Queen Victoria was after Prince Albert died. It might have been better for his chances if they had separated. At least she wasn't married, though there could be a new partner. He had to find out but further questioning would need tact and sensitivity. 'And what's transpired since then?'

'In what way?'

'Have you found a replacement?'

She smiled. 'You make it sound like I'm on the lookout for a new plumber or electrician. But I suppose I know what you're getting at. Well I've had the odd fling, some of them very odd, but nothing serious.'

'Good.'

'What's good?'

David shuddered having hardly recovered from the mess up at the start of their meeting and now this. "Good" was about his chances of a relationship so what could he say?

'I mean it's good of you to tell me a little bit about yourself because last time we met it was all about me.'

Over another coffee in the now deserted venue they discovered a shared interest in the arts, finally moving on to non-mainstream cinema classics.

'And then there's *Fried Green Tomatoes at The Whistle Stop Café,*' Bridget enthused.

David had disengaged, his focus being on how to engineer another meeting. With the pause in conversation Bridget glanced at her watch. 'Gosh, I didn't realise the time. I'm going to have to go, I promised the kids I wouldn't be home late.'

She had pushed her chair back ready to stand up. David had to think fast. A film, a concert, a visit to an art gallery? He was struck by inspiration. 'Bridget, Thursday week is Guy Fawkes and we're going to have a few fireworks at home. Would you and your children like to join us?'

'We usually go to the big event in the park.'

'I've been trying to get my lot to do that for years, but they won't have it. They insist on a small display at home. We get snacky food in like sausages. Why not join us for that, too?'

'We're all vegetarians.'

'Then we can eat snacky veggie things. My kids

will be just as happy.'

Now standing, Bridget looked down at him, noticeably paused, then nodded. 'OK, I'd love to.'

David gave details of address and starting time and they parted with a firm hug, though without the kisses he had hoped for.

~

The following day after work David announced the Guy Fawkes plan to Rachel and Sam.

'But Dad, we go to the big event in the park,' Sam complained.

'I know but this once we're going to have to do it at home. Bridget's children prefer a quieter fireworks display.'

'How can you have a quiet fireworks display? What's the matter with them?' Rachel mocked.

'Scared of big rockets and all the other people,' Sam added.

'No need to be like that. Be friendly, that's all I ask.'

At the dinner table the jokes continued.

'I've got a great idea Dad, we can get mini sparklers for those kids,' Rachel started.

Sam joined in. 'Yeah, but we'll need to provide extra thick gloves so they can hold them safely.'

David cleared away the half-eaten plates of ravioli. Rachel had opened up every parcel in search of tomato and Sam had cut the edges off each envelope in the same way he removed the crusts from slices of bread. Once he'd done that there wasn't much left to eat. David was running out of ideas for meals – should he insert a cookery course onto a long term action plan if he ever bothered to write one?

Rachel reappeared and helped him stack the dishwasher. 'How was Grandma when you told her that Mum had left us?'

'She already knew, Mum told her.'

'But what did she think?'

'Well, I wasn't happy because she insinuated that it had to be as much my fault as hers.'

'Ridiculous.' Rachel ran hot water over a cloth, squeezed it and began to wipe the table. 'So, you're going to divorce Mum?'

'That's what she wants and I can't see any point fighting it. She and Jim are going to get married.'

Rachel, her back to him, was wiping the work surfaces. 'Do you like this Bridget? Are you going out with her?'

'We've only just met. She's nice though.'

David had never seen such a display of cleaning from his daughter, now on her hands and knees sweeping the floor with a brush and pan. 'You will let me know if things develop, won't you?'

'You'll be meeting her next week.'

'And who is Jabulani?'

'Rachel, you've been reading my stuff!'

'You read *my* action plan so why shouldn't I read yours? Anyway, if it's secret don't leave it lying around.'

She smiled and planted a kiss on his cheek.

'I can't wait to read your long term plan.'

11

David discovered his sheet of paper on the coffee table in the lounge next to his mobile. He must have left it there when he'd called Bridget so Rachel could hardly be accused of high level espionage. She had teased him about long term plans and true enough, the heading was there with nothing written underneath it.

Aware of the banality of what was so far written, coupled with the embarrassment of Rachel having seen it, he nevertheless decided to push ahead. At the very least the exercise would provide a time-killer ahead of *News at Ten.*

The first objective was easy because he'd decided on it at dinner time.

1. Take a cookery course

Now he was stuck, staring at the sheet with the single item, clueless what next to add.

He made a cup of tea. He took out the rubbish. He emptied the washing machine. He hung the clothes on the drier. He took the sausages for tomorrow's dinner out the freezer and put them in the fridge.

None of these activities was providing inspiration. Was that single item the sum of his longer term ambition?

Ambition. Career. He thought of work and realised that being line managed by Mary had intensified his discontent. The job was tolerable with a guaranteed good pension, but in his mid-forties surely a good pension shouldn't be the sole reason for staying put.

2. Quit my job

It wasn't just the job, it was the occupation he'd had enough of. He added: *and pack in accountancy*.

What other work was possible? How bold could the list be because something had been on his mind for ages and he was tempted to put it down.

A café, an arts café like some he'd visited during holidays. He would be his own boss, getting away from sitting in front of a computer screen all day, able to meet new people, to create a high street hub that he could be proud of.

3. Open an arts café

Only fifteen words so far (heading excluded) but such dramatic ones. If only!

Long term
1. Take a cookery course
2. Quit my job and pack in accountancy
3. Open an arts café

This unexpectedly courageous approach to list-writing got his pulse racing as he considered The Bridget Statement.

Infatuation had set in big time and he couldn't stop thinking about her, lustfully at night and slightly less lustfully during daytimes. On any other evening he might happily have written something like "Develop a loving and long-lasting relationship with Bridget", but now, light-headed and filled with bravado, he opted for a rather more direct statement.

4.   Have sex with Bridget.

The frivolity brought a smile as he noted that he was on the way to making this a SMART objective. What he had written was Specific, Measurable, Attainable (hopefully) and Relevant. All that was missing was Time. He randomly picked his birthday.

4.   Have sex with Bridget by February 20ᵗʰ

Now in full happy-go-lucky mode he added a number five for good measure.

5.   Have more sex with Bridget by the first week of March

This sheet of paper must not be discovered by Rachel. He folded it into a tight rectangle and placed it inside his brown coat pocket. He'd take it to work and leave it there, locked in his filing cabinet. Or better still, he'd word process and password protect the document and shred the hard copy.

~

A clear picture of his colleague Jabulani's background had emerged piece by piece as their friendship developed. He had been a senior accountant in Zimbabwe's Ministry of Agriculture and Rural Development. A true patriot, he was proud of his country's independence though dismayed by the government's policies. With economic mismanagement came hyperinflation, unemployment and food shortages, the difficulties entrenched irrespective of who was in charge. As a result of joining a peaceful opposition coalition he lost his job in the ministry and his wife, Jestina, lost hers as a teacher. It was still worse for his brother, Farai, taken in by the police, questioned and beaten.

Farai decided to stay and fight on, Jabulani was advised by a friend who worked at the Ministry of State Security that it would be best for him to leave. On arrival in England the family were amongst the few lucky ones to be granted asylum seeker status.

It was a harrowing story but Jabulani's optimism and humour shone through in the telling of it.

'My application interviews,' he explained to David. 'We laughed so much. I knew more about Britain than the immigration officials did – I could name the entire touring English cricket team; I could tell them which Ealing Comedies I liked the best.'

He reckoned his knowledge of and passion for all things British helped him to qualify but his optimism about starting a new life was somewhat dampened by the struggle to find decent accommodation and a good job.

'I would not be proud to invite you to my home, David.'

'Where do you live?'

'Queensbury. Do you know it?'

'Vaguely, I've driven through once or twice.'

'I think the Queen would be embarrassed to have her name associated with the place if she ever drove through it.' Jabulani had a broad grin as he said this, his striking smile infectious and David laughed.

'I bet it's not cheap either.'

'It takes most of my salary to pay the rent so Jestina's income has to cover everything else.'

'She's a teacher, isn't she?'

'Yes, but she can't teach here, her Zimbabwean qualification doesn't count. She works as a learning mentor for refugees.'

'It all seems so unfair.'

'Perhaps. But on to more exciting things, that tea at the Ladurée café in Harrods.' He paused. 'David, I don't wish to take a liberty but would it be possible for my wife to join us on Saturday?'

'Of course she can, that would be lovely.'

'And do you think my children could come, too?'

'Why not? Bring everyone.'

This reply was greeted with another beaming smile. 'David Willoughby, you're a very good man, a very good man indeed.'

They arranged to meet outside Harrods at 3 p.m.

~

It was the last day of October. Autumn had well and truly arrived with a grey, chilling mist hanging over the city. Knightsbridge was bursting with affluent shoppers carrying designer label bags. The aged and infirm were in grave danger as insensitive shoppers pushed past in their race to the next shop. There was a steady flow of customers in and out of Harrods.

Having agreed to include the children, David had scrapped the idea of going to the rather sedate Ladurée café. The plan now was to take them to what he considered to be a more suitable choice, Café Godiva.

Jabulani emerged from the Underground station

exit, his wife by his side and four young children in an uneven line between them. The men shook hands and Jabulani presented his family.

'My wife, Jestina.' A handshake.

'My eldest, Chenzira.' A boy, about ten years old, extended his hand and David shook it.

The process was repeated as Maiba, Rufaro and Sekayi were introduced – there were two boys and two girls. Now that they were by his side, David could identify the children's matching fleeces with their red shield and gold cannon badges.

He must have looked aghast because Jabulani spoke with concern. 'What is it, my friend?'

'Oh, nothing.'

'But yes, something is bothering you.'

'The fleeces, they're Arsenal.'

'Yes, our team. The magic ones, they play the most beautiful football in the world.'

'I support Spurs.'

'Then may the Lord forgive you.'

David looked away from the badges to the faces, first the youngsters then up towards their father. Five identical broad smiles.

Having led them to Café Godiva inside the store, the children devoured chocolate drinks and chocolate cakes while the adults drank coffee and had bites of the children's choices. Conversation turned to the huge differences in lifestyle between London and Harare. The tales of considerable hardship were interspersed with laughter; being in the company of this optimistic, closely knit family was uplifting.

Having said their goodbyes, momentarily David was hit by a wave of despondency about the disintegration of his own family.

And then his attention turned to Bridgit's forthcoming visit.

12

Thursday November 5th. Guy Fawkes Night.

Bridget, Kay and Andy were due to arrive around five-thirty for snacks followed by the fireworks display. David planned to leave work early afternoon to pop into Waitrose to get the food. He'd decided it was only fair for his family to avoid meat and had used part of the morning to search online for appetising ready-made veggie choices.

There was loads to choose from. His list included french bread, couscous, marinated tofu, hummus, various cheeses (make sure vegetarian ones), pitta bread, olives, dolmades, dried apricots, mixed nuts, tortilla crisps, salsa dip, fruit, ice cream and yoghurt. That was probably enough but if something took his fancy when in the supermarket he could always add it.

A little after one o'clock, just as he was completing a final task before leaving the office, his phone rang. Diane transferred the call from a teacher at Sam's school. There had been an accident, nothing serious, but Sam was in A&E having his leg checked over.

David's first thought was of the effect this might have on Bridget's visit, concern for Sam in guilt-ridden second place. Well, the teacher had said it was nothing serious.

'I'm going to have to dash,' he told Diane having explained the situation.

'I hope he's alright,' she called out as David strode into the foyer.

'Thanks,' he acknowledged as he glanced back towards her, unaware that Mary was about to pass him. She managed to keep her balance as they collided but the coffee she was carrying tipped over her tailored brown jacket.

'Look where you're going for God's sake.'

'Sorry. At least it's brown.'

'At least what's brown?'

'Your jacket. When it dries you probably won't see a mark.'

She glared at him.

'It was a joke. Don't worry, I'll pay for the dry cleaning. It was entirely my fault.'

'Yes, it was.'

'I've already said it was.'

Her look remained ferocious but David was learning how to cope with her tirades and returned an expression of defiance.

'Where are you going?' she asked. 'I have some cases to work through with you.'

'Sorry, can't now, Mary. My son is in A&E.'

David didn't hang around to see or hear a reaction.

~

He drove to the hospital deep in thought. Would that evening's rendezvous be able to take place irrespective of Sam's condition? I am a dreadful parent, crossed his mind.

On arrival at A&E he spotted Sam in his shiny navy blue track suit with one trainer on, the other foot bare. A teacher was by his side. Both were reading tattered *Top Gear* magazines.

'Hi, Dad.'

'Hi, Sam.'

The teacher stood up. 'Thank you for getting here so quickly, Mr Willoughby. He was playing football and fell heavily. As you can see, his leg has swelled up quite a bit. We put an ice pack on but thought it best to come here.'

'My leg's got bigger, too.' Sam said as he pulled up his trouser leg.

'What did the doctor say?'

The teacher took over. 'A nurse has had a preliminary look but we're still waiting for a doctor. Apparently it's unusually busy.'

More like as usual busy David thought. 'Well I'm here so there's no need for you to stay, Mr …'

'Barnes, Noel Barnes.'

'You might as well head off, Noel. Thanks for bringing him.'

'Yes. Thank you, sir,' Sam added.

'I will go then if that's all right. Good luck, Sam, hope to see you back in school tomorrow.'

It was another hour before the X-ray was taken and a further hour before being seen by an enthusiastic, moon-faced doctor who looked far too young to be a medic. Fortunately, there was no break, just a bad

103

sprain, necessitating another wait until a nurse applied a bandage. David was on edge; it was getting nearer and nearer to Bridget's arrival time.

They reached home gone five. There would be no time to get food, let alone prepare it, before Bridget arrived.

When the doorbell chimed on the dot of 5.30, David was raking through the kitchen cupboards in the vain hope that Jane, an ardent carnivore, had left behind a hidden supply of vegetarian delights. A tin of baked beans and a packet of frozen chips was all he could find.

'Can someone open the door?' he called out, intent on cramming everything back onto the shelves before Bridget reached the kitchen.

Sam couldn't; he was sitting on the sofa in the lounge with his left leg propped up watching TV. Rachel wouldn't; she was in her bedroom listening to Justin Bieber while doing homework.

Leaving the kitchen in a mess he rushed to the hall to let them in, calling up to Rachel to join them. She sauntered downstairs, her greeting ice cold. They trooped into the lounge to meet Sam who was cheerful enough as he explained what had happened. *Pointless* was on and David suggested the children watched TV while he and Bridget went to the kitchen to sort out the food.

'The trouble is,' he informed her as soon as they were alone, 'there isn't any.'

Observing this beautiful woman it struck him that just like the previous occasion, he had by-passed any attempt at a normal greeting. No handshake. No hug. No cheek-kissing.

Bridget either didn't notice, didn't care, or was good at hiding her feelings. 'Not a problem. You've had a hectic time. Stay here with the kids and I'll get the food.'

'But I'm meant to be the host.'

'Well you didn't reckon on Sam's accident. It's no big deal, I saw a Waitrose round the corner, I'll pop in there.'

'If you're sure you don't mind. I'll get my card.'

'No need. You got the fireworks so it's only fair I pay for the food.'

She was making her way to the front door before he could protest. Mind you, it did seem a logical solution. For starters, she would know what the best veggie options were. Would her choices be the same as his guesses?

He called after her as she stood by the front door. 'I made a list, it's in my coat pocket on the coat rack. The brown one.'

Bridget took the sheet of paper from his coat and dropped it into her handbag. 'Got it. Tell Andy and Kay I'll be back in a few minutes if they bother asking.'

David went into the lounge where stony faces and silence prevailed except for Lisa's saxophone playing at the start of *The Simpsons*. 'Bridget's popped out for food,' he informed them.

'What's she getting?' Sam asked.

'I'm not sure. I suppose things like hummus,

couscous, pitta bread.'

Rachel reddened. 'I hate all that muck. Why can't we have proper food?'

'What do you mean by proper food?' the until now silent Andy asked.

'Stuff that tastes good and has lots of protein.'

'And you're the expert, are you?'

'Yes I am. I know what's good and what tastes like shit.'

'OK brainy, define what's good.'

If looks could kill Andy was close to death as Rachel growled, 'Meat of course – sausages, bacon, ham, chicken, pork. Anything except bloody veggie stuff.'

Andy held his ground. 'Well isn't that a healthy diet. Before you know it you'll be as fat as the pigs you eat. And riddled with cancer, too.'

Rachel stood up. 'Fuck you, veggie boy,' she muttered as she exited.

David's role, looking after the kids, wasn't going well. He hoped Bridget would soon be back. It was Kay who took on the role of peace maker, breaking the icy silence by chatting to Sam about his leg. She had her mother's pretty features, high cheekbones, blue eyes, light brown wavy hair. It would be hard to identify Andy as being from the same family. He was tall and gangly with a narrow face, piercing eyes and longish jet black hair that was wild and uncontrollably curly.

The crisis seemed over as the three youngsters chatted away about favourite TV programmes, civility at least until Rachel reappeared.

The doorbell rang and Bridget came in balancing cardboard boxes of pizzas in one hand and three plastic bags in the other.

'Here, let me help.' David took hold of the pizzas and they went into the kitchen, followed by Kay and Andy with Sam limping after them.

Rachel rejoined the group as the boxes were being opened. 'I thought I could smell pizzas. What happened to the Greek muck?'

'I reckoned you'd all prefer pizzas,' Bridget said brightly. 'There's a roasted veg and a margarita for us, which you can share of course, and I've got one ham and one pepperoni for you lot. The crisps and Cokes are in the bags.'

She had gained a giant brownie point.

'*The Simpsons* is on pause. Can we finish watching it before the fireworks?' Sam asked after they had finished eating.

'I'm OK with that – I'll do a quick clear up and we can get started in about half an hour.'

'Fine by me, too. Let me help you.'

It was like a blissful domestic scene as David and Bridget disposed of the empty cartons, loaded the dishwasher and drank a glass of wine while the four children watched TV.

'That was a big hit,' David said. 'An inspiration to ignore my list.'

'I'm not sure I took the right piece of paper,' Bridget replied with an expression of absolute serenity. She opened her bag and handed David his action plan, not altering her demeanour as David blushed more than he ever imagined would be possible.

Running away was the only option. 'I'll check the fireworks,' he mumbled. Bridget was left standing alone in the kitchen as David fled out the back door and into the garden. Inside the shed where the fireworks were stored he considered not stepping out until the visitors had departed, but there was no choice because the audience had assembled.

'Can I light the first one, Dad?' Sam asked. He'd put a plastic bag over his slippered foot.

'OK, as long as you're careful. Which one do you want?'

'A rocket, of course.'

David picked one up in the shed and carried it out with the empty wine bottle and box of extra-long matches. Kay stood next to Sam as he placed the rocket inside the bottle, lit the match and held it against the twist of paper until it caught.

'Quick. Run!' he called out to Kay as he hobbled towards the others.

In her rush to escape, Kay's foot clipped the bottle which fell to the ground. The resting place couldn't have been more accurate if she'd tried. The rocket took off at a shallow angle and with a piercing whistle and sparkles of red and green light, shot straight through the open shed door before bouncing around in a vain attempt to escape the confines of the building. There was a brief pause before the rat-tat-tat of bangers. Then the whole shed was illuminated by a shower of pastel pink sparks as a fountain ignited.

This happened in seconds, enough time for David to consider a range of possible remedial actions but insufficient time for him to implement any of them. With all now quiet he edged towards the shed. Before he had taken more than a few steps there was an almighty explosion as the whole collection of rockets was set off. One flew through a window with an almighty crash, sending a shower of glass onto the lawn. Another shot out the shed door, staying low as it drove on towards the spectators. They scattered to dodge the missile.

'Wick-ed!' Rachel yelled.

'This is so cool,' Andy added.

By now in addition to a cacophony of noise and an explosion of colour, the shed itself was alight.

'Have you got a hose, David?' Bridget called out.

'Yes, I do.'

'Should we get it?'

'Can't. It's in the shed.'

'What about buckets?'

'There are a couple in the kitchen, under the sink.'

Rachel and Andy ran in to collect them but their feeble attempts to throw water from too far a distance did little to diminish flames coming through the roof. The last fireworks to go were jumping jacks which scuttled out of the shed, bouncing along the lawn. A discussion ensued about whether to call the fire brigade, David deciding against it as the shed was well away from their own and their neighbours' houses so wouldn't spread to other buildings. They watched transfixed as the fire waned and the light dimmed.

'Well, that was the best fireworks display I've ever seen,' Andy exclaimed as they made their way indoors.

'Good, I'm glad you enjoyed it. I never much liked that shed anyway,' David said, making light of the incident but aware of an almighty problem that lay ahead.

13

David and Jane were sitting at the kitchen table looking out to the charred remains of the shed. It was Saturday.

'I still don't see why you had fireworks here. We always went to the park.'

'I thought it would be nice for the children to have a quieter event at home,' David suggested.

'But they like the crowds. And the noise,' Jane walked across to the fridge and took out a carton of milk. 'Since when have you been drinking this?'

'It's called milk, you've seen it before.'

'Not organic red top.'

'Less fat is healthier. And organic is safer.'

'Have you got a heart problem?'

'Absolutely not, I'm fine.'

David glanced at Jane. Did she look disappointed? He was uneasy about how she'd come in as if she owned the place, though admittedly she did own the half of the part not held by the mortgage company. She used her key without ringing the bell and with the merest of nods to acknowledge his presence, headed straight to the kitchen and switched on the coffee machine.

Sam had informed her about the shed fire and she was there to see the damage.

'It's a complete wreck, you must have had a hell of a lot of fireworks.'

'It is wooden, Jane.'

'*Was* wooden, David. What else was in it, apart from fireworks?'

'Just the usual stuff.' David was fighting off panic.

'If the insurance doesn't cover it you'll have to pay for a new one since you burnt it down. That's only fair.'

Jane tilted her head to catch the last dregs of cappuccino foam. There was a thin line of frothed milk above her upper lip. It made her appear less threatening, comical. She took hold of the cup. 'I think I'll take these, they're rather nice. You use mugs so I'm sure you don't mind.'

Opening the unit above the dishwasher, she removed the three remaining cups and saucers and set them down on the table before opening a base unit to get a plastic bag.

'The Times now,' she remarked as she wrapped a cup using the newspaper as yet unread on the kitchen table. Having carefully placed the cup in the bag she took hold of a saucer. 'Mail not good enough for you?'

'Never has been. I like a newspaper to have some news in it,' he sniped, uncomfortable as he watched her swan around in the kitchen, knowing where everything was kept. He would rearrange things as soon as she left.

'I didn't really come over to see the burnt shed. I'm here to collect some warmer clothes now that the weather's turning.'

This was it!

She moved towards the hall. 'Are the kids upstairs?'

'Jane.'

'Yes?'

'It was impossible to keep your clothes in our bedroom. The thought of them in the wardrobe near our – my – bed was desperately upsetting so I took them out and bagged them up ready for you to come over to collect.'

'Well, I'm here now so I'll take them though I would have preferred it if you'd left me to pack them, to make sure they were folded properly which I'm sure you haven't bothered to do. Never mind. Where are they?'

'You'll understand that I was pretty angry about what's happened.'

'Let's not go through that again. Where are they?'

'I didn't want them in the house so I left them outside. In the shed.'

There's often a moment of silence before an outburst. The calm before the storm. The streak of lightning before the clap of thunder. The release of the missile before the explosion on impact. The …

'You absolute bastard, David!' she shrieked. 'You absolute fucking tosshead bastard.'

'I didn't burn them on purpose.'

'You make me sick you pathetic moronic creep.'

Rachel was by the door. 'Well I rather like him.'

Jane spun round and managed to change tone. 'Rachel, dear, it's nice to see you. Do you know what your father's done? He's burned all my clothes.'

'Oh dear, how sad,' Rachel said with a broad grin.

'And I can see he's corrupted you. You haven't even tried to understand how I feel.'

'How's Uncle Jim, Mummy?' she asked, emphasising the last word with a childlike stress.

'He's fine, thank … you're being sarcastic, aren't you?'

'Of course not, my sweet considerate Mummy.'

Jane turned to face David. 'Every penny of damage you're going to pay for, and more for the stress you've given me.' She turned, ignoring Rachel as she stormed past her en route to the front door.

'Don't forget your cups and saucers, Jane,' David called out. He adopted a calm and pleasant tone, one that might be used if he were suggesting it would be prudent to take an umbrella on the off chance that it might rain. Lifting the bag, he lobbed it high in the air. It landed with an almighty crash on the wooden floor by her side.

Jane stormed out of the room, slamming the front door shut.

Rachel was still smiling. 'Good for you, Dad. This calls for a song. What shall we do, the Queen one or *Fiddler*?'

'I think I'll go for Queen please, Rachel.'

Sam had avoided the conflict, but now downstairs

he watched in wonder as the unlikely duet commenced.

~

Never mind Jane because there was the disaster with Bridget to reflect upon. She would want nothing more to do with him having read that his intention was to have sex with her by February 20th. What could he do? Call to apologise?

He was considering this option late afternoon when there was a knock on the front door.

It was Jim. 'David, we must speak.' David contemplated slamming the door in his face. 'Please let me in,' the rat implored.

Jim was in before David had a chance to decline the offer and was holding up a bottle of red wine. 'It's a Prince de Courthezon 2007. Rather special.' He strode on into the kitchen where he took out two large glasses from the unit to the right of the hob before opening the cutlery drawer to get the bottle opener.

He knows where things are, David realised. He's done this before with Jane.

David shuddered as he thought about their opportunities, perhaps last Easter when he and the children were in Birmingham with his mother. Jim invited him to sit down as if he were the host.

Jim. Such a good friend, always concerned about others, ever willing to offer advice or to help out in a crisis. Jim. Sincere and wise. The devious bastard.

The man was pouring out the wine. What did Jane see in him? Perhaps it was his soft blue penetrating eyes. David felt inferior to this tall and lean man looking down at him; he could appreciate Jane's choice.

'I think a glass of wine always helps break the ice at times like this,' Jim said as he lifted his and clinked it against David's glass which still rested on the table.

'Done this before then, have you?'

'What do you mean, David?'

'You said "at times like this". I was wondering whether you've made a habit of stealing other men's wives.'

'Don't be silly, Jane is very special. Unique. But never mind me. I want to know how you're feeling. Can I help in some way?'

'I don't need your help.'

'Having set fire to Jane's clothes suggests that perhaps you do.'

'That was an accident.'

'I'm sure it was, David.'

David explained what had happened, stressing that the incident took place during a visit by his new friend Bridget and her children which Jim didn't appear to pick up.

'Was smashing the cups and saucers an accident, too?'

Jim didn't respond favourably to David's comment about it being light-hearted fun.

'Jane was shocked. In retrospect, don't you think it was a terrible thing to do?'

'I've said all I want to say, it's time for you to go.' He lifted up the bottle. 'You can take this with you.'

'Let me warn you, your behaviour is going to make

things a lot easier for Jane's solicitor.'

'What do you mean?'

'Think about it.'

This was the final straw. David stood. 'Off you go, Jim.'

Jim stood. 'Have you understood my message, David?'

'Absolutely. I won't set fire to any more of Jane's clothes and I won't smash anything she thinks she can take without asking.' He looked him in the eye. 'You know where the front door is. If you don't mind you can show yourself out.'

'Very well.'

With Jim gone David began to rearrange things in the kitchen while considering whether there remained any chance of a relationship with Bridget.

14

David's deliberations about when to call Bridget and what to say turned out not to be needed because it was she who called him two days after the humiliating Guy Fawkes fiasco. Having established that he wasn't devastated about the shed burning down, Bridget thanked David for such high entertainment.

'My kids haven't stopped talking about it.'

The conversation turned to Jane's visit and by the time he was owning up to the destroyed clothes she was chuckling away. 'Why didn't you tell me they were in the shed?'

'I suppose I was worried you'd think I was a complete and utter idiot.'

'No, I wouldn't think that. The fire was an accident; you didn't deliberately burn them.'

'True enough though Jane intends to make me suffer for it. She's texted to let me know that having spoken to her solicitor she'll be making a claim for £5,000.'

'For clothes! You need to contest that.'

'And then there was something else.'

David described the cups and saucers incident.

'Bloody hell, you didn't.'

'I did. I was annoyed that she was taking things without any discussion.'

'So you decided to smash them!'

'Yes. No, not really. It wasn't planned, it just happened.'

'Burning clothes. Smashing plates. I'm beginning to wonder about you.'

'I…'

'I think I'm joking. Actually I called to see if you'd like to have dinner out. I'll be paying. I've just received a big bonus for the September sales so any objections to my offer will not be tolerated.'

'I'd love to.'

'I was wondering where we should go but the answer's obvious – Greek.'

'Why?'

'So you can practice your crockery smashing technique.'

'Ha-ha.'

'Actually they don't go in for that in the place I'm thinking of, but the food's great.'

~

They were sitting at a cosy alcove table in the Bouzoukia Restaurant in Muswell Hill. On the uneven white brick wall to their side was a giant poster of the Acropolis.

Conversation was flowing easily, interspersed with much laughter, possibly as a result of the bottle of retsina emptied at great speed while sharing a starter of the very foodstuffs David had planned to get for the

Guy Fawkes snack – hummus, goat's cheese, pitta bread, olives, tzatziki and dolmades.

'I wish there was a film of your plate-smashing episode.'

'Well, you won't believe this, but in addition to the claim for her clothes she's also claiming for the cost of the crockery. I've engaged a solicitor, it's too tricky to handle everything myself and I want the divorce sorted quickly.'

'Ah yes, that was one of the things on your famous list, wasn't it?'

David reddened, something he seemed to be doing rather a lot in front of her. Since his list hadn't been raised during the telephone conversation or the early stage of their meal together he was hoping that it was forgotten. Fat chance! 'Look, Bridget. That list …'

'Yes, David?'

'Nothing.' He paused. 'OK let me explain. I was just messing around when I wrote it. I had a few minutes to spare so I jotted down some daft things which I was all set to throw away because Rachel had seen my short term objectives and teased me which made me realise –'

'So everything you wrote down was daft, was it?'

'No, not …'

Torn between providing a serious statement or one of self-mockery, Bridget eliminated the need for either. 'Actually, I'm quite forgetful. Maybe I should write lists, too.'

He sensed that APLTO4 (action plan long term objective 4, the first Bridget one) had moved a step closer.

The waiter had brought their main courses. David was pushing a piece of lamb off his kebab while Bridget sliced her vegetable moussaka.

'Good to see you eating lamb again,' she noted.

'Yes, I think I'm much more at peace with what's happened.'

She took hold of his hand and gave it a gentle squeeze. 'I think you are, too.'

'Thanks, Bridget. Shall I order more wine?'

'Blimey, no, I'm already halfway under the table. We can get some for you though if you like.'

'Nope. I'm fine, too.'

There was a lull in the conversation. David plucked up the courage to ask. 'We always seem to be talking about me. I wish I knew more about you.'

'Sure. What?'

'Maybe this is an odd starting point, but you said your husband died in an accident. What happened?'

'I'm OK to talk about it if that's what you'd like. Let's get some coffees, maybe ouzo too.'

She called the waiter over and placed the order.

'I told you about how I ended up in the art gallery that exhibited his works.'

'Yes. I remember you saying that.'

'It was great at first, until Roland's sculptures stopped selling. I saw a different side of him then – resentful, depressed, using alcohol and drugs in an attempt to lift his mood. I was subjected to all that "No one understands me" stuff that people involved in the arts think they have the sole right to say. I tried to be supportive but he was taking his frustration out on me. To be honest, he became abusive. Cruel.'

She turned to what at first seemed unrelated, her love for her parents. Unfortunately, they played an indirect but important part in her husband's death. Sensing the tension between Bridget and Roland they suggested the pair took a break to sort things out, offering to pay for the holiday and look after the kids. Bridget accepted their kind offer and searched for the ideal place to inspire Roland to rediscover his creativity. Hopefully, to improve their relationship, too.

They flew to Inverness, hired a car, and drove to a remote cottage at Fanagmore in the far north-west of Scotland. It was a beautiful place right by the sea with stunning cliffs. There wasn't a shop for miles around, the nearest a general store eleven miles away that made a Tesco Metro seem like a hypermarket.

'Every day we'd go for a long walk, either setting off on foot from the cottage or driving along tiny lanes to deserted coves. The scenery was dramatic as was the weather; one minute blazing sun and the next, dark storm clouds throwing down a torrent of rain.

'One day towards the end of the holiday I was driving with no idea where we were heading but we ended up by an amazing lunar-like landscape of bare rock. I'd never seen anything like it, jagged outcrops stretching a huge distance towards a fierce sea. I can still visualise the scene. I often do.'

The waiter arrived with two tiny cups of coffee and glasses of ouzo. Bridget knocked hers back in one gulp then took a sip of the thick black espresso.

She described their walk that day, heading out towards that wild sea, gingerly treading over the slippery rocks laden with barnacles and seaweed, stepping into small clear pools. She and Roland were getting on a little better; perhaps their relationship had a chance after all. At some stage she stopped to remove a pebble lodged between her toes. Sitting on a large boulder, she took off her trainer and looked back towards the red sandstone cliff. As she turned, sunbeams struck it, producing a view of such beauty that she gasped in admiration of its grandeur. She was set to call out for Roland to look when she was interrupted by his shout.

'I turned to face the sea. He was smiling, a rare event over recent times. "Look what I've found," he yelled. He was perched on a high outcrop of rock holding a large crab. "Here, catch it." He pretended to throw it across to me but as he did so, he stumbled backwards.

'It looked really funny, him losing his balance, hovering like in a Buster Keaton movie, swaying with the crab in his hand. The expression on his face, the puzzled look of "Should I let go of this crab now?" He tumbled sideways and went crashing down.

'I stopped laughing when I reached him. There was a large gash on his forehead and he was out cold. Having escaped his hold, the crab was scuttling away in the pool of reddening water. There were tiny crabs, too. I forgot, what do you call a collection of crabs?'

'A cast, I think.'

'Another ouzo, please,' she called out to the passing waiter. 'Do you want one, David?'

'No, thanks. Yes, alright.'

'We never took our mobiles on the walks, we'd decided nothing should disturb us, though we were probably out of reception there anyway. It was all my fault. Getting as far away as possible from civilisation had been my suggestion. There I was with an unconscious husband and no way of contacting anyone. It was over an hour's walk back to the car and then a drive to God knows where to reach help.'

Bridget described how she'd edged him out of the pool before making her way back as quickly as the difficult surface would allow.

They knocked back their second ouzos.

'It was an hour and a half later before I was with the rescue team. When I told them the location they looked at me with such pity. What an idiot I was. The tide, the fucking tide. I should have realised. They found him two days later, his body washed up a few miles down the coast in a sandy cove. I'd left him there to drown.'

She had been looking down as she spoke, but now raised her head to meet David's gaze and he saw intense sadness in her eyes.

He took hold of her hands. 'There was nothing more you could have done, Bridget.'

'Surely something. I should have dragged him up to higher ground or yanked him step by step all the way back. God knows what injuries that would have caused, but at least I might have saved him. Or died in the attempt,' she added solemnly.

'Sir, madam. We are closing soon. Can I give you your bill?' Bridget nodded as David looked past the waiter to the otherwise deserted restaurant.

'Well, that's the story. My parents felt dreadful since it had been their suggestion we went away. Dad came up for the inquest; I couldn't have coped without him.'

The waiter had returned. Bridget lifted her credit card out of a lilac and pink striped purse crammed full of cards and receipts. 'Remember, I'm paying,' she said as she tapped in her pin number.

'I can't think of anything to say to console you, other than how sorry I am to hear about such an awful experience. If I can do anything to help …'

'Thanks, David. And I know you're genuine about that. Hey, you came by car didn't you?'

'Yes.'

'Well you can't drive back in your alcoholic state. Didn't you say yours are staying at friends? There's a spare room at mine if you'd like.'

'I wouldn't want to trouble you.'

'No trouble. Come on, let's go.'

She took hold of his hand.

15

Who would have thought that holding hands walking past youngsters noisily hanging around outside bars and late-night food stalls in Muswell Hill Broadway could be so wonderful? Even seeing a girl dressed as if she were a midsummer's evening fairy staggering before vomiting right in front of him was bliss. And hearing a short stocky boy with a knife in his hand yelling "I'm gonna get them cunts" didn't seem to matter.

'It's getting worse and worse on Saturday nights,' Bridget apologised. 'I'm struggling like mad to keep my two away from this. Andy's happy enough to stay in, he's quite a loner really, but I don't think there'll be any stopping Kay in a couple of years' time. She's one for adventure and dares.'

'Where are they tonight?' David asked, feigning a casual enquiry though with a strong hope that they would be staying over at friends.

'At home.'

'Oh, that's nice.'

Leaving the high street, they turned into a tidy road of Victorian houses, terraced but rather grand with turrets and ornate brickwork. Bridget led David along a tiled path, through a navy blue door with a large brass knocker, and into a narrow hall with emerald green walls. The lighting was subdued; it was like walking along a canopy of rainforest trees.

The interior décor of this home could not be more different to his own which suddenly seemed rather dull and austere. His wall colours, chosen by Jane, were "spot the difference" shades of white with names like almond white, orchid white, jasmine white, barley white, nutmeg white, vanilla white, blah, blah, blah. Here there were violent explosions of dark, rich colours – scarlet, turquoise, orange and violet. Bare polished floorboards were partly covered by oriental rugs, the tops of carved Indian cabinets and tables were heaped with books and magazines. There were sculptures, too, smooth stone abstracts and skeletal metal torsos. David assumed they were Roland's works.

His own pristine kitchen (though less so since Jane had gone) was fitted from floor to ceiling with units that hid everything except for the precisely placed (though less so without Jane) toaster, kettle, microwave and exhibition piece retro coffee maker. The kitchen where he now stood had three unmatching pine dressers and a table stacked with crockery, bottles and spice jars. A haphazard row of saucepans suspended from hooks ran a considerable length along one of the walls.

'Sorry it's a bit of a mess,' Bridget apologised. 'Leave the kids alone for one evening and this is what you get.'

No two children, not even teenagers, would be able to create this anarchy in one evening. David watched as Bridget shoved a couple of recipe books to the side to make room for the cafetiere and mugs.

Andy came in and acknowledged David with a nod before dropping an empty crisp packet and bottle of Red Bull into the bin. Kay followed him in, putting her unfinished Coke in the fridge before turning to Bridget and David.

'Hi Mum, hello fire man. Have you had a nice time?'

David smiled. 'Hello. Very nice thanks.'

'You should be in bed, Kay,' Bridget ordered.

'Yeah, I know. I'm on my way, but I do have a request, David.'

'Sure, what is it?'

'Could you burn down my school?'

'Don't forget to say please,' Andy added.

'Tell me where it is and I'll give it a go.'

'Enough requesting for tonight,' Bridget intervened. 'Bed. Now.'

'OK. Night, Mum.' Kay kissed her mother then turned to leave.

'Manners, Kay. Say goodnight to David.'

She kissed him on the cheek. 'Goodnight to David.'

'You'll see him at breakfast,' Bridget continued, 'he's staying over.'

Andy stayed put, hovering awkwardly.

'What have you been up to tonight?' Bridget asked.

'Bit of TV, some computing. Nothing much. I'm

going upstairs, too. 'Goodnight both of you.'

They sat drinking coffee and chatting, David's frustration at work coming up. He was about to mention his café idea when Bridget yawned.

'Sorry. Jeez, I'm shattered. Time for bed.'

He followed Bridget upstairs, mesmerised by the sexy view. She led him into a room with a black ceiling with tiny specks of silver. 'Roland's idea,' he was told. 'Apparently the dots are the star constellations but I've never been able to see any resemblance. The bigger splodges are supposed to be planets. I'll get you some stuff.'

He continued to gaze at the ceiling while Bridget was out the room. The splodge with the circle he assumed to be Saturn. Bridget returned with a toothbrush, towel, and an oversized t-shirt which she held up. 'I don't stock men's pyjamas; would you like this?'

'No, I'll be OK thanks.' The embarrassing morning after the reunion came to mind. 'Actually, yes.'

'We're lazy on Sunday mornings, breakfast's at around ten. But of course come downstairs whenever.' There was a dramatic pause. 'Best to wear trousers as well as this when you do though.' She was grinning broadly as she handed him the T-shirt and other items. Their hands touched and his grasp was reciprocated. It was Bridget who let go. 'The bathroom's second on the left. There's a dress code there too, I'm afraid.'

'Yes, I get the hint.'

'Seriously though. I've enjoyed this evening.'

'Me too. And thanks for the meal. I wanted to

protest about paying but knew I'd have no chance of getting my way…'

Bridget had put her arms round his neck and was about to kiss him. He decided to refrain from further talking. It was a gentle kiss, lip to lip, lingering though it was Bridget who pulled away when he would have liked to have remained locked in that embrace for approaching eternity.

'Bridget?'

'Yes?'

'About my list. I don't think I explained myself well enough first time round. Not everything I wrote down was daft, in fact none of it was.'

'Well at least they were to the point, there's no room for misinterpretation.'

'I suppose not,' David agreed, missing the tease until he looked up to her teasing smile.

'See you in the morning, David.'

How could he sleep with Bridget so close by, this a repeat of the night of the reunion though there would be no relieving of his erection. He caught the sound of the click of her light switch in the next door bedroom as he lay in semi darkness, a nearby street lamp casting subdued shadows across the star- speckled ceiling.

Logical thought disintegrated as the night dragged on. He endeavoured to push lustful thoughts about Bridget to the side. What could he do to improve the relationship with his boss? For the sake of the children might there ever be a degree of rapport with Jane? A brief doze ended with a start from a dream of the five of them, Jim, Jane, Mary, Bridget and he having a huge row at the side of a hotel swimming pool. He wished it had ended with him pushing Jim, Jane and possibly Mary into the water.

He looked at his phone. 01.29. It was impossible to focus on Mary and Jane when all that mattered was Bridget. The kiss, instigated by her, was promising. However, she was drunk so perhaps it was comparable to the random snogs between the youngsters they'd seen on Muswell Hill Broadway. No, Bridget wasn't a teenage reveller, she was a mature, cultured woman. Surely it meant something.

01.59. How much was she still in mourning over the tragic loss of her husband?

02.07. If her children hadn't been at home he might be in bed with her this very minute. To stifle his arousal he thought about the recent painful visit to the dentist. The drill had hit a nerve not reached by injections that had left his mouth, chin, tongue and left ear numb for hours after the root canal treatment. The focus on pain did the trick.

02.44. What next with Bridget, a meal, (he would insist on paying this time), something cultural – she liked art so perhaps an exhibition? Was she interested in a relationship? Should he turn off his phone?

02.58. The stars looked like they were moving, it must be the clouds reflecting against the street light. A black ceiling, whatever next? But why not? He needed bolder colours in his own home, not black though. He would do it, starting with the bedroom or maybe the lounge.

03.01. Stop thinking he was thinking as the items on his list came to mind. Three of the short term objectives had been accomplished, leaving sorting out the divorce as outstanding. Why wait for Jane to take the lead? They would need to divide their assets. He began two lists, one of assets for him, one for her.

It was a bit like counting sheep.

He fell asleep.

16

Rachel was standing by the lounge door. 'What have you done with the telly?'

'Good morning. It's under the dust sheet. Mustn't get paint on it.'

David was carrying a large pot of emulsion, a tray and a roller. He edged past his daughter. The furniture was stacked in the centre of the room, plastic sheeting covered the floor and a ladder was open close to the wall where the television had stood.

Rachel watched David lift the lid and tip dollops of paint into the tray. He climbed onto the ladder platform, the roller and tray balancing in one hand. Having dipped the roller into the paint he ran an untidy line across the wall close to the ceiling.

'Are you mad?' Rachel exclaimed. 'It's orange.'

'Burnt umber actually.'

'Well it's orange as far as I'm concerned.'

'Read the label on the tin. It says burnt umber.'

'Sam!' Rachel called out. 'Quick, come here!' They heard a scamper downstairs then Sam entered the room. 'What colour is this?'

Sam frowned, confused by the simplicity of

Rachel's question. He looked over to David, anxious not to give an incorrect answer.

'Orange,' he declared meekly.

'Not according to Dad. He reckons it's burnt something or other. Which of course is hardly the point. Our living room is being turned into, I don't know, a headache-inducing ethnic hideout. Dad, stop painting. Listen!'

David paused, roller at the ready. He'd already covered a considerable spread of wall; it was surprisingly quick to do, but it would be needing a second coat. A big decision was still to be made – whether to paint just the one wall in this colour or all four. He looked down at Rachel. 'I'm listening.'

'Why are you doing this?'

'I feel like a change.'

'But why not one of the colours we usually have?'

'I didn't realise how boring you are. I want to be bold, to try something completely different. Why not make us all tea?'

He applied another line of burnt umber. The previously applied paint was already drying – it was darkening.

'No I fuc – no I won't. I'm going to have to watch telly on the computer.' She left the room with a dramatic stamping of feet.

'I'll make the tea, Dad.'

'Thanks, Sam. Maybe some toast, too.'

David continued with the painting, humming favourite songs as he worked. He'd do all four walls to recapture the spirit of Bridget's house with its dark colours and moody, shadowy spaces. He had just started on the second wall when Sam came back with tea and toast.

'I'm not sure about this colour.'

'To be truthful neither am I, but never mind.'

He set the roller down onto the tray and sat on the floor with his son.

'I suppose we'll get used to it,' the diplomatic boy suggested.

Having finished his tea David sprang up. 'Thanks, Sam. I'd better carry on before the roller dries out.'

He was about to start the fourth wall when the doorbell chimed.

Rachel called out. 'I'll go, it'll be Daisy for me.'

It wasn't Daisy, it was Jane. David heard her tell Rachel that she'd forgotten her key. He didn't hear a response from their daughter, only the footsteps up the stairs.

'I'm in here,' he called out.

'What are you doing? Have you gone quite mad?' Jane cried out as she joined him.

'No I haven't gone mad but thanks for your concern.'

'You're ruining our lounge.'

'Since you don't live here it isn't really partly yours anymore.'

'I still own half of it. If we sell who's going to buy a house with an orange lounge?'

'It's not orange, it's burnt umber.'

'Well it looks orange to me.' She watched as David obliterated the final traces of the previously Almond

White wall. 'Can we talk?'

'As you can see, I'm rather busy.'

'It is important.'

Although David didn't want the roller to dry out he had yet to escape the habit of doing what Jane wanted when she wanted it. He got off the ladder and wiped his hands across his jeans, creating uneven burnt umber stripes.

'Ridiculous,' Jane fumed before leading him into the kitchen and switching on the cappuccino machine. 'Coffee?'

'No thanks, I've just had tea.'

He watched Jane glide from cupboard to cupboard collecting the necessaries. He'd started to rearrange things in the kitchen; he resolved to complete the task at speed.

They sat at the table, Jane taking a deep breath before speaking. 'To begin with, Rachel's appalling behaviour. She's refusing to speak to me and I think you're responsible for that.'

'Me? I don't see how.'

'You could talk to her; she listens to you.'

'She's your daughter as well as mine. It's you she's angry with so it's up to you to sort it. I'm not getting involved.'

Jane frowned; she wasn't used to defiance. 'Anyway, that's a side issue. The main reason I'm here is to let you know that Jim and I have decided to get married as soon as possible. So I'd appreciate it if we could get a move on with the divorce.'

'That's fine by me, the sooner the better,' David

declared, drawing satisfaction from having the opportunity to accomplish the final short-term objective on his list.

'Good. Thank you for that. We need to sort out finances so I've drawn up a list of what I think are our assets. My solicitor suggests a straight fifty-fifty split.'

David scanned the judiciously crafted inventory which pointed to input from Jim or her solicitor or both because Jane had never shown enough interest in financial matters to cite ISAs, government and corporate bonds, stocks, shares and Self Invested Personal Pensions. However, her involvement was evident when it came to house contents. Her list was comprehensive with estimated values added in a second column.

David read a final statement: *House. Occupancy by David until children reach school leaving age. Thereafter two options. [1] Sell, settle the mortgage and share the remaining income 50-50 OR [2] Don't sell, David to reimburse to Jane a sum equivalent to 50% of the value as agreed by two independent estate agents.*

The author of the document became clear as soon as Jane continued. 'Jim thinks it's all fair. He also says that you have a duty to add anything we own that's missing from the list. It's a legal requirement.'

'I'm not sure what Jim has to do with it.'

'He's my partner; he's helping me.'

David concealed his anger. 'A couple of things come to mind. Do you intend to contribute towards paying the mortgage and to the cost of bringing up the children?'

'Not for Rachel the way she's behaving.'

'I'm not sure you can pick and choose.'

'I'll need to speak to my solicitor about those points.'

'Yes, you do that. And I'll show this document to mine.'

'You have a solicitor?'

'Of course.'

'I thought we could do this amicably.'

'But you have one. It's only fair.' The expression on Jane's face suggested fairness wasn't high on her list of considerations. 'Look, I must press on before the roller dries out,' David continued. 'I'm hoping to get started on the bedroom today.'

'The bedroom! Why? We only decorated it last year.'

'It needs a richer colour than Apple White. I'm going for Redcurrant Glory.'

'Red!'

'No. Redcurrant Glory.'

With a shake of the head and a sigh Jane left him to it.

David hadn't decided to decorate the bedroom, let alone chosen the colour.

It had been fun to wind Jane up but his high spirits evaporated as he reflected on the imminent end of his marriage. With little enthusiasm he rolled on the second coat of paint, to be left to observe a room that was dark and overwhelming. Why had he done it? To be like Bridget? To win her over based on his choice of wall colour? It's not as if they were seeing much of each other – a week and a half had gone by since the meal and his overnight stay. During the pleasant enough telephone chats she claimed that children and work issues were preventing any socialising. Was that true or an excuse?

A post from Official London Theatre popped up in his email Inbox. The advert was promoting *Chicago*. David took the risk and purchased two tickets before calling Bridget.

'What a lovely idea, I'd love to come along.'

'Mind you, it's hardly high culture.'

'I'm fine with low culture.'

17

The musical was over and they were weaving their way towards the exit from the third row in the stalls, David's back aching having sat for two and a half hours on the narrow seat with insufficient leg room.

'Thanks for the suggestion – and the ticket. I enjoyed it loads and I've been desperate for a break from work and kids. Don't you just love these old theatres?'

'I certainly do.' David was massaging the base of his back. 'Fancy a drink before we head home?'

'Best not to tonight, I don't like getting back late when the kids are alone. Also, it's going to be hectic at work tomorrow, we're setting up a new exhibition.'

Bridget had an impressive knowledge of the geography of Central London. With authoritative strides she led David through tiny lanes and alleyways as they made their way towards the Underground station. Kitt's Yard was like being in a time warp, the narrow passageway devoid of cars with two-storey brick warehouses that had seen better days on each side. The old-fashioned street lights provided a hazy, yellowish glow. Remarkable such a place existed,

David was thinking, only a stone's throw from the affluence and bustle of the West End.

They were strolling along in silence, comfortable in each other's company, content to soak up the atmosphere. David took hold of Bridget's hand.

'You two. Stop!' growled a voice. They turned to see a shape in the shadows, leaning against a dustbin that was overflowing and surrounded by loose rubbish piled high. His hoodie dispelled the Victorian ambiance.

Without the need for consultation, Bridget and David took the sensible decision to continue walking with a quickened step, but the tall, stocky man stepped out in front of them.

He stood against David, blocking his path. 'You 'eard me. I said stop,' he yelled, presenting David with an unpleasant combination of stale beer and body odour. 'I want yer stuff.'

David was affronted that their peaceful walk had been disturbed. Commendably, he had no fear of danger.

'What stuff?' he jibed.

'What d'ya mean "what stuff"? All yer stuff – money, phone, yer cards,' the assailant screamed into David's face. He turned to Bridget with a slightly softer tone as if in deference to her femininity. 'And yours.'

'Don't forget my watch, surely you want that, too? It's good quality. A Sekonda,' David mocked as he lifted up his wrist to reveal the silver timepiece with a black leather strap. He glanced at Bridget; she had a strange look of incredulity.

'Don't mess with me. Hand yer valuables over. Now!' His volume was somehow exceeding the previous scream.

'There's no need to shout.' David was enjoying his fearless flippancy.

'What?' he shrieked as he grabbed David by the lapels.

'I said there's no need to shout.'

David's attitude appeared not to be welcomed by Bridget. 'Why not let him have what he wants and then we can go?' she suggested.

'I'm only advising him not to shout, Bridget.' David turned to face the man, their noses touching. 'It's bad for your health.'

The attacker was somewhat taken aback by his victim's concern and their noses disengaged. David explained. 'If you behave like this it'll give you high blood pressure. Do you get heart palpitations?'

'Do I what?'

'Does your heart thump when you're robbing people? If you're not careful you could have a stroke. On top of that there's the potential damage to your vocal cords ...'

The last thing David remembered before hitting the ground was 'Don't you take the piss with me.'

Lying there, temporarily paralysed, he was vaguely aware of his jacket being opened and things taken out before being rolled onto his stomach to extract the wallet from the back pocket of his trousers. As he regained a sense of the now he saw Bridget surrender her handbag to the man.

They both looked down at David. 'Scumbag,' the man spat before giving David a light-hearted farewell kick to the ribs and heading off.

Bridget knelt down by his side. David was all set to tell her what a cheek it was being called a scumbag by a man who was one hell of a scumbag himself. He wanted to make light of the whole incident, to jump up and head off to the Underground in the hope that the thief hadn't taken their tickets. It was a disappointment to discover he was unable to sit, let alone jump up, and he couldn't speak.

Two observations flashed through his mind ahead of passing out.

This was the second time in their relatively brief period together that Bridget had seen him punched and floored.

And this punch was substantially more forceful than the one Ben Carpenter had bestowed at the reunion.

~

David regained consciousness as the ambulance was pulling up at the hospital. The left side of his face was excruciatingly painful, a dull thud running from his temple through his ear and down to his chin. Lifting his hand to his face he discovered a bandage wrapped around his head. It seemed to be fastened with a bow. Realisation of how ridiculous he must look and the cause came flooding back. He lifted his head to see if Bridget was still with him.

'Best to keep your head still, sir.' David glanced

sideways and saw the blur of a powder blue uniform. 'We're about to lift you out.'

'Gigget?' he enquired, now concerned for her well-being. His flippancy had put her in danger.

'Yes, I'm here. Everything's going to be fine.'

'Garldy, I gug look rigigulus.'

'No, you look fine.'

David was impressed with Bridget's linguistic skills. However he wasn't sure whether he was glad she was with him or not. It wasn't going to do much for his I-am-a-cool-man-who-you-want-to-have-a-relationship-with image.

By now the door was open and he was being stretchered off the vehicle.

'Gare ar gee?'

'What's he saying?' the paramedic asked.

'He's asking where we are. We're at University College Hospital, David.' Bridget's understanding again impressed him, but aware that he sounded absurd, he decided not to say anything else for the time being.

~

The A&E reception was immaculately maintained, the staff impeccably polite and efficient. The spanner in the works were the patients. Being late evening in Central London, the place was heaving with intoxicated and stoned citizens who, judging by appearances had overdone it to the extent of inflicting self-harm or subjecting others to their uncontrolled aggression. The two policemen on guard twice had to intervene when fighting broke out.

David was relieved to be called to the injury assessment booth.

'Good news,' he was told by the doctor having returned from having an X-ray. 'It's a dislocation, there's no fracture.'

'Guy is gat getter?'

'Pardon?'

'He's asking why that's better,' Bridget translated.

'Because we can snap it back easily enough.'

The next half hour was not pleasant despite the two numbing injections. A doctor juggled with his cheeks until there was a loud click. He was told that this was to get his face back to the right shape. There was a cut on his forehead so on went a new bandage with the bow.

The doctor outlined next steps – a course of anti-inflammatories and muscle relaxants. He handed Bridget a sheet outlining the recommended regime of liquids and blended soft foods for the next two weeks. Even yawning and sneezing were covered with the doctor, a stout bearded fellow with a Welsh accent, simulating a yawn to demonstrate how David needed to support his jaw with a hand to prevent over-stretching. And there was Bridget, witnessing all this embarrassing dialogue. Would he be covering pooing and farting next, David wondered?

But that was it and the doctor stood. 'I'm done. Time to tackle some of the lovelies waiting out there.'

'Gank oo. Go I neeg to cun gack?'

'Pardon?'

'He's asking if he needs to come back.'

'No, his GP can sort it from here on.'

David was aware of a further embarrassment. Because of the numbing injections he was unable to prevent saliva from gushing out his mouth and down his chin.

Standing by the door to the cubicle, the doctor turned to David. 'You're lucky to have this good woman to look after you.'

The good woman took David home in a taxi and explained to Rachel and Sam what precautions would be needed. Finally, she ordered a taxi to take her home.

'I'll call tomorrow,' she said having heard the knock at the door.

'Gank oo, Gigget. Solly agout togite.'

18

Rachel took the day off school to look after David.

By the time he entered the kitchen she'd googled *Diet for dislocated jaw sufferers* and the room was a food factory. Orange juice, soda water, yoghurt, bouillon cubes and a large container of straws were lined up on a counter. The liquidiser was out on another work surface and next to it were potatoes, vegetables, cottage cheese, apple puree, two pots of organic baby food, bananas and a large cube of tofu.

'I've been to the supermarket.'

'Wow, ganks, Gachel.'

She lifted up the tofu. 'I wouldn't dream of touching this muck normally, but I read that you need lots of protein and this is good because it's soft. We can invite Bridget and her geeky kids round, it's bound to be one of their favourites.'

'Very gunny.'

'Seriously though, I'll need to blend everything because you can't open your mouth too wide. Breakfast is tea and a fruit smoothie, then maybe vegetable soup with tiny potato cubes for lunch and mashed pasta for dinner.'

After breakfast David sat in the lounge feeling sorry for himself. The fierce burnt umber walls weren't helping his thumping headache and sore jaw; the painkillers didn't seem to be working.

Mid-morning there was a knock at the front door. Rachel came into the lounge followed by two police officers, a man and a woman. They were from the Mill Hill Constabulary and had come to interview David about the attack, the hospital authorities having reported the incident based on their conversation with Bridget.

It was exasperating because having ascertained that he couldn't speak properly, he had to write down answers which the policewoman copied onto a tablet. He was given a crime investigation number, surely a waste of time as the chances of catching the man were nil.

David led them to the door. 'Gank oo.'

He was convinced that they were smirking as they left.

Time dragged on over subsequent days, the large pack of straws used up in the consumption of mushy concoctions manufactured by Rachel. She was taking her role seriously, gradually thickening the consistency of the meals to enable him to move on to eating using a teaspoon by the end of a week that had included visits by Bridget (twice), Jabulani and even Jane.

Ten days after the assault and he was back at work with Rachel's intricate instructions about what he was allowed to consume.

The serene return to work was about to come to an end three days later as he trekked along to Mary's office for his annual staff review. He was more indifferent than dreading it. The others had given Mary a *French Sophisticate* label that day based on the navy and beige hooped jumper and chocolate brown pencil skirt that she was wearing. Her hair was in a tight ponytail.

Her office said quite a bit about Mary. At an exact forty-five degree angle on the corner of the desk was a single framed photo of herself in ski gear. No children. No husband. No boy or girlfriend visible. Just her.

There was a row of five equidistantly placed cacti on her window ledge. A fitting plant for her – prickly, aggressive, arid. David considered sneaking in one day to shift them, varying the spaces. She'd notice that.

Council office walls displayed the wide preferences of the occupants – reproductions of Private Eye covers, Rothko's stripes, Mondrian's squares, Constable's countrysides, Stubbs's horses, Turner's trains, Hogarth's hell on earth. On Mary's wall hung two certificates, her first-class degree diploma from LSE and a Price Waterhouse Coopers Employee of the Month award.

As he sat down, David had the urge to sweep his arm across the tidy stack of A4 sheets in front of him.

'I hope you've fully recovered from your shocking incident.'

'Yes, ganks. My speech isn't gite gack to normal,

I'm worried about opening my mouth too wide and gickly.'

'Yes, well do your best. Shall we start?'

Mary droned on about the purpose of the staff review, how it gave both parties the opportunity to step back from everyday activity to reflect on the past year's achievements and to consider objectives for the following year.

I do know all this, he was thinking. I have conducted staff appraisals for over twenty years. 'Nice gacti,' David remarked looking across to the windowsill during a pause in her monologue.

'Thank you. Well, shall we begin. I forgot to say, this is very much a two-way process and you're welcome to provide feedback about my performance.'

Mary began by listing two concerns about his effectiveness. Was he managing his team well? Were family issues impacting on performance?

David kept his answers short, in part because he was disengaged but also because he was self-conscious about not being able to speak properly.

Did he think his team had a good understanding of budget restraints?

'Yesh, I gink so.'

Could family issues be kept out of the workplace?

'I gink they algeggy are.'

Perhaps he should report her to Human Resources because this line of questioning was out of order.

Finally, the following year's objectives were reached. An in-house training session *Dealing with Awkward Customers* was on her list for him to undertake.

It's more a case of dealing with awkward line managers, he was thinking. 'Mary, I'm fine with customers, they're never awkward when I speak to them.' He'd risked opening his mouth wider to say that and was pleased with the return to normality.

'I think you're wrong there, David. When informed that they won't be getting funding they can be very awkward.'

'That's because the rules aren't clear, they keep changing. And there's less money to go round.'

'Which takes us back to budgetary control. We aren't a charity.'

'But we're not a profit-making organisation either.'

After a frustrating forty-five minutes the meeting came to an end. Mary didn't look up, she was taking notes as she spoke. 'I will be including the customer interface training as an objective. You do need to do it.'

There was an obvious candidate in the room for a course on interpersonal skills and it wasn't him. As he watched her finish her note-taking, her handwriting neat and tiny using black ink, he thought of the turquoise swirls and loops on the get well card that Bridget had given him. The front cover had been a picture of a man swathed in bandages, only his left foot exposed bar the tiny gaps for mouth, eyes and the base of the nose. A doctor was by the side of the bed, speaking to a nurse as they gazed down at the foot. 'Good to see so much improvement in only a week.' Bridget had written *To David, my hero – but perhaps best not to take on a mugger next time! Love, Bridget.*

'David, I'm talking to you. I forgot one of the questions. Is there anything you'd like to cover regarding my performance?' She glanced at her watch before turning to her computer screen. Her invitation seemed to be a box-ticking obligation, nothing more.

'Actually there is, Mary. To be truthful, your line management is dreadful. You are more patronising than I would ever dream of being to my own children. I know you've been on loads of management courses because you're forever telling me. I'm surprised that with all your training you don't recognise that you can get more from your staff by motivating rather than bullying them.'

Mary was pleasantly speechless. David continued. 'I'd like that comment recorded in your notes, please.'

'Yes, of course. It has come as a surprise but thank you for your frankness. If I seem a little forceful it's because so much needs to change here.'

Her response confirmed an inability to listen. There seemed little point pursuing the point so David stood and extended his hand. 'Thank you for your time, Mary.' Grabbing the hand offered, he deliberately shook it with considerable force.

He went into the kitchen to make a much needed coffee. Jabulani rushed up to him. For a man who always carried a broad smile, this one was gargantuan. 'My news is wonderful. I've been waiting for you to come out of your meeting.'

'What is it?'

'My brother is safe! We received a call yesterday

evening from France.'

'Fantastic news. How did he manage to get away?'

'It was solved with money. One of his work colleagues bribed a prison guard. For others it is not so happy; I'm ashamed of what goes on there.'

'What will your brother do?'

'Join us here. An English doctor he knew in Zimbabwe can organise everything so he can work at his London hospital. In Stepney, so we'll be neighbours.'

'Stepney to Queensbury isn't quite neighbours.'

'No, but it is more of a neighbour than Zimbabwe is to England or heaven to earth.'

Jabulani had often spoken of his love for his brother, of their childhood in happier times. 'We sang, we played guitar, and now we will be able to make music together again.'

'I'm so pleased for you. Let's catch up at lunchtime, but I'd better get back to work or else I'll have Mary after me.'

'Of course, it's your review day. What happened? And you're speech – it's back to normal.'

'I'll tell you everything later.'

As David reached his desk his mobile rang. It was Bridget. 'Want to see *Brief Encounter* at the Phoenix on Saturday?'

'Yes, I'd love to.'

'Great. I'll get tickets and then we can sort the details.'

'Thanks. Remember Jabulani, the colleague I took for tea at Harrods? Well, his brother has managed to get out of Zimbabwe and he's coming to England.'

'That's good … hey, you're speaking properly.'

'I'm experimenting with opening my mouth fully.'

'It sounds like it's a success. Wasn't your staff review this morning?'

'Yes, 'fraid so.'

'And?'

'I told her what I thought, I reckoned what the hell. If it ends up with me being pressurised to leave I don't care. In fact, I have an idea about opening a café.'

'The café. I was wondering about that when I saw it written on your piece of paper. You can tell me all about it on Saturday but I'd better go now, we have a customer.'

19

David wiped away silent tears with the back of his hand as the credits rolled for *Brief Encounter*. He looked across at Bridget, who was dabbing her eyes with a tissue.

She gave him a watery smile. 'Daft, aren't we?'

'It's powerful stuff.'

They left the cinema, crossed the road, stepped into The Five Bells and immediately exited the packed and noisy pub. The Alexandra, across the road, was quieter with an older clientele, far better for chatting.

'My two are out tonight,' Bridget said when David was back with the drinks. 'Andy got a rare invite to a party, he was over the moon, and one of my social animal daughter's friends is having a sleepover.'

'Mine are also at friends.'

'Then you could invite me over to see the new colour in your lounge.'

Did this mean what he thought it meant? 'With pleasure.'

They had a second drink before taking the short walk to East Finchley Underground. Mill Hill East was a few stops away on the Northern Line with one change needed.

The train wasn't busy, it being too early for the pubbers and clubbers to be heading home. They watched as a shabbily dressed elderly lady sitting opposite them rummaged through her large, paisley handbag with a sense of urgency. She pulled out a buff-coloured envelope and lifted out the letter inside.

A letter, David was thinking, you hardly see one that isn't a bill or an advert these days. This one was three sheets filled with neat script. There were tears as the woman read. Bridget crossed the aisle and sat by her side. 'Are you alright?'

'Not really, dear, but thank you for asking. It's something I have to deal with all by myself.'

She started to tell Bridget her story, reminding David of how comfortable he had been talking to Bridget about Jane. Somehow Bridget's kindness and compassion were immediately an invitation to open up. This letter was written by the woman's husband as the poor man wasted away in hospital. He had died that morning, on the very day of their sixty-seventh wedding anniversary.

'I made a carrot cake, his favourite, to celebrate. But by the time I got there it was too late.'

Bridget consoled her with talk of the power of memories, mentioning the love for her own father and the pain of the loss.

'Is that your husband?' the elderly woman asked, looking across at David.

'No, but he's a good friend.'

The train slowed and the woman prepared to alight.

'Home I go to start my new life.'

'You make sure you look after yourself.'

'Thank you, dear, you're very kind.' She turned to address David. 'You're a lucky young man to have this woman.'

'Yes, I know.'

Bridget sat back down next to David. The carriage was deserted.

'No need to sit, we're at High Barnet, it's the terminus.'

'I thought your stop was the last station.'

'It is, but on a different branch. We needed to get off and switch trains a while back.'

'Oh God, sorry. I got carried away chatting to the poor soul.'

'It was worth it. I could see that your kindness was helping her.'

'I don't know about being kind,' Bridget said as they stood on the opposite platform. 'I didn't like seeing her upset. Usually no one speaks on the Underground. I hate the way passengers ignore each other. If you try to say anything people look at you as if you're mad.'

David was unsure why her comment brought on intense desire but it did. He drew Bridget close and they kissed.

He loved this woman, her physical beauty, her personality. The gentleness was coupled with a strong will and noble morals. She knew what was right and what was wrong with the world and wasn't afraid to assert her views.

There were pauses for kissing on the walk from the station to David's house, playful like young lovers.

'Love it!' Bridget exclaimed when David switched on a lamp in the lounge. 'Orange is one of my favourite colours.'

'Actually, it's burnt … oh, never mind, I love it too.'

'I bet your kids think it's great.'

'They're getting used to it. I've started decorating the bedroom, so far only one wall because I'm not sure whether to do the others the same colour or whether that might be oppressive.'

'Well, we'd better have a look then, hadn't we?'

Up the stairs they went, David's heart pounding. On entering the room Bridget praised his choice of red.

'Actually it's Redcurrant Glor … oh, never mind.'

'If you want to know what I think, I like it loads but the one wall is probably enough.' She was looking at the bed. 'Lovely. You can gaze at the rich colour when you're lying down.'

David wasn't sure how they got there, who instigated it, but they were on the bed kissing.

During a pause for breath Bridget sat up and took off her cardigan. 'Let's get undressed.'

David began to unbutton his shirt.

'Here, let me help.' Bridget took over, flicking her tongue over his chest as she undid each button. Jane had never done that. It was very nice.

'My turn.' As David unbuttoned Bridget's blouse, he mimicked the licking. With the blouse removed he planted delicate kisses on the erect nipples visible through her bra.

As he was undoing his belt there was a vibration inside his trouser pocket. He'd set his phone on silent before the film and his inclination was to ignore the call, but he felt duty-bound to look at the screen in case there was a problem with one of the children.

Bridget was down to her underwear, her knickers matching the pretty, lacy bra. As David lifted the phone out of his pocket she unhooked her bra.

'Hello, Sam,' he said as the bra fell to the floor to reveal miraculous development for the woman once known as "Titless". The sight of her breasts added to his erection though the impact was counterbalanced by having Sam on the other end of the telephone. If a penis could ever have a mind of its own and get confused then this was it.

Sam had had a massive bust up with Adrian. They had come to blows.

'Can't you make up, Sam, at least stay there until the morning ... the problem is I can't drive because I've been drinking ... that's kind of Adrian's mother ... you've already left ... in Cranbrook Drive. OK I guess I'll see you in about five minutes then ... bye, Sam.'

Having caught the gist of the conversation Bridget was getting dressed. David must have appeared distraught, disturbed, distressed, dismayed, demoralised, defeated because she burst out laughing. 'Poor you, but it's OK, there will be another opportunity. Actually I quite enjoyed doing a striptease while the audience is on the phone to one of his children. Is there a spare bed for me? Perhaps show me where it is before Sam gets back.'

They were in Rachel's room putting on new bedlinen when the front door opened. 'I'm up here, Sam,' David called out. 'Bridget's with me, she's staying the night. We'll come down.'

Bridget rested a hand on David's shoulder. 'Persevere and you'll get me,' she whispered, this followed by a motherly peck on the lips.

Alone in bed, his eyes glued to the Redcurrant Glory wall, David considered sneaking into Bridget's room once Sam was asleep. He decided against it, knowing it was merely a matter of time before he accomplished the all-important APLO4.

~

David woke early and sauntered downstairs to prepare breakfast. He heard the front door open, surely too early for Rachel's return.

Jane joined him and handed over an envelope. 'It's the settlement terms. I agree with everything you've put down. My solicitor suggested to speed things up that I come over to get the papers signed.'

'Sure. Leave them in the hall and I'll look at them later.'

'I meant sign them now then I can take them back.'

'Sorry, no time.'

'You haven't changed your mind about anything, have you?'

'No. I will sign but I haven't got time now.'

'What's so urgent to stop you?'

Bridget was standing by the kitchen door. She was wearing the Simpsons T-shirt David had given her. The family were in a line smiling. Homer was holding baby Maggie who was looking up in admiration at her frazzled father.

'Probably me.' She stepped into the room. 'You must be Jane. I've heard so much about you.'

'Who are you? This is my house, you're in my house.'

David laughed. 'That's ridiculous bearing in mind the circumstances.'

'Are the children here?'

'Sam is.'

'Well then this is different to my situation. Having a woman here isn't fair on Sam.'

'I'll be the judge of that. He knows Bridget, they get on fine. Perhaps it's a good idea if you leave.'

'God, you've changed, David. And I don't like what I'm seeing.'

'Well you didn't like the old me either. What's new?'

Bridget stepped forward and took hold of David's hand. 'I like him. And I'm starving, any chance of breakfast?'

Jane stood her ground for a few seconds, looking from David to Bridget then back to David again. 'OK, I get the message, I'm going.'

'I will look at your papers later if you leave them here.'

There was a thud as the thick envelope was dropped onto the table, followed after a short interval by the slamming of the front door.

'She's nice,' Bridget declared with a mischievous grin.

20

Bridget was keen to get home before her children so David drove her back straight after breakfast. On the journey they chatted about the night before and that morning's confrontation with Jane. Bridget saw the funny side of all that had happened. David didn't.

Having pulled up outside her house David moved up close for a kiss but Bridget edged away. 'Not a great idea if you don't mind. I've got some very nosy neighbours.'

'See you soon?'

'You bet.'

David's thoughts were all over the place as he drove home. There was pleasure, lots of it; despite last night's frustration a relationship with Bridget was surely imminent. To some extent it had been a Jane versus Bridget confrontation that morning. When Jane spoke of it being her house it had brought a surge of sadness about loss because for years he and Jane had been very much in love.

They'd met at a dinner party at his friend Bill's house. Jane was a work colleague of Bill's girlfriend and it was more or less a matchmaking blind date. It worked; they hit it off straight away and within six months were living together. House-proud Jane had a great eye for design. Their first home used Laura Ashley wallpaper and was filled with Habitat furniture. Having fallen pregnant with Rachel, on their way home after the first check-up Jane declared. "A child with you is my greatest dream come true." David had never forgotten those words.

When Sam was born they moved to the house that Jane was now calling hers. This was true beyond the financial tie; her choices of décor and furnishings were there for all to see, though now excluding the Burnt Umber and Redcurrant Glory walls.

David couldn't deny that during much of their time together Jane had been the ideal partner, a light-hearted counter to his rather serious self. He could understand her resentment in seeing another woman there, but hold on a minute, it had been her decision to leave.

He struggled to figure out when there had been the first indication that all was not right with their relationship. They'd been on the same wavelength until … until when? David had thought things were still fine during their holiday in Brittany.

~

At work David discussed his confusion with Jabulani.

'Are you missing her?' his friend asked.

'No, that's what is so peculiar. At times, not that long ago, it was as if we were telepathic, our relationship was that strong. Now she's like a stranger and the detachment hasn't gradually happened, it's as sudden as falling over a cliff edge. How on earth can that be so?'

There was a pause for thought before Jabulani replied. 'I think people are like onions. We have a multitude of layers, in our case layers of personality. You think you know someone inside out, then they strip off a layer or two and you don't know the person at all.'

'Interesting and I'll tell you something, I think that applies to oneself. At my age I'd expect my ways of doing and thinking things to be set, but in this new situation with a new woman I'm behaving completely differently.' At this point, licking Bridget as he undid each button of her blouse came to mind. He refrained from providing Jabulani with the illustration.

'There are an infinite number of layers, David. You will carry on shedding them until the day you die. And you can put one back whenever the need arises.'

'I hope so.'

'I assume you're thinking about your new woman.'

'Not quite my new woman yet, but close to it.'

'You deserve happiness.'

~

That evening David was all set to tackle APLTO1: *Take a cookery course*. It was hardly compensation for the delay over the Bridget objectives, but better than nothing.

There was a final meal to prepare before embarking on a culinary adventure.

Ahead of getting it ready he joined Sam to watch

an Attenborough nature programme, the pair of them mesmerised as the male penguins huddled together in the freezing Antarctic, eggs balanced on their webbed feet, in anticipation of the return of their mates.

'Amazing. How can they get such brilliant films?' David said as the titles rolled.

'I'd better go up and start homework. Oh, I forgot to tell you, Rachel phoned. She said don't make dinner for her because she's staying over at Hannah's tonight.'

'Thanks for letting me know. You go up and I'll call you down when it's ready.'

'What are we having?'

'I thought Welsh rarebits.'

'Nothing else?'

'You can have it with salad and there are plenty of desserts to choose from. I need to be quick though because guess what? I'm joining a cookery evening class.'

'I think that's a brilliant idea.'

'Except I thought Rachel would be here to look after you. Will you be OK by yourself?'

'Don't be silly, I'm thirteen, I'll be fine. I've got loads of homework to do.'

Two slices of bread topped with cheddar cheese was hardly gourmet, leaving David confident that he had made the right decision in signing up for the *Learn to Cook – Anyone Can Do It* course.

The promotional information had convinced him that this was the right one. It seemed to be a start from scratch course, intent on providing confidence to purchase good ingredients, understand all about proper preparation, and discover high-quality cooking tips, topped off with how to serve up in style. There was a theme for each session with catchy headings like *Great Grilling*, *Simple Italian*, *Cup Cake Champion* and *Fantastic Fish*.

He drove to the local further education college, an impressive new build. He was the first to arrive at the kitchen area having passed rooms buzzing with gatherings of evening class enthusiasts.

Before long there were eight of them waiting outside, four men and four women. Conversation unsurprisingly centred on the question "What made you decide to sign up?" Two of the men were in a similar situation to him, newly separated or divorced. Stephen was keen to widen the variety of what he could provide his two children. Luke's two stayed with him every other weekend. He claimed their mother had brought them up on a diet of pizza, beans and chips, and he wanted to improve on that. The fourth man was Nathan, a giant with tattoos covering his arms. He was a car mechanic keen on a career change to be a chef.

The women varied in age from sixteen to sixty something. The teen, a confident girl called Tanya, talked about how much she enjoyed cooking, claiming that what she learnt at school was dead boring. The oldest lady, Mildred, was looking for a new interest having retired; once she got talking there was no stopping her. The others, two Janets, were tired of serving up the same old stuff for their families.

In the short time that they were waiting together in the corridor a camaraderie developed which David appreciated. Being totally at ease in the company of such a diverse set of people got David thinking about Jabulani's onion layers.

Robert was the professional chef engaged as the course tutor. He was an instant hit, relating hilarious stories of disasters when he first started cooking.

'So if you feel culinarily challenged at any point during the course, join the club. You're prepared to do something to improve, that's the important thing. You'll be going home to amaze your dinner companions, whether it's a would-be lover, a rowdy gang of kids or,' he looked across to Brenda the pensioner, her grey hair permed with a hint of lilac rinse, 'to prove you're never too old to try something new.'

They set to work preparing the meal, seasonal vegetable soup with cheese croutons, pan-roasted free range chicken with tarragon and crème fraiche sauce, and a blueberry tart to follow.

They worked non-stop for the two hours, ending up with an impressive meal to take home.

'You could freeze it all, but it's best to put it in the fridge and serve up tomorrow,' Robert advised, this followed by a deserved round of applause for the way he'd raced round the kitchen to help everyone.

~

The next evening, with a degree of pride, David set the table with tablecloth, napkins and the best cutlery before calling the children down.

'What's going on?' Rachel asked.

'Dad learnt to cook last night,' Sam explained.

'One sec,' their father said, returning with the first course. 'Voila mes enfants, le diner.'

'Merci, Papa, c'est delicieux.'

'How do you know? You haven't tried it yet.'

'Let Sam practise his French, Rachel.'

By the end of the meal Rachel was happy to add her praise. 'This is fu…flipping amazing.'

'I'm going to tell Mum,' Sam told them.

'What would you want to do that for?'

'So she knows that Dad can cook.'

'Who cares what she thinks? Anyway, I'm popping over to Hannah for a bit.'

David began clearing up. He was in high spirits, the cookery course was working out, a relationship with Bridget was (surely) certain, and every one of his short term objectives had been achieved. Despite early doubts about the value of such an exercise he was now convinced that the process had given him direction. That being the case, it was time to consider the remaining long-term objectives bar those associated with Bridget.

Long term objectives

2. *Quit my job and pack in accountancy*

3. *Open an arts café*

He recognised the need for a business plan, and what with his accountancy background, had a sound financial knowledge. One thing was missing though, advice from an entrepreneur. He knew where to find one. Ross.

David had known Ross since their university days. While still a student his friend was moving from money-making project to money-making project. By no means were they all a success but Ross was indefatigable. "If this doesn't work I'll dump it and try something else" he'd say when confronted with David's list of what-ifs. The man was a millionaire despite twice being declared bankrupt.

They had last met about six months prior to Jane leaving. Ross was in the process of setting up an online pet food company.

'Why would anyone want to buy their pet food online, Ross?'

'It'll be cheaper.'

'But what about delivery costs.'

'They won't see those until check out and people rarely cancel once they've got that far.'

David could never work out whether he liked or despised his ex-university friend. Ross could be ruthless, aggressive and insensitive, but it was fun to spend an evening with him and at times he could be extremely kind-hearted. Like when he managed to get sought-after tickets for Rachel during her short period of obsession with Little Mix.

He called Ross and replied to the "How's it going, mate" with the news that Jane had left him.

'All for the best, mate, I've always thought she's a stuck-up frumpy. Don't you worry, us oldies attract younger women. It's a man's market out there, you'll be fine.'

As far as Ross was concerned this wasn't

conjecture, the ages of three wives and several mistresses testimony to that. This was not what David had contacted him to cover so he hastily shifted themes to outline his idea for a coffee bar.

Ross laughed. 'You're hardly going to make your millions with that.'

'That's not the point.'

'Then what is the point? Setting up a new business is risky even if it's only a piddly little café.' David didn't fill the silence. 'If you're serious I'm happy to talk it through with you, but I can tell you now, it wouldn't be a good use of your time. Or your money.'

David intended to take up Ross's offer, but in advance of any meeting he recognised the need to flesh out his vague plan.

Where to start though because he had no knowledge of how to open and run a café? His reason for this career change, at the outset obvious, was now unclear. He liked cafes but so what? He also liked films but that didn't make him competent to act, direct or own a chain of cinemas.

He began by reflecting on demand. Most cafes closed soon after the shops did. For a while town centres were occupied by youngsters moving between near-identical bars. As the evening progressed the bouncers appeared and the music blared, hardly a welcoming environment for the old – he reckoned "old" meant anything over forty. Pubs for this older clientele were often run down and uninviting. Of course there were restaurants but wouldn't it be great to have a coffee bar open throughout the evening, a place to visit after going to the cinema or theatre, or for a longer stay if it were a venue for concerts, poetry readings, book clubs and art exhibitions?

David decided to run the idea past Bridget.

He was saving his draft document when there was a ring at the doorbell.

21

It was approaching eleven o'clock. The ring took him by surprise. Rachel was out but had a key. No one else was expected at that hour of the day. Surely not Jane having forgotten her key and needing to collect something. Bridget? That would be nice.

A policeman and policewoman, the pair who had interviewed him after his mugging, had Rachel propped up between them.

'Good evening, Mr Willoughby. We've brought your daughter home,' the young woman said as the three of them edged in, the snow on them melting and dripping onto the floor as they stepped indoors.

'This way,' a shocked David gestured, noticing Sam on the landing peering through the wooden slats of the banister.

They led Rachel into the lounge. Letting go, she slumped down onto the couch.

'Don't push me. How dare you throw me down like that, I'm fragile,' Rachel growled. 'Hi there, Dad.'

She looked around the room, momentarily puzzled. 'Oh, am I home? But fuck these bloody orange walls, they'll make me be sick again.'

David turned to face the two police officers, standing, dripping, observing Rachel with a look of contempt. 'What happened?' he asked.

'Your daughter was seen staggering along the High Street barely able to stay upright and exhibiting the sort of lewd behaviour that we don't tolerate,' the policeman reported.

His companion continued. 'We were close to making an arrest bearing in mind how aggressive she was when we questioned her. It's fortunate her boyfriend was more cooperative. He told us their names, which she'd refused to do. This young lady –'

'I do have a name, you know. And anyway, I wasn't doing anything wrong, there's no law against having fun.'

'Be quiet, Rachel,' David ordered. 'You told me you were going to be with Hannah. Who's this boyfriend of yours?'

'I'm not a kid, I can have a boyfriend. And if these stupid idiots had left me alone then –'

'Quiet!' he snapped.

'There's something I have to ask them. Mr and Mrs Police, what colour are these walls?'

'Don't be silly.'

'It's a reasonable question.'

'Rachel!'

The policewoman removed her cap. Her jet black hair was in a tight bun. With a tissue she wiped water off her brow before continuing. 'That's good advice, Mr Willoughby, because if she carries on like this we still have the option of pressing charges.'

Despite her comatose state Rachel might have sensed the potential seriousness of the situation because she fell silent.

The policeman, a middle aged I've-seen-it-all-before type resigned to wasting his time with such incidents, indicated to his colleague that they should head on. He spoke as they edged towards the door. 'It's a great pity we're distracted from more important duties by this sort of behaviour. As my colleague has indicated, there will be no charges on this occasion but,' now he looked down at Rachel, 'if we catch Rachel in this state again she will be in trouble.'

The policewoman looked across to David. He wondered whether they had a standard script as she took over. 'We have identified that she's a minor so you should be aware that the responsibility to look after her rests with you, Mr Willoughby.'

'I can only offer my apologies. She told me she was at a friend's house.' He regarded Rachel who was staring ahead of her with no sign of remorse. 'Clearly that wasn't the case.'

'Clearly not,' the policewoman responded with an accusing tone.

As soon as he'd shown them out he returned to Rachel. 'What's been going on?' he asked.

'Not talking now,' she said as she tried to stand. Failing, she dropped back onto the couch. 'I won't be sick again, there can't be anything left to come out. I just want to sleep.' She was more successful at the second attempt to get up and was commencing an unbalanced struggle towards the door when Sam appeared.

'I'll help her upstairs, Dad,' he offered.

David watched the two of them leave the room, wishing Jane were there to advise him how to deal with this. Or Bridget, she'd know what to do. He called her.

'Hello?'

'Hi Bridget, it's me.'

'What do you want?' She wasn't her usual bubbly self.

'Only a chat.'

'A chat? Do you know what time it is?'

He looked at his watch, it was well gone midnight. 'I didn't realise it was so late. I'll call back tomorrow.'

'Well, I'm awake now. Chat away.'

'What I made at the cookery course was a great success with the kids.'

Bridget interrupted when he'd begun to describe the main course. 'I'm glad it went well but perhaps you could tell me the rest when we meet.'

'There is something I want to ask you about.'

'Yep, I'm still here.'

'Rachel got brought home by the police this evening.' David listed the collection of misdemeanours – lying about who she was with, not telling him about a boyfriend, getting blind drunk, obstructing the police, out-of-character aggression.

'She wasn't in a fit state to speak which is for the best because I need time to think. The problem is I haven't got a clue what to say. Any ideas?'

'No, not really. I don't know Rachel well enough to

suggest what tactic might work. Perhaps be open, tell her that at the very least you expect honesty. Have you considered asking Jane for help?'

'No. Should I?'

'Possibly. Yes. I'll call tomorrow evening to see how you've got on.'

'Oh, one more thing.'

'David, it is a bit late. I've got a hectic day at work tomorrow.'

'Perhaps not now but soon I want to tell you about my idea for a café.'

'Your list!'

'You've got a good memory.'

'Hard to forget. Yes, I'm happy for you to tell me about it. And I haven't forgotten some of the other things you wrote down. Having you in bed with me right now is a nice thought.'

'Sequentially it fits in after the café, but a change of order is definitely a possibility.'

'Well, let's both have sweet dreams about the sex. Mmmm, mine is starting now. Night-night, David.'

22

David checked on Rachel before going to bed. She was sprawled diagonally across her own bed, fully dressed and snoring, a bucket on the floor by her side. A rancid streak of yellow-brown on the carpet around it indicated that she had partially missed her target. Having shifted her so that her head rested on the pillow, he covered her with the quilt like a dad tucking in a small child. Only this child was now a young adult with actions and thoughts that she kept to herself. He emptied the bucket down the toilet, washed it out in the sink, and reinstated it in Rachel's bedroom just in case.

The next morning he left her to sleep off the hangover, leaving a text.

Off to work. Disappointed – expect honest explanation later. Text me if you want picking up after Fiddler. I assume you'll get to school later.

He was glad not to have seen her because he needed more time to decide whether to take up Bridget's suggestion of involving Jane. There were pluses. After all, she was still her mother and she was good at this sort of thing. There was a minus though,

Rachel didn't want anything to do with her.

Deep in thought as he drove into the local authority car park, he scraped his car on a concrete column. Inspecting the damage, he noted the symmetry of matching striations on each side of his vehicle. In anger he lifted his foot and kicked his front tyre, this setting off the alarm on the neighbouring vehicle. It was Mary's BMW. He fled.

There was a Post-it from Mary on the corner of his computer screen. *Please come to my office as soon as you can.* The relationship with Mary had improved since his staff review, her emails were noticeably more conciliatory. He'd responded with feigned enthusiasm for her proposals for departmental improvements despite believing them to be unworkable.

He had no idea why she had called this meeting. He was greeted by something remarkably similar to a smile. Perhaps he was misinterpreting a sneer, scowl or snarl, but her facial expression continued to resemble a smile. It made her look quite different – almost pleasant.

'Is everything alright?'

'Of course. Why do you ask?'

'Nothing in particular.'

It wasn't only the smile, there were a range of modifications to note. Mary's soft curls had gone, replaced by a severe asymmetrical cut, the hair on the left side brushing her shoulder while on the right barely reaching the bottom of an ear adorned with a dangling silver earring. One earing – surely executives were meant to wear two. The previously brown hair had been dyed a much lighter colour. When she stood to greet David, this also a first, he stopped in his tracks. She had on the identical maroon and lime green skirt with beige cardigan that Bridget had worn the previous Saturday. Was this a coincidence or was she stalking him as a weird punishment for his harsh words at the staff review?

He was so taken aback by her transformation that he remained rooted to the spot. Mary looked good, very good, her lips scarlet, her mascara thick and black.

'You don't have to wait for my permission to sit down. Fancy a coffee?' she asked, lifting the cafetière from the top of a cabinet.

'Yes please,' David squeaked in response to the new softer, slower, seductive voice.

He sat watching her prepare the drinks, her back to him, an attractive back. He'd never thought of her femininity before, she'd just been his unpleasant boss.

Mary set down two mugs, a milk jug, the cafetiere and a plate of dark chocolate wafers on the desk between them. 'The real stuff,' she said as she poured. 'I'm a bit of a coffee snob.'

'Me too.'

'Look, I owe you an apology. In my obsession to make changes I wanted to start by letting everyone know that I was in charge. That was a childish power grabbing ploy. It was wrong and I'm sorry.'

She picked up a wafer and took a bite. The chocolate melted against her warm coffeed lips, the smear blending with the scarlet lipstick. This generated erotic thoughts which in turn brought on a sense of disloyalty towards Bridget.

'Working for the council is different to my experience of the private sector but that doesn't make it worse here.'

'No,' David agreed, barely listening.

Was Mary aware of his state of mind because she was smiling as she licked the chocolate off the top of the wafer, her delicate pink tongue moving from side to side? 'Mmmm, these are good. I hope you can forget the past and we can move on as a unified team.'

"Mmmm." Bridget had uttered that same sound the night before. 'Yes, I can.' David was struggling with confused thoughts about Mary and Bridget.

Back in his office any work was impossible. He tried to replace fantasy with accountancy, diving into spreadsheets created to establish procedures to prevent future budget difficulties.

All this came to a sudden halt when he remembered that a confrontation with Rachel loomed. Jabulani came into his room at the point when this realisation had hit home.

'Oh dear, not a happy face. Another bad meeting?'

'What?'

'With Mary.'

'No, she was fine. I don't know what's got into her but she's completely different.'

'Long may it last. Then why the gloomy face?'

'Oh, my daughter. She was brought home drunk by the police last night.'

'I'm sorry to hear that.'

'I'm sure I can sort it,' David replied, more in hope than expectation.

'She's sixteen, isn't she?'

David nodded.

'Well at least I've got a few more years before having those worries with my own children. I came in to give you this.'

David took hold of the flyer. As he read it Jabulani announced: 'You are to be an honoured guest at our first gig in England.'

He and his brother, their wives and three other Zimbabweans had formed a band called Kanjani and they were performing at The Duchess of Devonshire the night before New Year's Eve.

'Brilliant. I'd love to come.'

'Will we see your new woman?'

'She's not that, but we are getting on well.'

'Bring her and then she'll be an even closer friend.'

David smiled. 'I will.'

'Excellent. And how are your onion layers? Have you stripped any more off?'

'Actually it's more a case of putting some back on; I'm much happier now. What made you think of using onions to explain personality? It's neat.'

'I made it up though I'm probably not the first with the idea. I could have chosen carrots or sweet potatoes. Onion happened to be what I came out with.'

'Carrots and sweet potatoes don't have layers though.'

'True. What a wise man you are. I'd better get back

to work, see you at lunchtime.'

As soon as Jabulani left him David called Bridget to get her to add the date to her diary. Her reply wasn't what he had expected to hear, in fact it was dreadful. The family would be spending Christmas and the New Year with relatives up in Scotland.

'You'll miss the gig.'

'I'm afraid so. I'll be back the second or third of January. Sorry I haven't told you but I suppose it's only now that we've reached the point of sharing diaries. I guess we are sort of dating, aren't we?'

'Well yes, I suppose we are.'

'I haven't forgotten a missing deed which I want as much as you do. I'm not going to write it down though! And there's that chat about your café to have, too.'

'Yes, both though one of them takes priority.'

'And on the subject of priorities, have you decided what to do about Rachel?'

He'd gone round and round in circles wondering how to approach this. Past conversations had dealt with homework, menus, the dangers of smoking, everything trivial compared to issues like the risks associated with abuse, STDs, contraception, alcohol and drugs.

'I'm going to ask Jane to join me for this,' he announced, as much to himself as to Bridget.

'I think that's a good idea. Let me know how it goes.'

23

David was making the right decision. Yes, Jane had left them, but she'd been at the heart of every child crisis for sixteen years. He needed her now.

When he called to explain what had happened she was eager to take part in the evening meeting. 'I appreciate including me. Thank you.'

Rachel hadn't gone to school that day. In an attempt to move on she'd cleaned her bedroom, gone food shopping and cooked dinner. Although obliging and friendly, there was no reference to the evening before, no apology.

After dinner, with Sam out the room, David announced the meeting. 'We must discuss last night. Mum will be joining us.'

'We don't need her.'

'It's a serious matter. We do.'

'What do you mean by "it"?'

'Several things.'

As if on cue they heard the front door open and Jane joined them in the kitchen. 'Hello David. Rachel.'

Rachel offered a cursory nod as her mother sat

down.

David began. 'We're all aware that there are family issues but I hope we can put those aside for a while to find out what's going on. Agreed?' With no acknowledgement from Jane or Rachel on offer, he pushed ahead. 'The first thing is that you told me a lie, Rachel. You said you would be at Hannah's.'

Rachel admitted that she'd been out with Joe, her boyfriend.

'I didn't know you had a boyfriend.'

'Nor did I,' Jane added.

'How serious is it?'

'I think what David is asking is are you sleeping with him?'

'His parents are usually around so I sleep in the spare room. But I'm not a child. Sometimes I'm in his bed.'

'You are a child, Rachel. You should not be *in bed*, as you put it, with a boy at your age.'

'I'm sixteen, Mum, it's legal.'

'That's not the point. We don't even know him. Who is he?' Jane continued.

'Someone at school.'

'Perhaps we should meet him. At least have the address of where you're staying; that's a basic safety precaution,' David suggested.

'I can't see what meeting him has got to do with it. He hasn't got to be approved by you.'

'If I were still here I wouldn't allow you to go out with him until we'd met.'

'Well you're not here and your obsession with

meeting him is absurd. I *have* met Jim, is that supposed to make it easier to know you're fucking him?'

A furious Jane let fly. 'There's a lot for you to think about, Rachel, starting with some respect. Questioning my behaviour is a bit rich having heard how your father was summoned to school to be told about bad behaviour. After what happened last night if I were your father I wouldn't trust you to go out.'

'Thankfully you're not my father and it's nice to have one parent who cares about me.'

'Don't you ever forget all I've done for you, all the sacrifices I've made. That's true isn't it, David?...No, Rachel, don't try to answer back because I haven't finished...Where do you think you're going, I haven't finished? Come back here this instant. Rachel!'

Jane and David were left alone.

'I was hoping to resolve things a bit more amicably,' David said.

Jane got up and headed over to the storage unit to the left of the sink. 'I need a coffee, do you want one?'

'Yes, why not.'

She opened the cupboard. It was full of tins, bottles and jars. 'The mugs have gone.'

'They haven't gone, they've moved.'

'Why?'

'I felt like a change. I put them in there,' David said, pointing. 'The milk's still in the fridge though,' he joked.

The holiday snap was on the fridge door, the one with everyone smiling. She paused to examine the picture before replacing the milk. 'That was a fun holiday, wasn't it?'

He didn't reply; she must have started her affair with Jim by then. He sat in silence as Jane manufactured two perfect cappuccinos.

'Thanks for asking me over, even though it was a bit of a disaster. I shouldn't have lost my temper.'

David realised he was no longer bitter about what had happened, it was all about layers of onions. They chatted on for a while as they drank their coffees, agreeing that their lawyers had earned enough money and it was time to resolve unfinished business.

At the front door Jane seemed geared up for a hug but David stepped back. As soon as she'd left Rachel came downstairs.

'Sorry, I shouldn't have got angry.'

His daughter was changing. In the past, engulfed in a whirlwind of emotion, she would explode with rage. This would be followed by tears and remorse for her behaviour. Now she was calm, detached, hard.

'Yes, it would have been better not to. That applies to both of you.'

'Yeah, especially her. Fucking bitch!'

'Rachel!'

'Only joking. Shall we sing the Queen song.'

'No.'

David called Bridget to relay the evening's events. She was preoccupied with getting things ready for their trip. When she told him that there wouldn't be time to see each other before she departed he had the horrible thought that she was no longer interested in him.

~

The last days at work before the Bridgetless Christmas break were quietly festive. Colleagues put up streamers and displayed Christmas cards on desks and window sills. David wanted to sidle away on the final afternoon but at Jabulani's insistence he joined in with tea time mince pie eating followed by the pub for a drink. The new Mary was at the heart of the festivities, laughing away and drinking rather a lot.

On Christmas morning Sam got his model racing car and Rachel got new earphones – both outrageously priced. They also each got a sack full of this and that, a tradition that had survived since early childhood.

Jane would be seeing the pair over the New Year. Ahead of that was an undesirable but necessary duty.

'I'm not sure which is going to be worse,' Rachel stated as they were driving up to Birmingham. 'Seeing Mum or this trip to Grandma.'

On arrival and with the hugging over, their grandmother gave the children £40 each. 'I've got no idea what young people want these days so money is best.'

'Agreed Grandma. Thank you,' Rachel said as she folded the notes into her phone cover, leaving David to tot up how many shots of gin or vodka that could buy.

'Here's ours, Gran,' Sam said, taking the neatly wrapped parcels out of the plastic bag. They watched impatiently as she opened the presents, explaining that she would be reusing the paper. She received three handkerchiefs with embroidered flowers on the corners, a bottle of sweet sherry, a box of chocolates and six luxury mince pies.

'What have you got for Dad?'

'He's too old for presents, Rachel.'

'But you've got presents and you're older than him.'

'That's different,' was the only explanation on offer. 'Sit in the lounge and I'll make tea.'

Charlotte and her family joined them, popping in on their way to her husband Donald's parents. By the end of their visit David wondered how the pair of them could be related. His sister showed no interest let alone sympathy regarding his separation from Jane. Rachel and Sam fared little better with their two cousins despite being almost identical ages. Donald sat in sullen silence.

'Great to see you all,' Charlotte said as she drained her second cup of tea. 'Must go though or else we'll be late for lunch.'

Their own lunch consisted of dried-out turkey, boiled to death Brussels sprouts and rock hard roast potatoes.

'This has got to be the best meal ever,' Sam proclaimed.

'I can't wait for Her Majesty's speech, Gran.'

'*The Sound of Music* is on soon, that's got to be my all-time favourite.'

'Morecombe and Wise, has there ever been anything funnier?'

Gran took great delight in such comments, failing

to recognise that her grandson's proclamations were steeped with sarcasm. Like Rachel, he's growing up fast, David observed.

Despite the drudgery they stayed on for two nights, trapped by the feeling of guilt nurtured by David's mother. Rachel was furious to be missing partying opportunities, but David insisted they remain, in part as a safeguard against his daughter getting into trouble.

On the day after Boxing Day they played countless games of cribbage before partaking in the final Christmas leftovers lunch – the turkey drier than ever, the Brussels sprouts mushier, the potatoes like cannonballs, and the depressing new addition of fat-saturated sausages.

'This is even better than yesterday,' Sam told his grandmother.

'I knew you'd like the sausages.'

Rachel volunteered to do the clearing up. When she failed to return to the lounge for over an hour, David checked to see what was going on. She was sat at the Formica kitchen table.

'What are you doing?'

'I'm watching the second hand go round,' she said, pointing to the clock on the wall above the birthday calendar. 'It's the most exciting thing on offer.'

'Can I join you?' At least that made Rachel smile.

When David's mother suggested that they stay on for another day a rebellion erupted while she was out the room making tea.

'If you say yes I'm getting the train back,' Rachel

declared.

'And I'll reveal my true thoughts about Morecombe and Wise. And her food.'

His mother came into the lounge and set the tray down. 'As soon as we've had this I'll prepare dinner.'

'Sorry Grandma, we can't stay. If I don't get my coursework finished they'll kick me out of school.'

David was relieved that Rachel had been the brave one. 'Yes, tea then I'm afraid we're off. It's been a great couple of days, hasn't it?'

'I'm sure you've got more important things to do than staying here.'

'Yes, we have,' said Rachel, mimicking her mother's method of tackling the guilt trip.

24

'Dad, everyone knows it's a drug den.'

'Well, everybody except me, Rachel. I went to hear the music.'

'Do you realise you're a marked man now, with a police record? You'll get the sack and no one else will employ you.'

'Very funny. Actually the police were extremely apologetic about keeping me there for so long, but I can see their point. They couldn't let anyone go before a search. The owners have been arrested for dealing.'

'Dealing – you're even using the right term. I bet you know all the slang for drugs, too. I'm not sure I'd have let you off if I was the police.'

'Ha-ha.'

'Seriously though, next time you score skunk get me some Black Russian or White Widow.'

David had called Rachel from the pub a little before midnight to explain the situation. He told her not to wait up, but unsurprisingly curiosity got the better of her. She was watching a re-run of *Buffy The Vampire Slayer* when he got home and refused to go to bed until he'd told her exactly what had happened.

That was over an hour ago.

'Enough Rachel,' David implored. 'I'm exhausted.'

~

Jabulani's gig was at the Duchess of Devonshire, a pub he'd walked past many times. It was a double-fronted mock Tudor building, shabby and run down. On the night of the concert, ravaged by frost, the row of hanging baskets were filled with the sagging black remains of dead flowers. A sign attached to the wall by the entrance advertised that night's specials – sausage with mash and cottage pie with chips. Would they be prepared to serve sausages with chips, he wondered as he moved up to the hand-written notice pinned to the door.

David was tapped on the shoulder. 'Hello there.'

He spun round to see his boss standing behind him. 'Mary! I didn't know you were coming.'

They read the notice together. *Tonight: Kanjarny from Zimbarbwe. Entrance £3.*

'Actually it's Kanjani. K-A-N-J-A-N-I. It means "hi there" Jabulani told me.'

'They're not too hot on the spelling of the country either,' Mary added.

They laughed together. That was a first.

Stepping inside there was no evidence of a band. A darts match was being screened on two giant TVs which no one appeared to be watching. Four boys of questionable drinking age were playing pool while vying for the attention of the two girls sitting on a bare wooden bench near them. An eczema-faced, greasy-haired youth cried out, 'Me ball's tight against the hole again,' this followed by shrieks of pretend laughter from the girls.

The only other customers were a middle-aged man and woman sitting at a table with half empty pints of Guinness in front of them. She was gesticulating wildly; he had turned away from her. As David and Mary passed them the woman leapt up.

'You ain't listening, are you?'

'That's 'cos I've 'eard it all before.'

'If you did somefin' about it I wouldn't keep goin' on, would I?'

'Yes you would, yer never stop!'

'I'm goin' home!'

'Suit yerself, I'm finishin' this.'

They watched the man tipping the remains of the one glass into the other before they approached the bar.

'This can't be the right place,' Mary uttered.

'But it said it was here on the note outside. This is like an *Eastenders* set,' David added, looking behind the bar at the buxom middle-aged woman with dark roots at the base of her bleach-blonde hair.

'What can I get you?' the landlady asked.

'We're here to see Kanjani – the band,' David answered, self-conscious of his posh voice.

The barmaid nodded towards a door at the far end of the room. 'In there.'

Four others from the local authority had joined them. Charlie, Mitch, Dee and Freddie worked on David's floor. They were the ones who made up the nicknames for Mary.

The world the six of them entered was very different to the room they had come from. Here lighting was subdued and the dark walls were filled with retro rock concert posters. Having paid they made their way towards the small lit stage in the corner to greet Jabulani who was shifting a speaker into place. 'You've made it, wonderful. This is my brother, Farai,' he said, indicating the man by his side. There were handshakes all round. 'We'll be starting soon.'

'Could we move away from this lot?' Mary whispered looking across at the others from the local authority. 'Their immaturity drives me up the wall.'

The room was filling quickly. David recognised a few other local authority employees, with the rest of the audience, judging by clothes and hairstyles, perhaps described as ageing hippies.

Having followed Mary to a rail of hangers and helped her out of her North Face Polar Protection coat, he struggled to avoid a gasp. If a name were needed to describe that night's attire it would be *Rock Chick*. If he were truthful, *Divine Rock Chick*.

Mary had on tight fitting jeans with rips across the knees; an equally tight fitting black T-shirt with a sequined jazz trumpeter, his instrument raised aloft; and a multi-coloured bead necklace. He had to have a second take of her feet. Each toe, exposed in high-heeled sandals, was painted a different vibrant colour.

Of course both takes happened in a split second but when he looked back up to Mary he knew that she was aware of his inspection.

'I think you deserve a drink on me,' she said, utilising her newly acquired slow and sensuous voice.

Taking hold of his arm she led him to the bar and ordered a bottle of wine. As she was filling their glasses the band came on stage. There were seven of them, three women and four men, dressed in matching kaftan tops and baggy white trousers. The shirts were white with a purple animal with horns as a motif.

The music started, acoustic guitar and two instruments Jabulani had told David about – the *mbira* and the *hosho*. It was highly rhythmic with hand clapping, harmony vocals and dancing. The appreciative audience swayed along. Farai did lots of talking between numbers, explaining the origin of the instruments and the inspiration for their songs. Briefly he referred to the political situation in Zimbabwe, too.

'Tatenda. Thank you,' he called out after one song. 'Now we put our instruments down for *Steam Train*. These trains were running in my country long after they had stopped here. Children were brought up with the shushing and the clattering noises. We would race along the side of the track waving to the passengers.'

As the hissing harmonies began the audience started to dance. Mary, having downed her second glass of wine, took hold of David's hand and dragged him onto the dance floor with a determination reminiscent of Bridget at the school reunion. They stayed put for a second song, this one slow and melodic. Mary put her hands on David's shoulders and he responded by laying his hands on her waist. She pulled him closer. He enjoyed the contact, offering no more than a minute degree of unnoticed resistance in deference of loyalty towards Bridget.

'God, I need another drink,' she said, leading him back to the shelf where their bottle and glasses rested. She knocked back her third glass. 'We're getting low, I'll grab another one.'

'Enough for me, I feel quite light-headed.'

'It's the dope.'

'What do you mean?'

'There's so much around you don't need to smoke it to get stoned, you just have to breathe.' She moved closer to him. 'You're quite an innocent, aren't you?' She moved closer still and their lips met. For an instant, actually for quite a bit more than an instant, he enjoyed the soft warmth of the kiss before drawing back.

'No, Mary, we can't.'

'Why not? You've separated from your wife; I thought maybe we…'

'Oh it's complicated, Mary. You see …'

Their conversation was brought to a sudden end as six policemen and women came bursting through the door. The band stopped playing and one of the policeman, the very same man who had visited David after his mugging and again when bringing the drunk Rachel home, climbed onto the stage.

'Everyone must stay in this room until they have been interviewed.'

It was an efficient operation. The audience was divided into five lines to be questioned by a designated policeman. The sixth officer, the policewoman he also knew from the two previous incidents, acknowledged him with a nod. Once the interviews had commenced some of the audience were passed over to her and she wrote down details of something or other. Might these be the ones to be arrested for drug offences? Did Mary have drugs on her?

No one was allowed to use their phone or leave until all the interviewing was over. Departures were then permitted except for seven who stayed behind with the police. David called Rachel to let her know he was on the way home. It was 1.30 a.m.

Mary and David left together, he hoping to avoid any follow-up to the earlier kissing. She grabbed hold of his hand as soon as they were out the building. 'Sorry if I was pushy or misunderstood your situation. Hey, it was a fun night though, wasn't it?'

'No need to apologise. It certainly was interesting. I enjoyed it.' Perhaps it would have been better not to have mentioned enjoyment.

'We've done rather a lot of apologising lately, haven't we?' she continued, taking hold of his other hand. 'There's my taxi, I'd better head on. Have a great New Year and I'll see you back at work.'

Mary drew David towards her and planted her lips on his.

In assessing the deed afterwards, several things crossed David's mind.

The duration of the second kiss was considerably longer than their first one.

As their tongues touched there was more than a

hint of arousal.

With his arms tightly wrapped around her, his erection must have been apparent as their bodies clamped together.

Turning back having waved Mary off in the taxi, he was aware of Charlie, Mitch, Dee and Freddie watching. There was plenty of scope for office gossip.

25

The following evening on the dot of midnight Bridget called David just as Jools Holland was starting the countdown. He left the lounge where Sam and Rachel were with him watching the show; he needed privacy. What would he be telling Bridget?

'Happy New Year!' was her greeting.

'And a Happy New Year to you!'

'Everything OK? How was Jabulani's gig?'

'Gig?' Because of what happened with Mary he didn't want to talk about the concert even though the police involvement was quite some story to tell.

'You did go, didn't you?' It wasn't as if he'd done anything wrong. All the chasing had come from Mary.

'Yes. It was fine.' Responding to the first kiss had only been out of politeness.

'Fine? You don't sound particularly enthusiastic.' The second kiss was a little different and he had been a tiny bit aroused. But that was no more than a man's normal physiological reaction.

'No, it was excellent.' Mary had looked great. Surely there's nothing wrong in appreciating another woman's attractiveness. 'It's just that there was a spot of bother with the police.'

'Police!'

'Nothing much, just a drugs raid. I'll tell you all about it when we meet.' Who knows what might have happened had there not been the police intervention?

'Do you do drugs?'

'No, of course not.' It was time to change the subject. 'When are you back?'

'Late tomorrow evening. You sound weird, are you sure you don't do drugs?'

'I promise not. When can I see you?'

'Sunday afternoon would be good; come over for tea. Actually, there's something I need to tell you about.'

'Great. See you then.'

What a relief, the conversation was drawing to a close without the need to mention Mary. The second kiss had been enjoyable, the whole evening had been enjoyable, but not in the same league as being with Bridget. And seeing Bridget ahead of having to deal with Mary at work on Monday was a godsend. He had no idea what to expect from his boss but knew how he would behave. Polite. Professional. Friendly. Detached.

'Bye.'

'Bye, Bridget.'

~

Sunday afternoon arrived and they were sitting on a sofa in Bridget's lounge drinking peppermint tea. David sensed reticence as he tried to kiss her and possible reasons were flashing through his mind.

Option One was that any anxiety was coming from him because he was nervous, intending to own up about Mary. Perhaps not the full story but at least that she had been there with him. Option Two was that somehow Bridget had already found out. Option Three was anything else, most likely that she was going to dump him (not that they were quite in a relationship) having met someone while away in Scotland.

Bridget pulled further away. 'There's something I need to tell you.'

'I'm listening,' he said solemnly as he gazed at her anxious face. Option Three was the front running explanation for the tension. Or maybe Option Two.

'There's something you have to know. Roland didn't die by accident, I killed him. You're in the same room as a murderer.'

David expected a smile but Bridget remained serious. She had a great sense of humour, dark and cynical. The punch line to a joke was about to follow. He allowed the pause to build up but nothing ensued.

He broke the silence. 'Don't be silly.'

'I'm not. It's true. I killed him and I was lucky to get away with it. I can thank my dad for that.'

'You're telling me you murdered Roland and your father helped you? I don't believe you.'

'Well my father wasn't there when I did it, but he made sure I got off scot-free. Let me tell you what happened.'

David nodded, still half anticipating an amusing twist.

'You already know a bit about what Roland was

like, not all the nasty details because there's no need. Dad and Mum were aware of how unpleasant he was, they saw it every time we visited. They hadn't liked him from the outset and warned me off marrying him, but who listens to their parents about things like that?

'One day, arriving at their house in floods of tears, I finally admitted just how sordid our relationship was, that Roland was a serial seducer of students at the art college. He hadn't come home the previous night and when he'd turned up in the morning I let him know that was it between us. He let fly, the cheek of it, blaming me for his infidelity.

'What I told you the first time round about my parents' suggestion of a holiday was true. They volunteered to look after Andy and Kay and to pay for it in the hope that there was a last chance to sort things out.

'I had no enthusiasm to go along with their idea because to my mind we were finished, but they urged me to try and I relented. You know what happened next, me searching online and finding a lovely cottage in the Scottish Highlands by the sea. I booked the flights and the car. Although we were all but estranged, Roland was always ready to grab a freebie so it didn't take much persuading to get him to come along.

'The trip was a disaster from the word go. On the train journey to the airport he was as deriding as ever and I knew even then that being stuck together in a relative wilderness for ten days was going to be a nightmare. True to form, the first week was hell and I was counting down the days to the return home. He was probably doing the same.

'There were four days left.'

~

'My turn to drive, Roland. Let's head north, the guide book says there are stunning views up that way.'

'I don't want another fucking walk. Can't we find somewhere with a bowling alley or a cinema or even one bloody shop?'

'Tell you what, let's make this the last day here. We can head back to Inverness tomorrow and spend some time there.'

'I'm bored. Why not leave today?'

Bridget grabbed hold of his hand in an act of friendship. 'Come on, one more and tomorrow I'll book us into the fanciest hotel in Inverness, one with a spa. Then we can lie around relaxing for a few days.'

He pulled his hand away and in silence they collected their boots, rainwear and the packed lunches Bridget had prepared. Their phones remained where they had put them on the first day, on the kitchen table. Since there was no reception there was no point taking them.

Bridget drove while Roland cursorily flicked through the guide book, looking thoroughly miserable. 'Where the hell are we heading?'

'I've got a rough idea though it hardly matters, it's all so beautiful.' And it was – the scenery was stunning. Spring sunshine illuminated the patches of snow nestled in the dips below the rugged peaks. Waterfalls tumbled and crashed against the rock faces.

Lower downhill the bare grey-brown rocks gave way to meadows filled with purple and yellow flowers.

It was outside of the mainstream tourist season and the scenery was theirs alone to savour along the traffic-free roads. Bridget turned into what was little more than a track and after a short while they reached an irregular rocky pavement stretching out towards the distant sea.

'Perfect. All set?' Bridget's smile and light tone failed to illicit any enthusiasm from her husband.

'If we must,' he uttered, avoiding eye contact.

Roland strode off, head down, lost in his own dark thoughts. Bridget trailed behind, crossing the uneven ground with care. Her husband kept going, not once turning back to check on her wellbeing. No attempt to wait for her. No conversation. No interest.

'It's over,' she muttered. 'It really is over.'

She stopped to remove a stone from her boot. Sitting on a slab of rock smoothed by centuries of battering, she took it off and rubbed her foot. She looked behind her at the line of spectacular cliffs.

Roland was calling and Bridget turned back towards the sea.

'Look…' was all she could make out against the roar of water; the tide was coming in fast and they should soon head back.

He was smiling as he came running towards her.

'Careful, Roland, it's slippery.'

He kept on and she could see what he was holding up in his right hand. A giant crab. His smile was a malicious one, well known to her.

'Catch,' he called out when still some distance away. He leaned back, swung his arm and hurled the crab towards Bridget. It landed with a crunch on a rock a few paces in front of her, its shell crushed to pieces, its pincers twisted. The noise of the crab landing was followed by a much heavier thud as Roland slipped from the rock he'd perched on.

Bridget remained seated for a few seconds, her wish for calm silence disturbed by the breaking of waves and the shrieking of gulls.

'Roland? You OK?' Bridget called out as she tied up her boot lace. With little urgency she walked across to her husband, to see him lying quite still on the edge of a rock pool. He was out cold. He must have landed on his head because blood was running from a gash at his temple. The left side of his face rested in the water, turning the water pink and sending a group of tiny crabs scurrying for safety.

As she gently shook Roland, trying to rouse him, Bridget considered the options. And one was so obvious and easy she couldn't resist it. His nose and mouth were partly immersed under water and she left him like that, watching as air bubbles escaped as he breathed out.

Bridget returned to where she'd left her things and took out a cheese sandwich from her backpack. The tide was advancing quickly so she'd have to get a move on or else she might get trapped. Removing the cling film from the sandwich and crunching it into a ball, she took her first bite as she set off to seek the help that she knew would be too late.

~

'What happened next was more or less what I told you the first time, the only difference being what was going on in my head. Instead of being panic-struck and dashing to get help, I strolled back to the car and set off towards the cluster of cottages we'd passed on the way. It took an hour or so before I was banging on the door of the first in the line. "My husband's out there," I screamed at the old lady who greeted me, playacting the terror. "He fell over, he's injured and out cold." She was a sweetie, phoning the emergency services and making me a strong cup of tea with loads of sugar and a tot of whisky.

'It took a while for two policemen to arrive. The older one, he looked close to retirement, told me that one rescue team had immediately set off by boat and another by helicopter, before gently pointing out that it would be a race against time because the tide was against them. I had a good go at gasping in shock and began to sob. "I've killed my husband," I cried out, regretting it immediately because whilst the older one was consoling me, I saw the quiet younger one frown with what looked like recognition of over-acting. I started to panic about the chance of being found out. All those TV dramas I'd watched about the police uncovering what the perpetrator had thought was the perfect crime. Do you want me to carry on?'

'Yes, do. Though you left him there, you didn't actually do anything wrong.'

'In this case not doing anything was as bad as doing it myself. Surely you can see that. You must hate me.'

'Of course I don't. I'm assuming it ended well since here you are rather than in a Scottish prison.' David was unsure whether his observation was to make light of it or merely record the fact. Whatever the purpose, if Bridget had allowed it to happen when she could have prevented Roland's death, this seemed way out of character.

'My father saved the day. Without him I don't think I would have been able to cope. That Scottish prison would have been true.'

Her father travelled up to Scotland, arriving the day Roland's body was washed ashore. When the two policemen returned to let them know, he ushered them into the kitchen, closing the door behind them. When they came out he announced that he would be the one to identify the body.

'I asked why. "Because it's nothing more than the remains of a body, fish have seen to that" he told me. I burst out crying, a genuine feeling of shock and remorse for what I'd allowed to happen. Had done. Later on my father explained that he had set out to upset me to allay any distrust the policemen might have had ahead of the autopsy.

'Being a forensic scientist he knew what to do to prevent suspicion. He befriended the coroner ahead of the session, reminiscing about past gruesome cases. I was instructed on what to say at the post-mortem, to describe everything as accurately as possible, even our arguments during the holiday, everything that is up to the point when I left Roland's head submerged in water.

'Accidental death by drowning was the verdict. Incorrect though because I'm a murderer. What do you think of me now, David?'

'Even if you'd lifted his head out of the water he would still have drowned. It's not as if you would have been able to carry him to safety.'

'Maybe not, but I made sure, didn't I? God, how it hangs over me.'

'I can understand that, but look, it doesn't affect how I feel towards you.'

David put his arm around Bridget and she managed a smile. They sat in silence for a while before Bridget sprang up. 'Perhaps it's best if you go.'

'No. Let me –'

'Please. You need time to think things through.'

'If that's what you want, but only if we can speak or meet tomorrow.'

'Sure.'

26

The four females central to David's life were stressing him out. This was an understatement – he was a bundle of nerves.

Only a few weeks ago his pathway had seemed one of pleasant simplicity. He was racing through his list of short and long term objectives with uncharacteristic determination. There had been an unfulfilled night with Bridget but certainty that it was only a matter of time before they would be in a relationship. His tyrannical manager's dreadful behaviour had cemented his decision to quit the local authority. There was a growing confidence that he could cope with single parenthood. There was a truce with Jane.

Unsurprisingly, top of the list in generating anxiety was Bridget. She had insisted he leave having recounted the events surrounding the death of Roland. "Death" was his choice of word. "Murder" was hers.

'It doesn't affect how I feel towards you,' he'd told her, but by the time he was driving home he was less sure. Yes, Roland probably would have died anyway, but Bridget had made certain. She had left his head partly submerged. She had taken her time to get help, possibly the delay critical. From the little Bridget had told him her husband had been a bully and a tyrant, but that didn't make it right to leave him there without trying to save him.

He switched on the radio to blank out all thoughts of Bridget's crime. The Radio 4 *Moral Maze* discussion was about deceit and infidelity. This got him thinking about Mary. Although there had been no infidelity, not telling Bridget about what had happened between him and his boss on the evening of the concert was definitely deceitful.

Putting the guilt to one side, how should he handle seeing Mary tomorrow, their first day back after the Christmas break? It was too risky playing it by ear. He needed a plan and one began to take shape as he drove. He'd start by seeing Jabulani to find out more about the drugs raid, providing a topic of conversation with Mary to sidestep any talk about the other thing. He remained unsure if all the flirting had come from her or whether he had contributed. Perhaps it all boiled down to tongues, specifically their tongues touching during that second kiss. If she had slipped her tongue into his mouth then she was solely to blame and there was nothing to tell Bridget. If he had offered his to meet hers then it was a shared responsibility. He still wouldn't tell Bridget but that would be deceitful.

The third female on his mind was Rachel. Tomorrow was the start of the new school term, his daughter's return after her drunken escapade. The boyfriend would be with her and there was nothing

David could do to stop that. Though why should he? Sixteen-year-olds date. But what was this boyfriend like? Was he treating his daughter with respect? Did she know enough about contraception and STDs? Arriving home David heard whispered conversations when he passed Rachel's bedroom. He assumed they were with that boy.

Finally there was Jane to fret about, ranked at the bottom of the priority list despite this being the woman he had known for longer than the other three combined. They were about to sign the divorce papers. David was hit by a bizarre cocktail of relief, remorse, regret, joy and failure as he contemplated the end of their marriage.

With the children upstairs he relaxed in the lounge listening to the music he and Jane had shared a past love for – Arctic Monkeys, Coldplay, Arcade Fire. He poured out a glass of Merlot and turned his attention to the café idea. For a habitually risk averse man he was quick to make the bold decision to give it a go. The reasoning was simple, he could either sit at a desk analysing spreadsheets for the rest of his working life or run a coffee bar that would offer exciting arts based entertainments. Even if he failed, thereafter known as the man who chucked in a great council job helping the elderly to set up a coffee bar that never had a chance of attracting enough customers to be a success – he'd still opt for the café.

It was time to start planning in earnest, but not that night; he was exhausted.

There are few situations more dismal than not

being able to sleep when in desperate need. Bridget was the problem, the usual erotic thoughts about her replaced by ones about what she'd told him earlier that day.

On meeting her at the reunion he'd been enchanted by her serenity and kindness. Owning up to murder challenged this view. OK, it was only a slight murder, though did the concept of "slight murder" make any sense? It wouldn't wash with the police, lawyers, judges or a jury.

What about justice though? Didn't Roland deserve what he got? There followed an internal struggle to make the case for this, but in the end David couldn't accept that cruelty merited death.

And then there was truth to consider, or more to the point lying, because Bridget had lied to him when initially talking about Roland. A bizarre thought struck David, that the account second time round was equally untrue. That Bridget was a compulsive liar and a third version of events would soon follow. One that involved plunging her husband's head under water and holding it down as he regained consciousness and struggled for survival.

What about his own morality? Did he have a moral responsibility, a civic duty, to turn her in?

During this half-awake half-asleep crazy reflection, even fear reared its ugly head. If she had at the very least facilitated a death once, might she murder again? Him?

Justice. Truth. Morality. Fear. Over the centuries philosophers and other great thinkers had dedicated their lives in addressing each of these huge concepts. He'd raced through them in a semiconscious state to reach his decision. Forget the doubts. He liked her. He fancied her. He wanted her.

Time to sleep.

~

It was a cold and grey January Monday morning when a weary David set off for work. He had barely sat down at his desk when his phone rang.

The name he didn't want to see flashed up on the display.

'Good morning, Mary.'

'Hi, David, could you pop in?'

'Sure, give me five minutes.'

'Great. I'll put the coffee on.'

He texted Jabulani. *If you see this call me NOW!*

There was no response so David had little choice other than to abandon his plan. He gathered his thoughts, his composure, and strode into Mary's office intent on orchestrating a professional, detached dialogue.

Mary was by the window pouring the coffee. His brain was ignoring the professional detachment strategy because he couldn't help but notice how attractive she was. Her legs, bum, tapered waist, upright stance, that quirky new haircut. When she turned round, holding two coffees, his disobedient eyes moved down from the striking face to the striking body and back up to the striking face. She was looking at him looking at her; he was in severe danger of giving the wrong signal.

'Quite an evening wasn't it,' she began.

'It was.'

'Did you get home OK?'

'Yes, the walk back calmed me down.'

'Look I'm sorry …'

'I hope you don't think …'

Their statements collided, followed by a silence in anticipation of the other person resuming. Then they laughed together.

David was first to speak, explaining that her understanding that he had separated from his wife was correct, but that he had met someone else since then, a woman he was very fond of …

'So are you in a relationship?'

'Well no, not yet, but we're on the verge of one.'

Mary frowned. 'Our kiss then?'

There was a pause as David considered how to respond before coming up with an utterly impulsive statement. 'I hope you don't mind me saying this, Mary, but I think you're extremely attractive. Quite beautiful.'

'Thank you. That's kind.'

'It's true.'

'I always miss out on the good guys, that's my life story.' Tough cookie Mary was shedding tears as she spoke. 'The ones I end up with think I'm bossy and can't stand it or they're equally bossy and we spend all the time arguing.'

'You, bossy! Surely not.'

David's tease dissolved the tears and produced a smile. 'So recently I've gone for submissive types, but their subservience drives me up the wall and I abandon them as lost causes.'

'What category would I fit in?'

'None of them. I respected you challenging me the other week, I deserved it. And your nicknames about my dress sense are quite funny …'

'They aren't mine! How do you know about them?'

'I do have ears. Idle chat in the kitchen. The thing I like about you is that you have a sensitive side but you're no pushover. It's a good combination.'

David was fighting a guilt-ridden affection for this woman. 'Thanks,' was all he could come up with.

'Something completely different. I was wondering how come you knew some of the police at the raid.'

'It's a long story, but nothing important.'

'Good. I wouldn't like to think we were employing a criminal!'

Mary stood, walked around her desk and faced him. 'There's lots about my behaviour that needs sorting. I think meeting you has helped. It's just a pity that …'

She rested her arm on his shoulder. Their eyes locked and David was happy to move a touch closer as she planted a kiss on his cheek.

'I hope you don't mind that.'

'Not at all. I'd best be going though.'

The feeling of her lips lingered as he walked back to his office. He had wanted to kiss her properly. He still wanted to kiss her properly.

He was making a half-hearted attempt to get started with spreadsheet scrutiny when Jabulani burst in. 'What was the urgency? I was going to call you straight back but saw you were in with her.'

'It wasn't important in the end.'

'You are a dark horse.'

'Shh, Jabulani, at least close the door.'

'You have more onion layers than meets the eye. I did spot your very close slow dance the other night.'

'Oh, that was only being polite, nothing more.'

'Maybe so, but Charlie, Mitch, Dee and Freddie are letting everyone know about something more. A kiss, I believe – a long kiss!'

'Typical of that lot. They work in the School Bus Transport department so I suppose they need something to spice up their lives.'

'But what is going on between you two?'

'Look, Mary is a bit fragile at the moment.'

'And you kissing her will help? She likes you, man, I can see that, and you seem pretty keen on her.'

'No. Bridget is the one for me.' As he said this David revisited his view of Mary's legs, bum, upright posture and quirky hair, this mixed in with thoughts of Bridget committing a murder. 'Great gig,' he continued, keen to change the subject.

David was full of praise about the performance, the singing and dancing, the musicianship, how the band engaged the audience.

'Thank you. What with the arrests we didn't even get paid. Never mind though, we've got other gigs lined up. I hope you'll come along to hear us again.'

'Of course I will.'

'Who with? Bridget or Mary?'

'Get lost, Jabulani!'

~

Early afternoon David picked up a text from Rachel asking him to collect her after the *Fiddler on the Roof* rehearsal. As usual she was sitting on a wall in front of the school gates when he arrived, but this time a boy was by her side. He was tall and lean with straight blond hair down to his shoulders. They walked towards the car together and Rachel opened the front passenger door.

'Hi Dad, this is Joe, alias Lazar Wolf.'

'Hello, Mr Willoughby.' Joe had a pleasant look to him.

'He's my boyfriend and a star in this musical of ours. Lazar Wolf's the second most important male in the show.'

Immediately Joe made the purpose of this meeting clear. 'I want to apologise for the other week. I don't make a habit of getting drunk and neither does Rachel. It was the end of term, we'd been to a party and things got out of hand. It won't happen again, I promise you.'

'Well I appreciate your willingness to meet me to explain. Thanks.'

Rachel was sidling into the car but Joe took hold of her arm to stop her. 'One thing though, Mr Willoughby. I love Rachel and I intend to do whatever I can to make her happy.'

How does a father respond to that? Bridget with Roland, Jane with Jim, Mary with who knew how many men? There was no reason why two sixteen-year-olds should be excluded from the mess called love.

'I'm glad to hear that.'

David could do nothing other than watch as Joe pressed Rachel against the car where they entwined for a protracted kiss.

'He's nice isn't he, Dad,' Rachel said as they departed.

Well, at least he's not a murderer, David thought.

He would call Bridget as soon as he got home.

27

David was an accountant and by nature accountants plan meticulously. They research to get the facts exactly right. They take notes and rehearse what to say. They guard against making false claims.

He would have preferred to speak to Bridget from the heart, not the head, but years of doing things a certain way couldn't be swept aside. Maybe down the line, when he was running the coffee bar, he'd grow a ponytail, have his ears pierced, get a tattoo and become spontaneous. But for now he was David the Accountant so he wrote down a script for the forthcoming conversation. A conversation with a light touch, introducing humour to make her feel at ease.

With the handwritten prompts by his side he dialled, to be greeted by one of those "The person you called is unavailable, please try again later" messages. Having reached the same point twice more he called their landline.

'Hello, Andy. Is Bridget around?'

'No, she's setting up some exhibition. She said if you phoned I should let you know that she'll ring you tomorrow evening.'

'Alright, but please make sure you remember to tell her that I called.'

'Of course I will,' Andy replied in an I'm not stupid voice. 'Must go. Bye.'

The following evening David received a text. *Hi. Still setting up this event, it's a nightmare, back v.late tonight will def. speak tomorrow. Sorry. B xx*

Frustrated having geared himself up for a difficult conversation, he turned his attention to the contents of the A4 envelope from his solicitor. Having scrutinised everything with due care and attention, the solicitor was advising him to sign the document. This was it then, the end of twenty years of marriage to Jane, now blandly referred to as "the other party."

David scrutinised the home possessions sheet. Seeing one of two names against each item was a soul destroying experience. They'd gone from room to room taking it in turns to choose.

'I think I'll have the sideboard.'

'In that case I'll take the sofa.'

'Which one?'

'That one.'

'OK, I'll have this.'

'I think this painting, please.'

'I love that one. Do you remember … Never mind. I'll have this one then.'

It had been far less traumatic dealing with money despite the higher value. Bank accounts, shares and ISAs were just bits of paper, not physical items that they once had shared.

David went online to pay the £2,326.58 to his

solicitor for work to date. The invoice included a twenty pence charge per sheet for photocopying, fifty pounds per telephone call, even the cost of postage was itemised. At least this envelope seemed to be free of charge!

Be positive, be positive, move on, he forced himself to think.

The café.

To start with there was a survey he'd given to work colleagues to process. He'd organised it before the Christmas break to test whether a market existed. The questionnaire results indicated enthusiasm for somewhere decent to go after a meal or a film for those not drawn to the bars frequented by the young. Further answers were equally encouraging.

Would you like to see more independent coffee bars on the high street?

Yes.

Do you currently frequent the coffee bar chains?

Yes.

If an independent coffee shop opened would you switch?

Probably.

Although promising, David recognised that to entice customers his café would need to be different – a venue, not merely a coffee bar. A venue with music, films, poetry readings and art exhibitions. A place that served inviting homemade sandwiches at lunchtime, upmarket cakes and pastries in the afternoon, and a glass of good quality wine or a coffee while being entertained in the evening.

On googling "How to set up a café" he was confronted with 17,454,545 pages. Since lists seemed to work for him he constructed a new one to enable him to narrow down his search.

1. *Buy or lease a property?*
2. *What size of premises?*
3. *Where to locate?*
4. *Process for obtaining alcohol and entertainment licenses?*
5. *Best suppliers of furniture, coffee machines, food and drink?*

That would do for starters.

It was approaching three in the morning when he decided to stop, a heap of notes surrounding him. He was keen to show Bridget what he had achieved but knew that a discussion about the death of Roland would have to come first.

The next day at work, this ahead of any conversation with Bridget, was not easy, beginning as it did with a meeting in Mary's office. They sat together to prepare the following year's budgets, close enough for David to feel the warmth of Mary's body and smell the subtle fragrance of her perfume. Her skirt had ridden up her thighs making it a challenge for David to keep his eyes on the shared screen. It's Bridget I want (despite the murder) he kept telling himself.

'You're not your usual self,' Mary said. 'Is something wrong?'

It wasn't as if Mary was her old usual self either,

not with that provocative look, the edge of her tongue resting on her lower lip. Pink, delicate, inviting.

'No, I'm fine. Let's press on.'

'OK. Office Sundries. I'm hoping you won't be ordering another trillion Post-its!' Mary patted David's thigh as she said this, a little more than a pat, more a caress really. He looked down at her bare thigh and imagined doing likewise.

'We might need a new printer,' he suggested, survival being his sole objective for this meeting.

He was glad to escape the room and buckled down to work until he could head home on the dot of five. Rachel and Sam were in good spirits; their school examinations had started well. They were eating raspberries and yoghurt when his phone rang.

'Oh good, Bridget,' David declared as he was leaving the room. He took out the prompt sheet as he climbed the stairs. 'Hi there.' He closed his bedroom door.

'Hi. Sorry I've been out of contact for a couple of days. We're launching a new artist and he's obsessive about how we have to display his work. And he keeps changing his mind.'

David had thought long and hard about his all-important first statement, the one to set the tone for the entire conversation. He'd revised it several times before coming up with something light, humorous and filled with passion. It was perfect.

'You must know how fond of you I am, Bridget. I don't care how many men you've murdered – I still want to be with you!'

There was a pause without the expected laughter from the other end of the line.

David broke the silence. 'Bridget? Are you there?'

'I'd hoped for a little more sensitivity. It wasn't easy plucking up the courage to tell you.'

'It was a joke.'

'Well, it wasn't funny.'

'Oh.'

'Apart from my parents you're the only one I've ever told. I can never get over what I did, you should be able to grasp that.'

'I do.' David was frantically scanning his prompt notes, racing past all the light and humorous lines in search of something to fit the mood and repair the damage. He found it. 'I've been doing research about the café. It's really exciting.'

'Don't change the subject. Don't you get what I'm saying? I can't have you joking about what happened.'

'You're right and I'm sorry.' This statement was off script. In fact the piece of paper with his notes had dropped to the floor and might as well stay there. Probably for ever because this was shaping up to be a final conversation.

There was an awkward silence with David speechless. Bridget broke the deadlock. 'Maybe speaking over the phone is giving mixed messages. Do you want to meet?'

David struggled to sound upbeat. 'Good idea, I'd like that. When?' He was thinking that what he'd considered as an unstoppable march towards a relationship was about to come to an end and he would be told so when they met.

'Sometime this weekend. You'll have to come here because I can't leave Kay. She's gone down with something that's doing the rounds at school.'

'Poor thing,' David said, in the hope that Bridget might appreciate his concern for her daughter. 'Do send her my best wishes. When do you want me there?'

'Saturday evening?'

'Sure, I'll see you then.' He was squeaking, not speaking. While wondering what else to say, Bridget ended the dialogue with a curt "Bye" and cut the call.

It would be an understatement to describe the conversation as a failure. Even calling it a disaster wasn't strong enough. He had antagonised Bridget beyond redemption.

Sleep didn't come easily that night as he rued the immature opening comment that had ruined everything. It was over. His thought that there was always Mary to fall back on was disgraceful – he had become a rake, a cad! Shocking Jabulani-generated onion layers were being revealed.

Despite knowing it was underhand, he was particularly nice to Mary over the rest of the week, complimenting her on her dress sense, making her coffee, bringing in a packet of Waitrose Luxury Belgian Chocolate Biscuits, and sitting so close that their thighs touched as they worked together. Mary responded with plenty of smiling and some platonic physical contact that was anything but platonic. It's amazing what message a hand placed on an arm can give, especially when the hand lingers and the fingers caress.

David was relieved when the week came to an end and he could focus on the Saturday evening visit to Bridget. He planned to start with an apology, followed by being friendly of course, but not too friendly until he gauged Bridget's mood. And in the unlikely event of her being forgiving, he'd move on to discuss the café.

Bridget greeted him at her front door with a kiss, a quick peck but nevertheless encouraging. She took hold of his hand, led him into the lounge, plonked herself down on the sofa and looked across at him.

'A big apology, I was dreadfully curt the other night. I'd been working twelve-hour days and the sodding artist was driving me mad. And then I got home to discover that Kay was ill. I had to be at work the next day and had no idea who'd be able to look after her. In the end Andy skipped school to assist.'

'Don't even dream of apologising, that must come from me. I was an absolute idiot saying what I did and I'm desperately sorry.'

'OK, but I do recognise how hard this must be for you to come to terms with. I wouldn't have the foggiest idea what to say if it had been the other way round. I appreciate you apologising though – so we're both sorry then.'

'I don't want to lose you.'

'You haven't even got me yet, have you?' Leaning across she kissed him, sharply pulling away. 'We shouldn't be doing this until you tell me what you've been thinking about Roland's murder.'

'Not surprisingly I've thought a lot about it. Were you right? Were you wrong?'

'That's easy to answer. Murder is wrong.'

'Agreed. I know Roland treated you appallingly which got me considering whether there could be different levels of murder, but I realised that was ridiculous. Mind you, I wouldn't call what happened in his case murder. If you'd lifted his head out the pool he still would have drowned what with the tide coming in. If you'd dashed for help it would still have been too late to save him. Look, whatever word you want to use to describe what happened, it's done. I think it was a mistake and I know you do. It's not in your nature to be unkind.'

'Thank you.'

'There's one thing I'm absolutely sure about – I want you to be part of my life.'

'And I want you to be part of mine. A huge part.'

Their conversation jumped between Bridget's memories of the day of Roland's death and its aftermath and David's account of his clumsy planning for the recent telephone conversation.

It was Bridget who brought the dialogue to the present. 'So I suppose we're back to your bloody list! Your café idea.'

'Actually, I've made another list.'

'Stop it!'

'No, I really have. Things to do with the café.'

Murder was forgotten as David outlined his plans.

'The start-up costs are huge. How would you fund

them?'

'By offering the house as collateral to get a loan.'

'Can you do that if Jane's a co-owner?'

'I'll need to discuss that with the bank.'

Bridget rested her head against his shoulder and for a short while they sat in silence, David even wondering whether the exhausted Bridget had dozed off. Then she sprang up. 'This café. Might you want a partner?'

'Why do you ask?'

'I'm fed up with my job and wonder whether you'd be interested in taking me on. I think I could help.'

'Well, of course yes, that would be wonderful. But the gallery, I thought you loved working there.'

28

A career change had been on Bridget's mind for quite a while but she had no idea what to do instead. A dislike of much that she was selling and contempt towards a significant number of her customers was making working in the art gallery less and less enjoyable.

Friday's experience had been typical. 'This isn't art,' she declared having sorted through the new exhibits.

'Don't be a dinosaur, Bridget,' her boss Bradley proclaimed as they regarded the frame holding an opened condom stretching towards a scrappy ink sketch of a vagina. 'It evokes the degenerate pursuit of short-term self-gratification in the twenty-first century.'

'You don't really think that, you can't.'

'Actually I read it. It's how Sean Holloway describes the piece.'

Sean Holloway was flavour of the month, an artist of working class origins who hadn't lifted a pencil or paint brush for his first twenty-five years. Then he was arrested for graffiti offences in Sidcup and the art critic in the Sunday Times claimed there was an intense energy in his art. A minor art college offered him a place following the newspaper article, no doubt attracted by the lure of publicity. He was kicked out after a term, described as a talentless no-hoper. Despite that rejection he started to sell and the bandwagon rolled.

Bridget had first met Sean when they were setting up his exhibition. 'The condom work must go next to the crushed plastic bottles one,' the pretentious fool had declared. 'The two materials are in harmony. Surely you can see that.'

'He can't draw, he's useless,' Bridget persisted as her boss hovered over her. 'Abstract artists must go through the discipline of drawing. You know that Bradley.'

'It doesn't matter what we think, we're a business. I got these for a good commission and I bet we sell them all before the end of the month.'

Bradley was wrong if the opening day, that Friday, was anything to go by. They'd be gone within a week. And good riddance! Ahead of her lunch break a young couple came in. He had on a pinstripe suit with powder blue shirt and silver tie. She wore the casual clothes of the rich young, a pseudo-destitute look with skimpy ripped jeans and frayed leather jacket. The designer labels gave the game away.

'You've got the Holloways in, let's see them,' the man asked with something close to a Cockney accent. Bridget took an instant dislike to him and had a strong urge to tell him off for not adding "please". She led them towards the ten exhibits on display and the man's first sighting was the condom artwork.

He roared raucously. 'Bugger me. Come 'ere doll. Look at this!'

Bridget, though not a snob, cringed on hearing "'ere". Was this the remnant of a past at odds with his new-found City wealth or the attempt of a posho to be seen as one of the lads?

"Doll" was manicuring her nails. She looked across. 'Blimey.'

'Fuck me, and this one,' City boy exclaimed, looking at a diaphragm surrounded by speckles of red and to its right a poorly drawn cartoon of an erect black penis. 'These are great,' he exclaimed. 'Aren't they?' he ordered rather than asked his girlfriend.

The young woman glanced up again, irritated by the disturbance. 'If you like them,' she muttered as she lifted a lipstick out her handbag, 'get them.'

'How much are they?' he asked Bridget. The prices were listed along with the titles and artist's name underneath the works. Perhaps he was illiterate; she couldn't bear the man. She pointed at the labels before summoning enough false enthusiasm to speak. 'Have you seen this sculpture, sir?' She had directed him to the plastic bottles. 'If you decide on the condom you must get this to go with it – the two materials are in perfect harmony.'

'Yeah, I see what you mean, they are kind of similar. Bit pricey though,' he added, having taken the trouble to read the large print labels. They were £24,000 each. 'Would you do a deal if I bought both?'

'This is an art gallery, not a supermarket. We don't do deals.'

Bradley was by her side. 'Apologies, sir, Bridget is having a tough day. We can take 10% off if you purchase both.'

The deal was done with Bridget loitering in the background as Bradley cast dark looks. She adjourned to the small kitchenette and ate her Marks & Spencer avocado and pine nut sandwich and tropical fruit salad. Bradley ignored her when he came in for his own lunch.

As soon as she returned to the gallery floor another customer came in, an older man, tall, rotund, with a thick mane of salt and pepper hair.

He was another of the pinstripe suit brigade, though not style-conscious like the previous customer. A crimson polka dot tie didn't sit well against the navy and white striped shirt. You're devoid of aesthetic taste so why bother purchasing art, she felt like asking him.

'I hear you have some Holloways in this treasure trove,' his voice booming, pompous. Bridget thought his smile was a leer and kept a physical distance. 'Oh, I see them.'

He pushed past her and walked across to the Holloway area, now with red stickers on the corners of the sold works. 'Two already gone, eh?'

'Yes, though in my opinion nowhere near the best ones,' she said, resigned to drumming up sales to boost her commission. They approached an appalling attempt to draw a table on which rested a syringe and a flattened can of Red Bull.

He examined the information below the work – this one was priced at £31,000. Since it was no more skilfully painted than the others, Bridget could only assume price was set based on size. She calculated that it came out at about £150 per square inch.

'I think they're awful but they are shooting up in value, eh,' polka dot man said. He took out a Filofax and turned to a page with jottings. Bridget glanced across, noting dates and prices. March £12,000. July £21,000. December £26,000.

'I'll take it,' he said. 'It'll be up to forty by next summer, eh.'

And that was that. This dinosaur, with his Filofax instead of a smartphone, took out a cheque book and Parker pen. As he filled in the details Bridget considered the meaning of the "eh" when upper class men spoke. Were they taught to use it at school?

'Jolly good value, eh,' she jibed as he was writing. She caught Bradley giving her a filthy look. She didn't care. Three pieces of absolute crap sold in an hour for over £70,000. A furious boss. A sizeable bonus.

'I don't feel great, do you mind if I go?' she asked when polka dot man had gone.

'A good idea if you do,' Bradley replied.

She left the building without casting an eye on the artistic offerings on display. She knew them well; the Holloways might be at the bottom of the talent list but there were some close runners up.

The Northern Line was down due to signal failure so she began walking. She was tired, tired of the daily commute, tired of what the West End had to offer, tired of selling poor quality, high-priced so-called art to buyers only interested in the shock of the new or the investment potential. Perhaps she was arrogant to categorise art as good or bad with such authority. Over a century ago many had ridiculed the Impressionists and it was left to pioneers to buy their works, possibly for the same two reasons as her customers. At school she had loved Impressionism but at college she'd been weaned off it by lecturers who considered the movement too mainstream and not sufficiently challenging.

Bridget had reached Trafalgar Square and fancied a shot of Impressionism. She spent an hour wandering around the late nineteenth-century rooms in the National Gallery. The colour, the movement, the sheer emotion of the works relegated the modern stuff to pretentious insignificance.

By the time she left, her spirits lifted, the trains were running. It was on the journey home that she realised that she had to find new work, and quickly what with two children to provide for. But what?

~

Fate? Because the very next day David was talking about his café with great enthusiasm, checking how serious she was in suggesting she join him. 'Do you really think your new career could be running a café with me?'

'Yes, at least a tentative yes, but obviously we need to think about how it would work.'

'Agreed. I've made a start on how it could work

once it's up and running. It's promising.'

'I bet it is and sorry if I'm sounding too cautious. I'm really excited.'

'Mum!'

'Yes Kay.' Bridget stood. 'I'll pop up to see what she wants.'

David was left to reflect on how good it would be to have Bridget working with him. She had commercial experience, an interest in the arts, a bubbly personality. That was his head thinking. He would be able to spend every day with the woman he loved. That was his heart.

When Bridget returned she suggested they call it a day. 'She's still got a fever, poor thing. I need to change her bed linen and nightwear, they're soaked through.'

'Of course. You look after Kay. We can carry on with this when she's better.'

The hug as he was leaving was short-lived, but as far as David could tell the crisis was over, the relationship back on track, and the opportunity to have Bridget as a business partner in place.

29

David's list was hidden in an office filing cabinet, tucked away between two sheets of the uninviting *Procedural processes for care homes failing to report the death of a resident* document. It was doubly secure since he was the only one who dealt with such occurrences and he had the one key to open the cabinet.

Absurdly, even though he knew to the word what was written, every so often he took it out to check on progress. Somehow it was comforting to hold the scrap of paper.

Long term objectives

1. *Take a cookery course*
2. *Quit my job and pack in accountancy*
3. *Open an arts café*
4. *Have sex with Bridget by February 20th*
5. *Have more sex with Bridget by the first week in March*

Although only one item on the list had so far been accomplished, his Saturday evening meeting with Bridget followed by extensive research about café ownership on the Sunday indicated that the others were well within his grasp. He replaced the sheet and set to work on local authority expenditure analysis, light-headed with the thought that this chore was coming to an end.

~

Rachel and Sam were hovering when David returned from work. His daughter looked concerned and David feared another school incident.

'Dad, we've got something to tell you. Well, to ask.'

Sam took over. 'Mum's got tickets for *Billy Elliot* on Saturday evening and she's asked if we can stay over – at Jim's. We don't know whether to say yes or no.'

Rachel continued. 'Part of me thinks it's happened and we might as well move on. But I don't want to upset you. Would you mind?'

'Not at all, I think moving on is right,' David replied with false generosity because on his mind was the opportunity this might present.

With the children out of earshot he called Bridget to invite her over for dinner that Saturday. Yes, she could farm her children out to friends; she looked forward to it.

The next evening, the Tuesday, he had a trial run of Saturday's meal. It was still early days on his cookery course and since he had doubts about his competence to reproduce the recent Tuscan and Sicilian delights, he decided to revisit the first meal he'd prepared.

The seasonal vegetable soup with cheese croutons was easy enough, but the pan-roasted free range chicken with tarragon and crème fraiche sauce was problematic because Bridget was a vegetarian. His suspicious children stabbed the soggy replacement ingredient with their forks.

'What is this, Dad?'

'Quorn. It's very good for you, Sam.'

'I don't think it's a winner,' Rachel said. Having tried it David had to agree.

After work the next day, the Wednesday, he scoured the supermarket shelves for a substitute.

'Dad, why are we having the same meal as yesterday?'

'It's not the same, Sam. The Quorn's gone, this is marinated tofu.'

'Another MasterChef disaster?'

'Not at all, Rachel. At least give it a try.'

As a reward for their resilience he cooked unadorned chicken on the Thursday and battered cod and chips on the Friday.

~

Saturday had taken ages to arrive.

David drove Rachel and Sam to Jim's place, a house he'd visited many times. How odd to think of it as Jane's home now. Out of curiosity rather than need he got out of the car and walked with the children up to the front door. Sam rang the bell. Jane answered.

'Hello everyone.' She looked at David intently. 'Thanks for letting them stay, I appreciate it. Want to come in for a coffee?'

David noticed the painting above the small table in the hall, the one of a man and woman at the seaside stretched out on striped canvas deckchairs munching ice cream cones. He and Jane had bought it in Brighton way back before the children were born.

'Thanks but I'd best head on. I've got a lot to do.'

'Anything nice?'

He didn't answer.

Jane continued. 'We were thinking of taking them ice skating at Somerset House tomorrow afternoon. Can we do that?'

'Sure,' David said. He looked across at his children and gave them a reassuring smile. 'Have a good time,' he added before heading off.

Full of nervous energy, David filled the morning with unnecessary garden maintenance. After lunch he showered and set to work preparing the meal, with all tasks accomplished on time ahead of Bridget's arrival at seven thirty.

He felt a rush of panic as the doorbell chimed. Help! What now? As he stood there set to greet her, the options flooded in. An affectionate hug. The affectionate hug followed by sitting in the lounge chatting about the café over a glass of wine. A passionate embrace. The passionate embrace followed by a dash to the bedroom for sex. An endearing kiss. The endearing kiss followed by small talk in the kitchen while he served up the meal.

Would there be discussion about the café?

Would there be sex?

Would there be a meal? Yes, of course, that was at least one definite.

He froze, probably only for a split second but it

seemed like an eternity before Bridget rested her arms on his shoulders and kissed him.

'The food smells good,' she said.

'I hope it tastes OK.'

'I'm sure it will. I guess it's eat first and then Objective Number Four!'

Thank you Bridget – with good humour she'd set the agenda. Food. Sex. Café. So simple really, why hadn't he thought of that order?

'A drink before we eat?' he suggested.

'Good idea.'

Dinner was a success with Bridget complimenting him. 'Is this one of your cookery course menus?'

He'd momentarily forgotten that cookery was on the list of objectives she'd seen. 'Sort of, though I've refined it a bit to be vegetarian. More?' he asked, holding up the bottle of wine.

'Yes, please.'

They were well into their second bottle of Vouvray when Bridget took a couple of sips from her newly filled glass and walked round to David's side of the table.

'Now, where were we up to the last time? I think this.' She was undoing his shirt buttons. 'This too, I seem to remember.' She was licking his chest as she opened each button.

David joined in, removing Bridget's cardigan, blouse and bra, replicating the licking. 'Shall we go upstairs?' he suggested ahead of any further stripping.

'Sure.'

The confident tone of that single word was at odds

with David's trepidation. How many lovers had she had since Roland? Was he about to embarrass himself due to lack of expertise and/or recent practice.

With Bridget leading the way upstairs he felt like a novice about to be seduced by an experienced lover. The wine was making him light-headed as he leaned forward to caress her naked back. He misjudged the distance, stumbled and ended up on his knees stroking a stair.

Bridget turned and gave him a puzzled look. 'You alright?'

'Yes. I thought I saw a tack poking through the carpet.'

'Perhaps sort that later?'

They reached the bedroom. He was as nervous as a first-timer which of course wasn't the case. There had been sex with Jane for many years, though before her only one brief affair. It struck him that Jane must have been having sex with both he and Jim for a while.

Bridget had removed her skirt. David undid his belt and pulled down his trousers. They got tangled with his shoes and he toppled down onto the bed. He'd even forgotten the order for getting undressed and Bridget was smiling at him.

'Let me help.' She crouched to untie his laces and remove his shoes before pulling off his trousers.

David had an uncomfortable flashback to when he used to undress Sam to change his nappy.

'You need breathing room here by the looks of things,' Bridget said as she slid off his boxers before running her hand against his erection. She'd taken off her knickers and they were on the bed naked.

'I've been wanting this so much,' he whispered, gazing into gorgeous soft blue eyes. With their bodies locked David caressed the small of her back before moving his hand round to stroke her. At last.

He felt Bridget's foot against his own. 'Err, just one thing, David.'

'Mm?'

'I hope you don't mind me asking.'

'No, what?' Was there to be a request for some deviant erotic act?

'Socks.'

'What?' Had he heard correctly? Not mask, handcuffs, whip.

'Socks. Your socks are still on; I should have pulled them off when I did your shoes. I've got a bit of a thing about having sex with a man wearing socks.'

David sat up with a start as did Bridget and their heads collided. After the initial shock and shot of dizzying pain they both laughed. He took off his socks, looked down at his shrivelling penis with intense embarrassment, and then up to a smiling Bridget.

'Come here you.'

They were soon engaging in blissful foreplay, his erection restored. On the verge of making love he paused, considering it a moral duty to raise the issue.

'Hang on, Bridget.'

'Why?'

'No condom.'

'What?'

'I haven't put on a condom.'

'Don't need it, I'm protected. That is, for contraception, not STDs. But somehow I don't think you're a risk and I'm not because this is my first sex for ages.'

David's fears about inexperience and inadequate technique evaporated. The conversation ceased, replaced by the sound of heavy breathing and gasps of joy.

He woke with an aching upper arm resting under Bridget's head. With the light still on in the landing he could see her face, a face that had enchanted him from the instant they'd met at the reunion. The quilt was tightly wrapped round her shoulders. He was hungry to see more of her so edged it down to expose her breasts. She giggled in her half sleep as he leant down to kiss a nipple. Turned on, he moved his hand down to her stomach, to the tight curls of pubic hair, to between her legs.

'OK, so obviously you're awake,' she said, shifting to glance at her phone. 'It's three-eighteen if you're interested. Obviously you're not,' she added as she stroked him. They made calmer more rhythmic love than the first time.

David struggled to get back to sleep. It had seemed like the most powerful, wonderful sex he'd ever had, though wouldn't he have felt the same when he'd first made love to Jane?

Finally he slept, waking late morning to see Bridget propped up looking at her phone. 'That was a lovely night,' she told him. 'And I suppose congratulations are due.'

'What for?'

'You've accomplished Objective Four *and* Five, both ahead of schedule. That leaves the café which is what I've been researching while you were asleep.'

'Perhaps take a break from that.'

'Blimey, are you allowed two Number Fives?'

30

David and Bridget were talking about the café while brunching in his kitchen. Bridget had produced two perfect cappuccinos using the espresso machine that until then only Jane had mastered. He'd only kept it because Jim had purchased a top of the range machine as a welcome-to-your-new-home present for Jane.

The bread popped up and David went across to collect it. Jane had taken the family toaster and he'd replaced it with the most expensive product he could find, an Art Deco black and silver work of art.

Focusing on the café wasn't easy because Bridget was wearing the same Simpsons T-shirt that David had provided during her first visit. Naked underneath, he could see the outline of her nipples through the material. To make matters worse, or better depending on how you looked at it, the garment had ridden up to the top of her thighs.

Bridget seemed blissfully unaware of his lustful thoughts as she chatted away about the possibly prohibitive cost of opening and running the café. 'The arts focus is exciting and I accept what you say about it providing a unique offer, but we have to sort out the money side before getting carried away with anything else.'

'Agreed. I think we need independent advice to make any analysis of costs meaningful.'

'So is there anything left to talk about now then?'

'The name. I have an idea – *A Street Café Named Desire.*'

'That's absolutely brilliant. I love it!'

'To be honest, it isn't my idea. My uncle came up with it; well, to be exact his business partner did. They were all set to open a café when his friend abandoned him to go to Russia to meet a woman he'd found on the internet. That's a story in itself. Apparently the man had never married nor been in a proper relationship but there he was in his late fifties off to see a twenty-something woman. You can bet what she was after and I can imagine how it ended. Anyway, the café idea was scrapped.'

'But does your uncle mind us pinching the name?'

'No. I asked, he's fine with it.'

'Great. What's next?' All that was on Bridget's pad of paper was the name.

'Perhaps location?'

Bridget wrote down the word ahead of their discussion. They agreed that there would be competition wherever they set up. Our café they decided, (already using "our"), would be charging premium prices so it had to be in an affluent area, ideally an arty place. Bridget reckoned another factor might be to locate where customers were likely to have an aversion to corporate chains.

'That's Muswell Hill all over,' she declared. Having witnessed the poor behaviour of the local youths on the night he'd stayed at her house, David was less sure but was happy for Bridget to investigate vacant premises and their rents.

They'd just started chatting about the events they could offer when they heard the front door open. Rachel and Sam came bursting into the kitchen.

'No ice skating. Jim's got a headache,' Sam explained before catching sight of Bridget.

There were awkward hellos and a brief exchange about the *Billy Elliot* performance before the children, sensing their father's embarrassment, headed upstairs.

'Bridget,' David asked. 'Is it fair to say we're in a relationship?'

'That's a reasonable enough assumption.'

'Then we should let Rachel and Sam know. It's not as if there's anything to hide.'

'I'm OK with that.'

'I'll call them down then.' David stood then paused. 'Jane left me four months ago, that isn't much of a gap before starting a new relationship, is it? Do you think they, particularly Rachel, might resent it?'

'I think they'll be pleased you're happy.'

'I'll get them back down then.'

'Let me get dressed first.'

'Me too.'

They went upstairs, Bridget going into David's room while David tapped on Rachel's door. He was told to wait and heard some scurrying around. When the door was finally opened he was hit by a blast of cold air, insufficient to dispel the smell of cigarettes.

'Could you come down in ten minutes?'

'Will do.'

He knocked on Sam's door and got another instruction to wait. When his son let him in David saw pie charts on the computer screen. A parent's sixth sense gave him the feeling that the current display wasn't what Sam had been looking at.

'Could you come down in ten minutes?'

'OK Dad.'

At the designated time the four of them were sitting in the lounge, all fully dressed.

Rachel beat David in starting the conversation, firing a question. 'Bridget, what colour are these walls?'

Bridget played along, pretending to think deeply as she examined them. 'I reckon they're orange,' she finally announced.

'Nope, you're wrong. Do you want to try again?'

'No, I'm happy for you to give me the correct answer.'

'You tell her, Sam.'

'No, I'm not playing.'

'OK, I'll do it. The answer is burnt umber.'

'Yes, I can see my mistake now. What an idiot for not spotting it.'

Before David had the opportunity to switch to the subject in hand, Bridget was naming the colours in her house which led to her talking about her background in art and the work she did at the gallery. They were getting on well with David and Sam sitting in silence.

'Anyway, I think your dad has got something to tell you.'

'Yes, I do. It's about Bridget and me. We've grown extremely fond of each other and intend to spend lots of time together. So she'll be staying here sometimes, sleeping in the same bedroom as me, and sometimes I'll be at hers. I'm sure you realise what I'm saying in terms of what this means for adults, which of course is what we are.'

David had been avoiding eye contact. Now, as he looked up, he saw three smirking faces.

'We're going out,' Bridget summarised.

'Well that's pretty obvious from this morning,' Rachel said. 'Cool, hopefully it'll make Dad a bit less of a misery.'

The children seemed so relaxed about things that David suggested going to a restaurant that evening to celebrate, all six of them. Bridget agreed and set off home to inform Andy and Kay about the new man in her life.

They were delighted to see that the children were hitting it off that evening. They appeared to be genuinely pleased about the relationship though David was somewhat disturbed on overhearing Rachel describing it to Andy as an "OAP fuck fest".

~

It was all one could ever want from a relationship – exciting, passionate, open, comfortable. The couple shared an ardent and adventurous joy of sex, but equally savoured lazy weekend mornings in bed chatting away about this and that. They took on board differences of opinion as they planned for the future. They had an interest in the wellbeing of each other's children.

On one of those lazy mornings Bridget spoke a little more about her childhood. At their school she had been ostracised as an outsider.

'It was because I was foreign, even though foreign only meant Scotland. Joining a year after everyone else after my father got his job in Oxford, didn't help. By then firm friendships were in place and I suppose I was seen as a threat.'

'God, children can be so cruel.'

'And the fact that I enjoyed schoolwork didn't help.'

Defiantly Bridget had refused to be bullied into concealing her interest in learning and, most of all, her love of art.

'If the memory is so unpleasant why on earth did you decide to go to the reunion? I'm glad you did, of course.'

'It was a set of coincidences, although who knows, maybe it was fate.'

David didn't believe in fate, does any accountant? But Bridget's explanation did make him wonder.

She'd had no contact with her peers of twenty-five years ago, unsurprising given how unhappy her school days had been, marginalised by the girls and mocked by the boys.

'Do you remember Miss Harris, the art teacher? She was my inspiration.'

Out of the blue in early September Bridget had

received an email from Pru White. "Friend" would be too strong a description to use, but the girls shared a keen interest in art and in the sixth form Miss White had taken them on trips to galleries. Pru was notifying Bridget that their favourite teacher had died. *BTW, are you coming?* the message had ended.

A flurry of communication followed with the decision that they would go to the reunion together. The plan fell flat when a last minute work commitment meant Pru couldn't attend. Bridget's first reaction was to drop the idea.

'My social life was pretty dire, I'd already organised for the children to stay with friends, it would be an opportunity to see my old home town again, it might be interesting to discover whether the people I'd despised had improved – they haven't – but all those half-reasons made me decide to go. And I'm glad I did.'

Bridget planted a platonic kiss on David's forehead. He would have been happy to move beyond the platonic stage but Bridget was already up and putting on a black kimono with little sprigs of pink and yellow blossom. 'You stay in bed, I'll bring up coffees.'

David was left to reflect on the random good fortune of their meeting. Or could it have been fate?

'To be honest,' she said as she got back, 'the boys at school weren't so much nasty as blanking me out. Except for one. His name was David and I was hoping he'd be at the reunion.'

'I do remember standing up for you when some of

252

the girls were calling you a lunatic for wearing odd socks and doing ink drawings on the back of your hand.'

'And do you remember checking if I was OK when you saw me crying in the playground.'

'I didn't want to see you hurt. I liked you. I wish I'd been bold enough to ask you out. All these years wasted.'

'No, not wasted. For a start if we'd got together then there wouldn't be Andy, Kay, Rachel or Sam. And it might have only lasted a week like most of the other school pairings.'

'I suppose so. Was Roland your first serious relationship?'

'More or less.'

'And am I your first serious relationship since Roland?'

'Definitely the first proper one.'

'Meaning?'

'Meaning that until you I've not been great at choosing.'

~

Bridget was not going to talk about past relationships – what was the point? But Jan had seemed serious at the time.

She'd met him having taken the morning off work to catch the Rothko exhibition at the Tate Modern. She'd been meaning to go for months and had left it until the final day. To avoid the inevitable crowds she was one of the first in and was able to stand well back from the giant canvases to appreciate them.

'Magnificent,' exclaimed a deep voice behind her.

'Agreed.'

'I've never been able to understand why an abstract shape can take on such a vibrant form. His colours flow like a river.' The accent was Nordic or Germanic, the grammar and intonation perfect, his comment a cliché. 'And these blocks of colour became a breakthrough in form. A hundred years ago people would have laughed at them. Don't you agree?'

'I can't say, I wasn't around then,' Bridget replied with deliberate detachment to waylay either pretentious tosh or corny chat up lines or a combination of both.

Reluctantly, she turned to face the man and liked what she saw. He was tall and lean with a narrow, attractive face and sharp eyes. His honey-coloured hair was unfashionably long; it suited him as did the stubble on his chin. Probably in his forties she was thinking, and he looked good for his age.

With the gallery still near empty, trekking round together seemed like the natural thing to do. Jan was a smooth talker, interspersing details of his life with observations on the art around them. She refrained from informing him that she had a fair degree of expertise when it came to art appreciation, letting him pile on the clichés and giving the impression that she was lapping up his insights.

She'd got it wrong, Jan was neither German nor Scandinavian. He was Dutch and regularly visited London on business, selling graphic art software. Whenever possible during these trips he took in a gallery she was told. Had she visited Holland? Only Amsterdam? The Rijksmuseum and the Van Gogh were wonderful but she should see the Mondrians at the Gemeentemuseum in The Hague. Did she think Rothko was influenced by Mondrian?

His knowledge of art wasn't as shallow as she had first thought and conversation flowed. Having coffee together seemed another natural thing to do. Then they walked over the footbridge to St Pauls, taking lunch at a restaurant at the old Billingsgate Market. Bridget liked the fact that Jan was treating her as a friend not a possible catch. He wasn't at all pushy and, she had to admit, he was a good looker.

'I'd love to see what you sell in your art gallery. May I meet you when I'm next in London?'

They exchanged numbers and two weeks later Jan met her at the gallery followed by a meal and theatre trip. Somehow he'd managed to get best seat tickets for Hamilton. His impeccable gentlemanly behaviour continued during three further visits, each one ending with no more than a snappy kiss on each cheek.

In the restaurant during the next visit Jan asked if Bridget would like to stay overnight at his hotel. Bridget didn't need any persuading, she was more than ready for a new relationship. For sex.

Four months into the affair Jan invited her for a weekend in Amsterdam. Without embarrassment he came out with it. His wife and children would be away visiting her parents in Brabant so it would be a perfect opportunity.

'Wife? You didn't tell me you're married.'

'I haven't told you I'm not, you've never asked.'

'I'm just your bit on the side then.'

'Bit of side?'

'Mistress.'

'Have you enjoyed our time together?'

'Yes.'

'Well, so have I. Isn't that what matters?'

'There is such a thing as morality, Jan.'

'Bridget, this is the twenty-first century. Adultery isn't a crime punishable by being stoned or burnt at the stake any more. I'm comfortable with my twenty-first century morality.'

'Well I'm still stuck in the past.'

Bridget ended the relationship there and then. It was a matter of weeks before the reunion and another one of the half-reasons why she decided to attend.

~

'That's plenty about me,' she told David, all thoughts of Jan pushed aside.

'It was nice to hear about you for a change though.'

'I suggest that's enough about our pasts for today. And now we have a huge decision to make. Which is it to be, sex or chatting about the café?'

'Let's do the café later.'

31

Extended family gatherings with the four children were frequent – meals together, cinema, bowling, Rachel's performance in *Fiddler on the Roof.* Although the children were getting on reasonably well this was particularly true between Kay and Sam, with Rachel tolerating Andy, categorising him as a bit of a nerd. Any teasing was gentle enough and Andy could give as good as he got.

'Ready for today's big outing, Andy?' she asked as they piled into the car.

They were on their way to Oxford, the younger children staying behind with friends.

'Remind me, exactly why *are* we doing this?' Rachel asked with dramatic emphasis on the "are" as they turned off the M25 and onto the M40.

David had already told her, twice, and was not going to go through the reasoning again. Bridget displayed greater patience. 'Look out there. Not a cloud in the sky, beautiful countryside, and you'll love the architecture. Your dad and I went to Oxford loads when we were your age.'

'Together?'

'No, we didn't know each other then.'

'I thought you were in the same year at school.'

'Well, yes, but we weren't friends.'

'Actually they hated each other,' Andy joked.

'Andy, you're alive, I was getting worried. Do you think they still hate each other deep down?'

'No, Rachel, we don't,' said Bridget. She stretched across to kiss David on the cheek.

'Not while I'm driving.'

'You are so romantic, Dad. Anyway Bridget, you can cut out the crap about this being a trip to rediscover your roots. We're here to be sold the university.'

'There's nothing wrong with that is there?'

'Maybe not for Andy, but not much point for lazy thicko me.'

'Lazy yes, thick no.'

'Thanks a million, Dad. Stick to driving will you.'

Rachel rummaged through her backpack, pulled out her earphones and scanned Spotify. She looked across at Andy playing a geeky game on his phone. He'd fit in perfectly with the other eggheads doing computing at Oxford. She turned up the volume to drown out Bridget and her father's chatting. She hated sitting in the back on a long journey, it made her feel sick. Her dad knew, but since Bridget had arrived on the scene the front passenger seat was hers.

She looked out the window as they passed through the steep cutting at Stokenchurch. It was OK seeing some countryside, the sheep scattered across the gentle hills. Cows always stuck together but sheep spread out. Why was that, she wondered? Her observation was proven beyond doubt on passing a herd of cattle squashed together in the corner of a field. Some were sitting; did they expect rain or was that idea as absurd as much else she had picked up from adults over the years?

They took the motorway exit to Oxford. The decision makers in the front had opted for Park and Ride. Rachel couldn't understand why they weren't going to drive straight into the city centre but decided not to argue the case. There would be more important things to contest.

It turned out that she should have argued because Park and Ride was inappropriately named. It ended up as: finally find a space right on the outer rim of the jam packed car park. Walk miles to reach the bus stop. Wait. Wait more. Stand up on the packed bus. Reach a place called Headington. Disembark when the bus breaks down. Wait. Wait more. Wait lots more. Stand squashed like sardines on the replacement bus which surely was illegally overcrowded. (Though with the benefit of being able to edge up against a dishy bloke with baggy jeans and a Glastonbury T-shirt). Ride. Stop in traffic jam. Ride. And finally get off at a bus station that looked like any other bus station, namely it was full of buses.

Bridget claimed to know Oxford well and marched them off towards a particular venue for lunch. Why they didn't go to one of the Prets, Starbucks, Caffé Neros, or Costas they passed en route was beyond Rachel's understanding, and she made her view known as they trundled up and down narrow lanes because Bridget couldn't remember exactly where her obsessive destination was located. And the university quest had yet to begin.

Eventually they found the place and the food was OK – they all opted for a pasta something or other – though her Diet Coke was lukewarm.

Bridget's great delight was an embarrassment. 'Do you know what, I think I'm sitting on the same chair at the same table as when I was last here more than ten years ago.'

A flood of sarcastic options to choose from emerged, but Rachel kept quiet, aware that David was eyeing her with suspicion. She contemplated whether she'd be saying things like that when she was older. Orgasmic ecstasy over a fucking chair. And Bridget wasn't even old and was relatively cool.

What must go on in the heads of even older people like the ones sitting opposite them?

Look at this teapot, darling. It's identical to the one we got as a wedding gift.

Do you think this is Linguine or Vermicelli?

You might be incorrect on both counts, sweetheart. I believe it's Fedelini.

It's just fucking pasta. It all tastes the same, just eat it!

Rachel's anger grew to boiling point. This was a complete and utter waste of a day and she'd been pretty well forced to come along because, as her dad had put it, "Andy is coming and he'd appreciate you joining him." His phone was what was keeping him company, not her. He'd reached about level eight million on his game and had hardly spoken to her. Nerd.

Now they were walking up The High. Bridget had made a point of telling her that despite the signage, "Street" should be omitted and "The" added.

They crossed into Queen Street. 'Here we are. The Queen,' Rachel tested.

'Yes, Queen Street.'

'I don't get it. Why bother with the street and knock off the the? Make it like The High.'

'Because when …' Bridget started before ceasing mid-explanation. Their walk came to an abrupt end, followed by whispering between David and Bridget as they watched two sneering men approach.

'What's the matter? Who are those two fatties?' Rachel asked.

'Ex-school mates,' Bridget said as the men moved in position to block their path.

The shorter man spoke. 'Well, well, well, if it isn't our David again.'

'Hello, Ben. Hello, Bill.'

The taller one, Bill, looked across at Bridget then back to David. 'You've managed to hook up with this tasty bit of skirt, you sneaky bugger.'

'I do have a name, though clearly your brain struggles to access two bits of information in quick succession,' Bridget stated with a fair degree of aggression. 'Still, congratulations for remembering it's David.'

David had a flashback to Bill's potential for

violence and his encounter with the mugger came to mind, too. The smell of beer on Bill's breath highlighted the danger of replicating the evenings at Henley and in Kitts Yard.

He opted for appeasement and hoped Bridget would follow suit. 'Ignore them. Let's head on. Could we pass.'

Bill stepped in front of Bridget. 'You were a mouthy bitch at the reunion. Maybe bits of skirt shouldn't be mouthy bitches. What d'you reckon, Ben?'

Ben appeared to be in a conciliatory mood. 'Come on, Bill. Let's go,' he suggested but Bill was having none of it.

'Go, why? I want to join the romantic couple for a Sunday stroll.'

Rachel and Andy had been ignored like they were a pair of walkers who only stopped because they happened by chance to be behind Bridget and David when they were blocked.

The conversation between Bridget and Bill was getting heated, with Bridget accusing Bill of being brain dead and Bill suggesting she must have had breast implants. David and Ben were making unsuccessful attempts to separate the antagonists.

Andy stepped forward. 'Stop being rude to my mother.'

'Who'a, a knight in shining armour. I'm really scared of you.' Bill said ahead of giving Andy a shove. Andy held firm.

'I'd rather you didn't do that.'

'Oh, would you rather I didn't do that,' Bill sneered as he gave Andy a stronger push.

Fearful for Andy's wellbeing, even survival, David was set to intervene when Andy grabbed hold of Bill and with what looked like little effort deposited him on the pavement. Bill leapt up, furious, his fists clenched.

'I'm goin' to kill you for that, you little bugger.'

The pedestrians who had run off desperate not to get involved had been replaced by a younger clientele of onlookers who formed a circle to watch Andy throw Bill over his shoulder and back to the floor. There was a loud cheer. This action was repeated twice more and Rachel clapped and cheered with the rest of the audience. A frazzled Bill seemed ready for more humiliation, but Ben grabbed hold of his staggering, cursing friend and led him away.

Andy had achieved instant superhero status. Spectators patted him on the back, shook his hand, declared "Well done mate", hugged and in one case kissed him before continuing on their quest for consumer gratification.

'Under-16 County Judo Champion,' Bridget explained as Rachel and David observed the adulation.

It would be fair to state that Rachel's opinion of Andy was elevated to Nerd Plus status that afternoon as they explored Queen's, Magdalen, and Christ Church, entering each of the colleges through uninviting gateways before stepping into a world of imposing ancient buildings, quads and immaculately landscaped gardens.

32

On their return from Oxford the focus was back on the café.

'I think the priority is to have a clear idea of how much it's going to cost and where we can get the money from,' Bridget said, having given David's list no more than a cursory glance.

David agreed. He needed to wear his accountant's hat for this venture and hats are worn on heads, not hearts.

'And it is scary,' David admitted as they once again ran through the figures on the business plan that they would be presenting to the bank. As they worked, a cruel slate grey sky was hurling rain, hail and sleet onto the windows. '£70,000 for decoration, furnishings and equipment seems massively high.'

'We've been through this and yes, we could do it for less, but not if we want a state of the art venue.'

Bridget had found the venue in question, a recently vacated restaurant a short walk from the bustling Muswell Hill Broadway. It was big enough to seat eighty customers with a large kitchen that they could split to accommodate an open bar area. It wasn't cheap though –£80,000 a year to rent.

'So let's re-check your figures for income to see if it adds up.'

'There's the big mark-up on coffee,' David said as they regarded the printout of the sales spreadsheet. 'If we sell a cup for £2.40 that leaves £1.70 gross profit.'

'Yeah, but don't forget staff costs and the leasing of the machine.'

David began to explain how accountants distinguished between gross and net income but the sketches that Bridget was doodling of coffee cups with steam floating upwards indicated that she had lost interest.

'OK, that's coffee. What about food?'

David handed over another spreadsheet. 'This one compares buying in against making our own sandwiches. Buying in is more expensive and we'd have to place a regular order so there could be waste.'

'And we wouldn't be offering food that makes us stand out from the chains.'

'Exactly.'

'OK, we'll make them. Next?'

'Don't you want to check the calculations?'

'Not really. Cakes?'

David could see that Bridget had great strengths, speed of decision-making being one of them, but close scrutiny of figures didn't seem to be a strong point. 'We should buy the cakes. Making them isn't like making sandwiches, it's a much higher level of catering. If we want to be like a Viennese coffee house then I think –'

'Fine. Alcohol next.'

'Here are the figures. They aren't guaranteed; there are risks.'

'Everything has risks. Alcohol's the big evening earner, right?'

'Correct. We'll need a licence and a Designated Premises Supervisor.'

'That'll be me,' Bridget joked. 'I'm the alcohol expert around here.'

'Yes I had noticed.' David topped up their glasses with the Rioja Gran Reserva. 'Here are the estimated mark ups for alcohol.'

He handed over a further spreadsheet.

'I can't do any more figures. But look at this.' Bridget opened a floor plan of the building. 'We can fit in a small stage by the bar. If we want performances we'll need a proper space.'

'How much would that cost?'

'According to the builder, £15,000.'

The specification for what they wanted was going up and up with costs spiralling. When David hit the sum icon on the laptop spreadsheet, £267,000 appeared as first year setting up expenditure, not counting the cost of food and drink. It would cost £112,000 in future years to merely keep the place open.

Bridget's excitement and enthusiasm came crashing down. 'Fuck. We can't afford that.'

'First year costs can be carried forward as tax deductibles for future years.'

'If there is a second year! All this effort and we

could have done a back of an envelope calculation to see how impossible it is.'

David had opened another spreadsheet. 'I'm not as negative as you. Look at this. We're talking about around a hundred customers a day to break even and that's with three distinct offerings – lunchtime sandwiches, morning and afternoon cakes, and evening entertainments.'

Bridget didn't look convinced.

David continued. 'We're seeing Ross, that friend I mentioned, before the bank appointment. He'll give good advice.'

'My head is utterly mangled. I feel sorry for you having to work with figures all day. I need more wine. Quick!'

'Here we are. For our Designated Premises Supervisor.'

'This supervisor is going to drink straight from the bottle. Come on, let's go to bed.'

One wall in Bridget's bedroom was purple, the others dove grey. The bed linen was off-white. It provided the perfect ambiance to forget about the café, the perfect place to make love.

It was only when Bridget was asleep that David's thoughts returned to the café. There was loads to sort out and Bridget's doubts about whether it had any chance of success were entirely justified. During a fraught night, spreadsheets entered and left his brain at the speed of light, the numbers lurching from low to high and between black and red.

'God, I slept like a log,' Bridget said the next

morning. 'How about you?'

'Great.'

~

A critical twenty-four hours had arrived, an evening with David's entrepreneur friend Ross, an appointment at the bank the following morning, and immediately after that, a meeting with Mary to hand in his notice.

It was Friday 1st – fittingly April Fools' Day.

They met Ross in a heaving Hampstead pub. His latest girlfriend was with him. As Ross got older his women got younger and if looks were anything to go by, this one bordered legality.

'Come with me, mate.' David followed Ross to the bar to order drinks. 'What do you reckon? She's a beauty, isn't she?'

Candy certainly was pretty. David deferred from questioning why Ross was dating a girl at least twenty years his junior; a previous interrogation concerning a former girlfriend called Hazel had created an uncomfortable atmosphere.

'I'll tell you what,' Ross continued, 'I think Birgit is a massive improvement on Jane. Well done, mate.'

'Actually, it's Bridget.'

'Yeah, that's what I said.'

By the time they returned, with wine for Bridget and a designer vodka for Candy, the women were chatting away, seemingly comfortable in each other's company. When the conversation turned to the café, Ross's view was that although the venture might be feasible, why would anyone bother to establish a business with so little potential for high profit?

'We'd be happy if it was a small-scale success,' Bridget asserted in defence of their idea.

'Not everything is about money, Ross. I'll come along and I'll bring all my friends,' Candy declared. 'Especially if you show those old films. I love the black and whites.'

'What would you come to see?'

'Anything, everything Bridget. *Casablanca*. *Brief Encounter*. Hitchcock films. And Dmytryk, he's my all-time favourite.'

Candy's probing about their proposal was spot on. David's bigoted perception of what could be expected from someone wearing snakeskin leggings and a polka dot T-shirt, with a body adorned with tattoos, piercings and studs was shot down as Candy talked about her undergraduate film studies course.

'Two things,' Ross said as they were ready to part company. 'The bank will need watertight collateral before providing any funds.'

'And the other thing?'

'If the purpose of this evening has been to get me to finance it, forget it. There's no *Dragon's Den* from me, mate.'

The following morning they were up early to prepare for the appointment at the bank. It was a Candy rather than a Ross suggestion that got them to amend their business plan. In the market research section they added that having interviewed a substantial number of young potential customers, a strong interest in old movie nights had emerged.

'It's not 100% true,' Bridget admitted, 'but she did say she'd bring her friends so it's fair to assume they all like the idea of a café screening films.'

This was the only dubious evidence in the document; the financial data was spot on.

'What do you reckon?' Bridget asked as she pirouetted in a chocolate brown two-piece suit, beige blouse with a frilly collar, and shiny black patent shoes with glittery gold bows. 'Do I look like a responsible investment candidate?'

'Absolutely. And you look gorgeous. It's like having a new woman.'

'Shut up.'

They were ready to set off.

'Well, here goes,' David said as they entered the bank following the short walk.

Your friendly bank was stated on a large banner across the frontage. Two life-sized cardboard cut-outs were by the entrance, a mixed race couple with perfect teeth and welcoming smiles. The real person who greeted them didn't quite match the warm affection of the cut-outs. They were led to an open plan space, such areas having long replaced the privacy available in rooms with doors that could be closed.

Peter Ridge gave the impression that the pair weren't to be trusted and his job was to get rid of them as quickly as possible. David provided financial information with all the accuracy that could be expected from an accountant and Bridget contributed in an attempt to generate enthusiasm, but the stony-faced young man gave no sign of interest and no hint of what he thought about their vision. After thirty-nine minutes of a meeting scheduled to last for forty, he spent the final minute summarising the bank's position. To be considered for a start-up loan, 20% of the sum had to be the clients' own money and in addition, collateral of at least fifty per cent would be needed.

Back on the high street they stopped at a café. It was lunchtime and it was jam-packed. Silently, enviously, they observed the queues to select food from self-service shelves, queues to order coffee and queues to pay. Every table was taken and they huddled together on bar stools by the window.

Bridget was the first to comment on their meeting. 'I hated that man. I'd rather have had hostility than indifference.'

'We knew he'd ask for collateral, we didn't need Ross to tell us.'

'Which you can't provide since Jane owns half your house. But I can, I'm the sole owner of mine and there's no mortgage. As far as the 20% contribution goes, I can do that, too. I inherited a fair amount when my parents died.'

'I wouldn't allow that; it's much too risky. Which is what you said last night.'

'Well, I've changed my mind. Or more to the point, what the fuck! Let's give it a go. Even if it didn't work out we wouldn't lose all the money, there'll at least be some customers. If the absolute worst came to the worst we'd shut down and return to boring accountancy and rip off art.'

'It's still too much we could lose. A hundred thousand, perhaps more.'

'That would be terrible, but I have got that in savings. I want to do it. Have your meeting with Mary and hand in your notice because that's what I'm going to do at the gallery this afternoon. Come on, finish your £2.20 cappuccino which only costs about 16p to make while I finish my £3.20 avocado, pine nut, pea shoot and hummus sandwich which by your reckoning cost them £1.60 to buy in.'

David sat in silence.

'No need to ponder, David. I'm serious, I've made up my mind. If you don't join me I'll just have to go it alone.'

Bridget chatted away at high speed as he walked with her to the Underground station. It was small talk, she was nervous. David went home to collect the car and set off to the council building. He was shedding tears as he reflected on the generosity and optimism displayed by Bridget. There was no going back, they were going to do it, but he wouldn't let Bridget put up the whole sum. He had savings too, theoretically put aside for Rachel and Sam's university costs. He'd work his socks off to make the café a success.

He'd arranged to meet Mary at half past three. The conversation wasn't going to be easy; they were getting on well and he was about to let her down.

She greeted him with a warm smile.

'I know you called this meeting but there's something I'd like to tell you first. You know me – always straight to the point. I handed in my notice today. I've been thinking about things for quite a while. You've been the catalyst, what with our initial difficulties and how we worked through them. I'm going to take some time out, travel a bit, then when I get back I want to work in the charity sector. I've been self-centred, downright selfish and now it's time to put something back. And I really mean put something back, not the bullshit I sprouted to get the job here.

'There's something I have to tell you, too.'

'Hang on. One more thing before you say anything. There's someone working here who is perfectly suited to take over my job and deserves it. That's you.' Mary waited for David's response. When it didn't come she continued. 'I've put your name forward and Stuart wants you to apply.'

'Thanks for thinking of me, Mary, but I won't be –'

'No need to answer now. Go away and reflect, I don't want another word until you've thought it through carefully.'

'But –'

'Not a word.'

'OK, I'll be back very soon though.'

David had to consider the new situation. He constructed a remain at council versus start a café list. He could itemise the reasons for staying at his current workplace with ease – an increase in salary, a generous pension provision, security, enhanced status. The reasons for setting up a café were shrouded in mist – maybe enjoyable to run (but a massive time commitment); maybe profitable (but the risk of huge losses); maybe recognition as a patron of the arts (but the danger of no one willing to perform at his café and insufficient customers even if he did manage to get artists in).

Heart beat head. With the list chucked in his bin he strode back to Mary's office.

'I'm leaving too.'

He told Mary about the café and to her credit she was encouraging. The council would be looking for two new recruits.

Jabulani was standing outside David's office on his return. He knew David was going to tell Mary that afternoon and was eager to hear how it had gone.

'I've done it, Jabulani. Can you keep another secret?'

33

'This looks great,' Sam said as David set down three plates of Portofino Lamb and Artichoke Risotto, the latest creation to come from his cookery course.

'Tastes good too,' Rachel added having taken her first mouthful.

'Let's see if it's as good as the one my tutor made,' David said as he lifted his fork.

His mobile rang as fork reached mouth.

'Leave it, Dad, it'll only be some fake sales call.'

David had enrolled with a telephone preference service to block unsolicited calls but they kept coming. He felt sorry for the call centre staff with their "I understand you've recently been involved in a car crash that wasn't your fault" statements, often said in a barely comprehensible accent. He was never aggressive towards them though.

Although the screen was displaying *Private Number*, since he'd already picked it up he decided to answer.

'Is that Mr Willoughby, Mr David Willoughby?' This accent sounded Indian.

'Yes it is, but I haven't had a car accident and I'm

not interested in buying anything, thank you.'

'I'm not selling.'

Yes I bet, David thought. Upgrade your computer virus protection. Buy a conservatory now that summer is approaching. Hand over your bank account details to verify authenticity ahead of some scam or other.

'Look, I'm not interested. Goodbye.'

A minute later the phone rang again.

Rachel held out her hand and with a degree of trepidation David passed it over. 'Thanks,' his daughter said as she pressed the icon. 'He won't call back after I've finished with him.'

'You are a disgrace! Take a hint and get lost! Goodbye.'

'Well done for not swearing,' David remarked as Rachel gave the phone back to her father.

It rang again. 'Can I try, Dad?'

'No Sam, it's not a game. But I'm not having this.' He pressed the speaker icon, intent on demonstrating to his children how assertiveness rather than aggression was the better tactic.

'Now listen here, will you. I want to know which company you represent and what your telephone number is. And I want to speak to your supervisor.'

'I am truly sorry to disturb you, Mr Willoughby, but it really is most urgent here.'

'Urgent? What are you on about?'

'It's your mother.'

Mr Gupta, his mother's neighbour, actually no longer his mother's neighbour, went on to describe the circumstances of her death. Mrs Willoughby hadn't put out her dustbins on Tuesday night for early Wednesday morning collection, a very unusual omission. When the Wednesday milk was left uncollected outside her front door all day he investigated. He was a key holder in case of emergencies and that is what it turned out to be. He found her dead, stretched out on the floor of her lounge, still in nightwear and dressing gown. Having called emergency services, the body had been removed to the mortuary, but now it was time to hand over to her family. Gupta had tried contacting Charlotte who apparently he had met a couple of times in his neighbour's house, but his calls went to voicemail. So now he was phoning David.

The news had been relayed to the whole family via speakerphone and when David had ended the conversation with an apology for their initial rudeness the three of them sat in shocked silence.

There was little time for reflection and none for conversation because Charlotte called. She had picked up Mr Gupta's five increasingly desperate messages. The brother and sister arranged to meet at their mother's house the following mid-morning.

David, Rachel and Sam stayed put in the lounge dwelling on their recent Christmas visit. There was a degree of guilt because they had been bored, impatient and sarcastic when they should have been warm and caring. The children asked what they could do to help but collectively concluded that the best thing was to go to school while David met Charlotte in Birmingham.

David gathered his thoughts on the drive to his boyhood home. He was feeling the loss, the severance, though with less grief than he considered worthy. Charlotte was by the front door as he pulled up and there was rare sibling hugging ahead of a reflection on their childhood.

'Mind you, she was a bitch and a half,' Charlotte said in between tears, 'but she was still our mum.'

David nodded.

They wandered from room to room looking at possessions one would expect for an old-fashioned woman in her late sixties who had made minimal effort to move on since her husband had died. Little had been replaced over all those years; only the flat-screen television and a mobile phone hinted at twenty-first century existence. There was no computer, no DVD or CD player.

'It's so sad,' Charlotte remarked as they entered her bedroom, its tea-stained candlewick bedspread, shag pile carpet and beige velour curtains striking in their ugliness. 'I can't see anything I'd love to have as a keepsake.'

'Nor me. Her worldly goods will end up in a charity shop or in plastic bags on a skip.'

They sat in the kitchen drinking lowest grade instant coffee from the cups and saucers that had been a long ago wedding present.

'Do you think our kids will feel the same about us?' Charlotte wondered aloud.

'Who knows? I hope not, though I haven't got the newest iPad, smartphone or car for them to inherit. I suppose it's just the money we leave that will count.'

'Yes, I guess so. Talking of money, this house should fetch a fair bit. I'm assuming she's split things fifty-fifty. Mind you, you always were the favourite so maybe all I'll get is this stained bedspread.'

'Well even if she's left this to me I'll be generous and let you have it.'

'Very funny. We'll need to see her solicitor, won't we? I think I know who he is, I'll give him a call. I vaguely know the local vicar too. I'll speak to him about the funeral.'

'Let's see the will first, there might be funeral instructions, a preference for burial or cremation and things like that.'

'She might want particular music or a hymn. Led Zep's *Stairway to Heaven*, that would be a surprise, although heaven might be wishful thinking as far as she's concerned.'

'Come on, she wasn't that bad.'

'She wasn't that good either. I don't believe in this heaven and hell stuff but if I did and I was in charge, being merely all right wouldn't qualify you. You'd have to have done something special to get in.'

'There wouldn't be many up there then.'

'Don't worry, you'd make it. You always were the family goody-goody.'

They were smiling. The death of their mother had brought them closer.

~

They arranged to see Mr Spratt, their mother's solicitor, the following morning.

279

David stayed over in the house, an eerie experience without the presence of the person who had lived there for all forty-four years of his life.

He popped out to buy fish and chips at the takeaway he'd gone to when a child. Now pizzas and curries were on offer in addition to the traditional fare. On returning to his temporary home, he sat in "his" armchair in the lounge, restlessly switching from channel to channel before another wander round the house. Distant memories were roused by each item of furniture or knickknack that he noted. His parents had collected junk during their travels – a Swiss cuckoo clock, a plastic Venetian gondola, and worst of all a battery-operated lamp in the shape of Blackpool Tower. He remembered when they'd bought it. He was fourteen and had fallen in love with the daughter of another family staying at the hotel. She was sweet sixteen and had led him along until an older boy had come on the scene. David saw them kissing one evening by the swings and was devastated. He could feel the despondency again as he touched the plastic casing of the tower.

Charlotte and David met outside a smart Victorian double-fronted villa in the centre of Edgbaston, close to the university and across the road from a park with giant oak trees, yellow forsythia and pink azaleas. A shiny brass plaque to the left of the door displayed *Clutterbuck, Sharpe and Spratt.*

'A bit posh for our mum, isn't it,' David remarked.

'I was thinking that, too. Everyone knows it's the most expensive law firm in the area.'

No expense was spared in the modern reception with its huge semi-circular desk, plush leather armchairs, zany chandeliers and vivid abstract oil paintings.

By contrast, Mr Spratt's room was like taking a giant stride back into the nineteenth century. His room was a parody of a solicitor's office and Mr Spratt a caricature of a solicitor. The furniture was dark oak, the desk and chairs covered with the mottled maroon leather that had once been popular. One wall was lined with bookcases and there were piles of paper and files on the floor. The only sign of modernity was a computer on a separate workstation in the far corner of the large, high-ceilinged room. Mr Spratt was the perfect Scrooge, peering at them above his half-moon reading glasses. He was dressed in a dark suit, crisp white shirt, and navy bow tie. His salt and pepper hair made it difficult to identify age – anything between forty and sixty was possible.

'Sit,' he instructed before shuffling papers on his desk and opening a folder. 'I'm sorry to hear about your loss, your mother was a fine woman.'

'Thank you for saying so,' David responded quickly, fearing a sarcastic put-down from Charlotte who was fidgeting on the uncomfortable chair.

Mr Spratt began by declaring that their mother had instructed that her assets were to be equally divided between her two children.

As he read on soon Charlotte was gasping and grabbing hold of David's arm.

Their mother was loaded. She had inherited the

fortune acquired by Joseph Kirby, a great-uncle jewellery manufacturer who had died when they were infants. During the 1960s and 1970s he owned one of the most successful businesses in Warstone Street, at the heart of Birmingham's Jewellery Quarter.

Mr Spratt explained that the sum their mother had acquired was managed by his firm's recommended financial consultancy. Despite the current economic downturn, the investment had continued to grow.

Charlotte was impatient. 'So how much? How much is there now?'

'I haven't got the current tax year figure to hand; I expect a statement soon.'

'How much was it worth last year then?' Charlotte persisted.

Mr Spratt lifted a sheet from the collection of papers in front of him. With a deep, austere tone he read. '£1,427,345.86.'

Charlotte let out a scream. Mr Spratt waited for calmness to be restored before continuing. 'This sum refers to Joseph Kirby's portfolio which has been kept apart from everything else. Your mother had additional assets –shares, a savings account, jewellery, and the house of course. There will be a hefty inheritance tax sum to pay.'

David was in accountancy mode, doing calculations as Mr Spratt was spelling out exactly what those additional assets comprised of. Not surprisingly he was linking the inheritance to the cost of setting up the café.

Charlotte's line of thought was at a somewhat

lower level. 'The miserable old witch. She never let on she had money. If she gave the kids £20 at Christmas she made out it was a major sacrifice,'

Once again Mr Spratt paused until calmness was restored. As the solicitor ran through the long list of assets, David continued totting up the total. For insurance purposes the jewellery had been valued at £200,000, savings were in excess of £300,000. The extensive portfolio of shares – British companies bought by his father years ago and many of them now major international players – would make a sizeable contribution to the total. He would be able to calculate the current value as soon as he had access to a computer. Finally, there was the house, located in one of the most fashionable streets in affluent Edgbaston.

'Just making a quick call,' David informed Charlotte on leaving the solicitor's building.

'Me too,' said Charlotte as she stepped a few paces away from her brother.

David pressed the Bridget icon.

34

Throughout early April they had enjoyed delightful blue skies and the first warm sun of the year. On the day of the funeral the weather turned and it was as cold, windy and wet as the most brutal mid-January day. The small group of mourners made their way to the graveside, their shoes caked in sticky brown clay. Wrapped in dark raincoats, they were struggling to hold on to umbrellas.

David and Charlotte led the group, walking alongside the vicar. They were followed by Donald, Charlotte's husband, and her children, Crispin and Emma. Jane was close behind them with Rachel and Sam by her side. Poor Sam, it was his birthday. Bridget, Andy and Kay were next in line along with the few acquaintances of David's mother, including Mr Gupta and his wife.

The rain lashed down as the vicar spoke, generic words of kindness followed by the traditional prayer. Briefly, the mourners watched as the grave diggers began to fill the hole, shovelling sodden soil onto the coffin, the harsh rattle of clay and small stones against the wood, before scuttling back for shelter.

At the family home the caterers had prepared sandwiches, cake, tea, coffee, sherry and wine for the mourners.

'We could have gone for champagne and caviar what with all our money,' Charlotte joked as she sipped from a glass of red wine.

'Let's keep quiet about that for now,' David pleaded as he looked across at Jane.

Charlotte noted his glance. 'Sure. Can you stay on for a bit afterwards to start sorting her stuff?'

'Yes of course. How long have we got the skip for?'

'No time limit. As long as it takes us to fill it.'

Rachel and Sam were hovering, keen to be with their father, happy to spend time with Bridget and her children, but feeling under pressure to stay with their mother since she was, as she put it, alone and uncomfortable.

However, before long it was Donald, not her children, by her side. Jane had always got on well with her brother-in-law and David observed them engaging in whispered conversation in a quiet corner of the living room.

Bridget approached him. 'Everything OK?' she asked, noticing his glance.

'I think so.'

'We're heading off now. Andy's got judo this afternoon and if we're lucky with the traffic we might also get back in time for Kay's dance class. Let's speak tonight.'

'Thanks for coming.'

'We wanted to. Bye guys,' she added, calling across to Rachel and Sam.

This seemed to be the signal for the other mourners to leave. One by one they queued up to offer their condolences, each providing a reminiscence about his childhood.

'I'm Vivienne,' the elderly lady said. 'Remember me? I lived three doors down.'

David did remember. The vibrant and vivacious teenager who had babysat.

Her speech seemed a little slurred. 'You were a good boy, that's for sure.'

'Thank you,' David replied in anticipation of what he'd already been told by two others.

'Not like that sister of yours. She was a right little madam.'

'Oh, I don't think so.'

'When she was a youngster she was, I can tell you. All that blaring nasty music. Punk, wasn't it called? I don't know how the rest of you put up with her.'

David didn't want to hear all this again. 'It wasn't like that; we loved our time together.'

'I'm only repeating what your mother used to tell me, God rest her soul.'

'Mother was always grumbling but she and Charlotte got on fine. In fact –'

'Talking about me?' Charlotte was by their side.

'I was just saying what a lovely family you were.'

Jane was approaching the group as David was coming to terms with Vivienne's two-facedness.

'I need to speak to you.'

Vivienne chipped in. 'Aren't you the wife who ran away? He was such a good boy.'

David faced his soon to be ex-wife. 'What do you want to talk about? I'd rather not now.'

'Only for a minute, though not here, please. Somewhere private.'

'OK, upstairs.' They left Vivienne and Charlotte together, possibly to talk about what an angel Charlotte had been compared to her difficult brother.

David led Jane towards his old bedroom, the venue for their clandestine sex ahead of getting a place of their own. It would be a poor choice given the circumstances so he did an about turn on the landing and they went into his mother's room. Clothes were piled high in cardboard boxes and the bed was stripped down to a stained mattress. They sat on it.

'What do you want to talk about?'

'I think you know very well. How could you?'

'How could I what?'

'Don't pretend you don't know what I'm on about. Donald's told me everything.'

'I have no idea. How could I what?'

'You were so keen to rush through the financial settlement, weren't you? Now I know why.'

Sitting together on the bed, David sensed the heat of her anger which was in an instant surpassed by his own fury. He stood and walked to the window, looking out over the large garden. The swing at the bottom was still there, though in a sorry state, the chains rusty and the wooden seat rotten. He'd spent many an hour on it as had his own children. The grass needed a mow; the March rain followed by the early April warmth had brought rapid growth. Flower beds housed untidy clumps of uncared for bushes. He wouldn't miss the place; they would put it on the market as soon as possible.

Having calmed down a little, he was able to turn to face Jane. 'OK, I get it and it's absurd. If you remember you were the one who wanted things settled quickly. A spring divorce and a summer wedding.'

'You knew your mother had a weak heart.'

'If you're implying that I knew she was about to die that's ludicrous.'

'Is the amount of money Donald mentioned true?'

'I've no idea what he told you and I'm not prepared to discuss it.'

David walked away from the window, stopping at his mother's dressing table. There was a large opal necklace and a pair of pearl earrings in a cut glass tray. Mr Spratt had informed them that all the expensive stuff was stowed away in a bank safe.

Jane had stood and was close by. Their eyes met. Anger, distrust and hate were reciprocated.

'What on earth are you going to do with all the money?' Jane asked.

'I'm sorry, but that's not your concern.'

'I disagree. For a start you'll have enough to finance all the children's maintenance.'

'I buried my mother today, Jane. This is not the time for a discussion about anything to do with money,' David asserted, nevertheless continuing. 'Loads will go in tax, then half to Charlotte and my half is for a business venture.'

'Your café? I've heard about that from the kids. Why on earth are you chucking in a good job to do something so daft? I don't understand.'

'Well, it's not for you to understand, is it? Perhaps more appropriate today is for you to offer your condolences.'

'You never even liked her. Your mother got on better with me than you.'

'True enough. Clearly you were more similar than I ever realised.'

'That's insulting.'

David returned to the window and faced the garden. There was a splash of colour, a clump of purple tulips with petals opened wide and drooping. Soon they would be rotting – like his mother.

The impasse continued, both waiting for the other to speak. Finally Jane left the room and he heard her stamp downstairs.

When Rachel came in he was still gazing out the window, wondering how past soulmates had arrived at such an unpleasant state.

'Dad? Everything OK?'

'Yes, fine,' he said as she moved closer. He smelt tobacco.

'Mum's stormed out. What was that about?'

'Just the usual post-separation hassles. She's tough, she'll get over it.'

'She was furious. She brushed straight past us without a goodbye.'

David shrugged.

'Would you rather be alone? Shall I go downstairs?'

'No. Actually take a look at Grandma's jewellery. See if there's anything you want as a keepsake although there will be more to choose from.'

'These are a bit not my style.'

'No, I suppose not. As soon as everyone's gone we'll get going with clearing out her stuff.'

'It's weird. I don't feel a strong sense of loss, but now that you've said clearing out her stuff, like chucking away evidence of her life, I think it's all very sad.'

When Sam came in to see what was going on, his father and sister were hugging.

35

David returned from the funeral furious following Jane's accusation. When his solicitor confirmed that she had no claim on the inheritance, his resentment was replaced by the sad reflection that everything had been shared during their marriage, but now it was a battle over who owned what.

Well, he was where he was and it was time to move on. He telephoned Bridget to tell her about the argument with Jane and the solicitor's response. She dashed over to console him, bringing a bottle of champagne, an expensive one in a gold container with fancy lettering and a heraldic shield.

'I know the separation is hard for you,' she told him.

Being in bed with the woman he loved was making it easy. His relationship with Jane was over. Full stop. He felt neither distress nor joy. The cliff edge that he'd described to Jabulani came to mind; now they were strangers going their own separate ways, both content with their new lives.

A week later, having signed the lease and gained possession of the café, champagne was again flowing as they stood in the property re-examining the architect's plans ahead of meeting the builder. Their excitement mounted as they discussed ideas for furniture, lighting and décor.

'Not having to worry about the cost is such a relief.'

'It's still a business though. Just because you've inherited the money it doesn't mean we should waste it.'

'You should be an accountant, Bridget!'

Bridget had strong ideas about the colours for the cafe. 'Let's look separately and see if we come up with similar choices,' she'd suggested on arrival at the property.

They'd sat on the floor leaning against walls on opposite corners of the room, using their iPads to google colours.

'I'm done,' David declared after fifteen or so minutes.

'Give me another five, I'm almost there.'

When they sat together it was apparent that they had vastly different opinions. Bridget had chosen light greys and beiges, David had gone for bold primary colours.

'But you love these vibrant colours, Bridget. Your house is full of them.'

'But this isn't my house. The café needs to be a place where people feel calm and relaxed.'

'They're like the off-white colours I got rid of in my place.'

'No, they're bolder than that. I've gone for

Scandinavian cool – that's popular now.'

'I'm not sure.'

'I am. You can't have navy and purple side by side on two huge walls.'

'It would make a statement.'

'Yes, it would do that, but not the one we want.'

The bickering developed into a bit of an argument, their first. A period of quiet reflection followed as each of them tried to imagine what the place would look like in their own and the other's choice of colour.

At six o'clock, with the light fading, Bridget broke the silence. 'Look we don't have to choose for ages. I'm absolutely shattered, let's head off and meet back here tomorrow afternoon after work.'

By the time David got home he had decided that Bridget was right about the colours. No need to call her, he'd let her know the next morning. With the children in their rooms he settled down to catch up on a TV drama about a group of factory workers who'd won the national lottery.

The doorbell rang. It was Jim.

Following the discomfort with Bridget the last thing he needed was Jim accusing him of treating Jane unfairly. He would not tolerate it; he was ready to do battle.

'May I come in please, David?' Jim always looked so earnest, so sincere. Perhaps it went with being a Philosophy lecturer. The rat.

'What is it? I've had a difficult day.'

Since Jane had moved in with Jim their only conversation had been the confrontation following the accidental burning of clothes on Guy Fawkes Night. And now the man was here for a confrontation about the inheritance.

'This can be quick but there's something you need to know,' Jim said. He had a countenance that exuded his mood and the one that evening suggested that the end of the world was nigh. David prepared his answer for what was to come. Having spoken to his solicitor there was no way Jane was entitled to any of the money left to him by his mother.

Jim had led David to his own lounge! The TV screen was frozen on a painfully thin woman wearing a factory overall. Temporarily static tears were rolling down her cheeks. David was unsure whether they were tears of joy or sorrow because despite the win not all was going well for the lottery winners.

'Could we …?' Jim suggested, nodding towards the screen.

'OK,' David conceded and switched off the TV. It struck him that when they had been friends Jim always got his own way. He had a knack of making it blindingly obvious that his preference was the logical one. He wasn't going to win this time. 'What do you want to talk about?'

'About Jane. Jane and me.'

'Look I know how she feels about my inheritance but I have to tell you –'

'It's nothing to do with money.'

'What is it then?'

'I've decided not to marry her.'

Jim had what seemed like a wonderful marriage

until poor Vanessa had died of cancer. She'd ignored the symptoms for ages and by the time it was diagnosed it was too late to do anything. Jane, David too, had helped as much as they could during the last few months of Vanessa's life and then afterwards in caring for Jim. Of course David hadn't been aware of just how supportive Jane was. Had Jim's love for his wife been so strong that he couldn't put her memory aside and remarry?

Despite it all, David had a helpful suggestion. 'Don't think about marriage now. Enjoy the relationship and see what happens in the future.'

'I don't only mean not marrying Jane. It's over between us, David.'

'What?'

'I've fallen in love with someone else.'

David remained silent.

Jim continued. 'A lecturer joined my department in January. We see eye to eye on everything, we spend hours in coffee bars and pubs chatting away on the same wavelength. It's incredible, it's like we're telepathic. Last week we discussed writing a joint paper on free will versus determinism. You see Descartes viewed the mind as pure ego, a permanent spiritual substance. Of course since then –'

'I don't care about bloody Descartes! I have similar ideas about the construction of balance sheets as some of my female accountancy colleagues, but that doesn't make me fall in love with them.' David brushed aside the thought of Mary.

'Fair point, David, though with Ursula it's more

than that. I'm in love and the feeling is mutual.'

'Does Jane know?'

'Yes she does. She's rather upset, David.'

'Rather upset! Honestly, what do you expect?'

'Fair point, David.'

'Stop saying "fair point" will you?'

'Fair … yes, sorry, David.'

'And stop saying "David" all the time, it gets on my nerves.'

'What do you mean?'

'How many of us are in the room?'

'Two.'

'Correct, so not a group. When you speak it's obviously addressed to me so why name me?'

'Fair point.'

'And stop saying "fair point", I've already told you that.'

'Sorry, David.'

'You really are stupid.'

Jim called up his hurt look. Head down, speaking even more softly than usual, he conceded. 'If it bothers you that much I'll try to remember.'

'Good, Jim,' David replied, Jim deliberately added to make the point, but he didn't anticipate what was to come.

Jim turned on his "Deep in Meaningful Philosophical Thought" expression as he scanned the room. 'I've not been here since you changed things. Jane told me how much she liked the new colours and I must say I rather agree.' Once again his demeanour transformed, now to an "I've Suddenly Had a Great

Idea" mode.

'You're soulmates, you two. Made for each other. David, why not take her back?'

'What?'

'Jane. Would you take her back? She still loves you, David.'

'I have a new partner who I adore. And unlike you with Jane, I intend to ensure it's long-lasting.'

'There's no need for that jibe, David.'

'I think there is. You've messed up her life.'

'I don't think so, David.'

'Cut out the "David"!'

'I'm sure Jane will be fine. She's an attractive woman and let's face it, there are plenty of fish in the sea.'

'Including sharks. Fortunately not everyone behaves like you. I think it's time to go.'

'Yes, perhaps I should, David.'

Jim stood. Some people think a handshake makes up for appalling behaviour. David remembered Jim attempting it when he and Jane had broken the news of their relationship. Now Jim was extending his arm once more. David refused to take his hand and marched Jim to the hallway and out the house.

Although shocked to hear the news and sad for Jane despite it all, there was nothing he could do. She'd made her bed and now she had to lie in it (although it wasn't to be the bed she'd made).

Returning to the lounge he switched on the TV and continued watching the drama. He was pleased to see that the factory worker's tears were tears of joy. The young winner who had bought a flash sports car was caught speeding. Offering a £200 bribe to let him off was not a good idea and the policeman was going to arrest him. This was a bit of a problem because his wife's waters had broken and he wasn't answering his mobile.

The drama was hotting up.

With the titles rolling, David decided to let Bridget know about Jim's announcement. 'Maybe Jane deserves it, but what a bastard he is.'

'Perhaps you'll have her back like he suggested!'

'I can't; not now you're a café partner!'

'And on the subject of the café, I'm sorry we argued earlier. Look, it's your place. You decide on the colour scheme.'

'Let's put that on hold, it hardly matters. I'd better go, someone else is at the door.'

'OK. See you back at the café tomorrow after work. Oh – and I love you.'

'I love you, too. Rather a lot.'

Opening the door, David was greeted by Jane in floods of tears. His good nature came to the fore as he put a consoling arm around her shoulders. She was blurting out the news in between sobs. David let her know that Jim had already been round.

The children were on their way downstairs. 'What's up?'

'I need to speak to your mum in private,' David told them. Leading Jane into the kitchen, he shut the door and poured out two glasses of red wine.

'He hasn't come home. No doubt he's at the club

again.'

'Club? What club?'

'Where he met his new woman.'

'No, she's a colleague at the university, a Philosophy lecturer.'

Jane dabbed her eyes with a handkerchief, downed the rest of her wine and held up her glass for a refill. She took a large swig before continuing. 'Hardly. I discovered the truth. He's a regular at *ComeInside*. All this time when he's been telling me he's got to stay on for a lecture or a meeting at university he's been going to a strip joint in Leicester Square.'

'Are you sure?'

'Absolutely. I found out when Ursula, his work colleague who I vaguely know, phoned the landline because his mobile was off. She had to speak to him about something or other. When the idiot got home and I asked why he was so late, he said he'd been with Ursula all evening planning for a conference presentation.' Jane was crying again. 'Got a tissue, please?'

'Yes, I'll get them.'

David rushed up to his bedroom – once upon a time their bedroom – and brought down a box. Jane took a handful and dabbed her eyes before continuing. 'That wasn't the first late night, and I mean very late. Until then I'd had no reason to doubt him.'

'What did you do after speaking to Ursula?'

'Initially nothing. I was hoping to unearth a reason to justify his lie. Then a couple of days ago I decided to confront him. As calm as anything he came out with it. Full of his bloody intense looks and "You see Jane, this…" and "You see Jane, that…".' There was a bitter laugh before she continued. 'I started yelling at him. "Stop fucking calling me Jane every few seconds." That drives me mad, he speaks like he's a counsellor giving me advice. There he was fucking someone else and my biggest grumble was his use of language!'

'So, if it's not Ursula who is it?'

'He's in love with Nadine, a hostess at the club, though despite what they call them, I think prostitute is a more appropriate word. According to Jim she's different from all the others, which in itself is an interesting comment since it implies that he has known several others. And "knows" in a strip joint has certain connotations. I hope I haven't picked up anything.'

Jane shot a glance at David, perhaps sensitive to the tactlessness of her remark. But the thought of Jane having sex with Jim no longer disturbed him.

'What now?' David asked.

'As I said, Jim's sure she's different, unhappy at the club but gallantly doing the work to make sure her daughter has a good quality of life. And now that she's found true love, la-di-da, she's going to quit *ComeInside* and live with him, I suppose as soon as I'm out of the way.'

She was crying again as she stretched out her arm for a top up of wine.

'It won't last, Jane. The man's an idiot.' David recognised that didn't solve Jane's dilemma; she would never go back with him.

There was a knock on the kitchen door; Rachel and Sam were both outside and Sam's question indicated that they had heard what was happening.

'Can Mum stay here tonight?' Sam asked.

David had considered this and was prepared to make the offer. He could sleep on the couch or even go round to Bridget.

Jane thanked Sam but insisted that there was no need. Jim had agreed to move out until she found somewhere else to live. She reckoned that "somewhere" might be with her mother for the time being.

There was an awkward silence as the four of them walked to the hall. Jane opened the front door. 'What the hell am I going to do now?' she said quietly as she left.

'I'm sorry, but that's her problem,' Rachel said after the door had closed.

36

David was filling in the details about Jane and Jim as he and Bridget drove to the café to meet the builder the following afternoon.

'God, what a mess. Let's talk more about it later because the builder's waiting; there's his van.'

They waved to him as they unlocked the door and Greg Trent followed them in. They walked round the premises discussing the order that things would be done, with Greg checking that their ideas matched his interpretation of what the architect had drawn up.

'Is your architect managing the project?'

'No, that'll be me,' Bridget said.

There was a pause and a frown as Greg looked across to David to verify that this was indeed the case.

'David's still working but I'm about to pack my job in so I'll be able to pop in every morning to check your plans for the day.'

Greg nodded. 'I must say though, this schedule is tight.'

'The reason we chose you is because you said you could do it to our deadline.'

'That's true enough,' he conceded, addressing his

response to Bridget. 'But one of my jobs is taking longer than I expected and I've got two decorators off at the moment.'

Out of the two of them, David was the procrastinator and Bridget was the get things done person. This was immediately evident to Greg when she addressed him. 'That's your problem. This work schedule of yours shows completion on time.'

'Things can quickly change in this industry. The schedule you've got is a couple of weeks old.'

'Where are the bottlenecks?'

'Knocking down this wall,' he said pointing, 'and the brickwork. I can't do anything else until that's done. And then, like I said, my problem is the decorators.'

'Surely you can get your team to do overtime for the wall and the brickwork over the weekend; they're hardly massive jobs.'

'I might be able to do that...'

'I'm sure you can.'

'Then there's the decorating, like I said.'

'Well, either evenings overtime or use freelancers to help you out. And we're both free to assist with the painting if need be, though if we do that you'd have to reduce the cost.'

With agreement about the way forward they sat on three chairs that had seen better days.

'You drive a hard bargain, don't you?' Greg declared, looking across at Bridget. 'You seem to know a lot about the industry for a woman.'

David prayed that Bridget wouldn't explode with

anger and sack Trent on the spot. To his relief she remained calm, smiling at Trent as she indicated that her job had involved setting up exhibitions which gave her a good insight into how builders operated.

'Seeing him every day is going to be fun,' she said when he left. 'Let's resolve our wall colour dispute, I've had an idea.'

'It's OK. Your choices are right.'

David was shattered after the meeting with the builder and he was finding it difficult to dismiss the news about Jane. After dinner he sank into an armchair to watch the final episode of the lottery winners drama. It was moving towards a happy ending for all involved.

The doorbell rang. Evening callers was becoming a trend. He pressed pause on the remote, opened the front door and greeted the policewoman.

WPC Zara Dixon was sitting on the extremely comfortable couch in this middle-class home located in one of the most affluent outer London suburbs. She was drinking Earl Grey tea served in a bone china mug. The startlingly bright orange walls were perhaps atypical, but everything else was appropriately respectable. The room was spacious with high ceilings; a maroon lacquered Chinese cabinet with big brass inlays stood by the bay window; two bold abstract art works hung on the wall opposite the Victorian fireplace; and a dark wood table in the centre of the room had coasters lined up at each corner. She set her mug down on the nearest, careful not to spill any liquid onto the Oriental rug with the swirling pattern that covered much of the polished wooden floor.

David lifted the plate from the tray on the table and offered her a second biscuit which she readily accepted. Chips of almond and pistachio were embedded in a light shortbread base and they were delicious.

Zara had transferred from east to north-west London almost a year ago and the contrast was stark. Back then she'd been involved in dangerous operations at high-rise blocks with their broken lifts, graffitied walls and harsh concrete terrains. Here she no longer had to break up feuding gangs or deal with associated brawls and even knifings, instead drunken teenagers, minor drug offences and dodgy insurance claims were the main demands on her time. And this family had scored for each of these three crimes despite their comfortable home, delicious biscuits and the other outward signs of middle class propriety.

'Why would I want to set fire to my own business premises before I'd even got started?'

'Why indeed, sir?'

'I've already told you, I can't be held responsible for my ex-wife's actions. We separated months ago and I have no idea why she would want to burn down the café. In fact we get on fairly well now.'

'Clearly not that well. May I?' Zara asked as she leaned across to take a third biscuit.

'Yes, help yourself.'

'You say your ex-wife but we have no record of a divorce.'

'Well we aren't divorced yet.'

'So she's not your ex-wife then?'

'Technically not, but to all intents and purposes she is.' David was being made to feel guilty when there was nothing to feel guilty about. 'The financial settlement was completed a while back and we're going through the final legal bit now.'

'To what extent is she involved in your coffee bar plans?'

'Not at all.'

'Let me get this straight. You've sorted out your finances so she has no interest in the success or otherwise of your business venture. She doesn't stand to gain or lose any money. So can you think of any reason for her action?'

They were going round in circles. David considered Jane's jealousy regarding his mother's death and his windfall inheritance. Then there was her distress at being dumped by Jim. 'I have no idea,' he declared.

~

At 12.15 a.m. two policemen in a duty vehicle had been making their way at no great speed along Muswell Hill Broadway to check that behaviour outside the pubs and clubs was not intolerable. As they reached the quieter end of the road, on glancing down a side street, one of them spotted a car parked on double yellow lines with warning indicators flashing. They stopped. It had been an unusually calm Saturday night and these two young policemen were missing the buzz of confrontation.

'There'll be a party on somewhere and that's a poor

parent who's been ordered to collect their little darling but instructed not to park too close to avoid embarrassment,' Robin surmised.

William laughed. 'No, it won't be a party and I'll tell you why not, it's approaching exam season so all the sixth formers will be busy revising.'

'What about the younger kids?'

'They've got exams too.'

'Do you think they really care enough to stay sober?'

'This is Muswell Hill. Of course they do, success beckons.'

'Yeah, maybe. Let's do a good deed and see what her problem is.'

'I'm telling you, it'll be a middle-aged lady waiting to pick someone up. Mind you, we could have a bit of fun – book her for stopping on a double yellow line. Why hasn't she parked further up the road?'

'You know what, I can't be arsed. Let's leave her in peace.'

'Agreed. Turn round at the roundabout and head back to the station. If we drive slowly enough we'll be off duty by the time we get there. I'm knackered.'

At the roundabout Robin drove all the way around and headed back down the Broadway at a snail's pace. This gave them plenty of time to observe the woman getting out of her car and staggering up to the last shop on the small parade, an empty plot. She peered through the letterbox.

William prided himself in recognising the potential for crime, although in this case it didn't take Sherlock

Holmes to appreciate something was up. 'Pull in for a minute will you, Robin, I want to see this.'

Robin stopped fifty or so yards from where the woman was standing. He switched off the lights and engine. She was too preoccupied to notice company.

Unsteadily the woman returned to her car, opened the boot, and lifted out a green metal container. It must have been heavy, she was struggling to carry it.

'That's a petrol can!' William exclaimed.

They watched in awe as this smartly dressed middle-aged lady stumbled back to the shop, pushed the stem of a funnel through the letterbox, opened the can, and began to pour out the contents. She was finding it difficult to control the manoeuvre and liquid was spilling onto her clothes. Setting the can down on the pavement, she put her right hand in her jacket pocket and pulled out a box of matchers.

'Enough of that,' Robin declared. 'Let's go.'

Within seconds their siren was blaring, their lights were flashing and the car was speeding the short distance towards the imminent arsonist.

'She's soaked; she'll be setting fire to herself.'

On hearing then seeing the advancing police car the woman raised her arms high in the air to indicate surrender. Her dramatic stance made William laugh out loud and he had to bite his lip to stifle it as he stepped out the car. He stopped smiling when he saw that she'd already lit a match.

'Don't you move an inch,' he yelled as he sprinted towards her. 'Not an inch!'

When he reached her he grabbed hold of her wrist,

brought it close to his mouth and blew out the match.

'Thank you, that's very kind of you,' Jane mumbled. The policemen's attempt to get any sense out of her was pointless given her level of intoxication. A flustered, incoherent Jane was taken to the police station. On taking the breathalyser test she used the logic of an alcoholic to explain that the drinking had been essential to build up the courage to carry out the destruction. She was locked up for the night with charges of attempted arson and drink-driving pending.

She spent a miserable night in a cell and was remorseful in the morning when she gave David's contact details to WPC Zara Dixon. Zara decided to visit the address provided, well aware she had been there before. Twice.

~

'I still don't understand something, sir. If, as you say, you are separated, why would Jane provide this as her home address?'

What was wrong with this policewoman; it was so simple. Once again David explained the situation. His soon to be ex-wife had been dumped by the man she had left him to live with. Although she was still a resident in Jim's house this was only for a short while until she found a place of her own although she might be going to stay with her mother for a short while first not that they got on particularly well but beggars can't be choosers so it was hardly a surprise that giving this address was the best option. Was it?

'Was it what, sir?'

'Was it hardly a surprise?'

'I don't think I can provide an opinion about that but what I would say is that finding somewhere to live wasn't the only thing on her mind last night, was it?'

They were back to square one. David decided to keep further answers brief. 'Apparently not.'

The policewoman asked if David intended to press charges.

He'd been expecting this question. 'No.'

'No?'

'That's right. No.'

Zara was beginning to think the work in east London, although much tougher, was rather easier to comprehend. She waited for David to explain his decision. It was a long wait.

'Could you elaborate please, sir?'

'She's going through a tough time. And she didn't end up doing anything wrong, did she? The premises weren't set fire to, no property or person was injured. I'm sure she would have realised it was wrong before taking the action.'

'Sir, the officers were fortunate to intervene just in time. There was a pool of petrol inside your door, she was covered in it, and she had already struck a match.'

'I'm sure all sorts of things were going through her mind at that point to prevent her doing it.'

'In her state I don't think much could have been going through her mind. We have a recording of her interview. She admits to getting drunk to give her the courage to commit arson.'

'People can say things in the panic of the moment,

things they don't mean. The fact of the matter is that there was no fire and therefore no crime.'

'Apart from driving when almost four times over the limit.'

'I thought she was parked when you apprehended her. Did anyone see her drive in that state?'

'Well that's not for you to pass comment on. Are you sure you won't be pressing charges?'

'I'm positive.'

'OK, I'll record that.'

'Is that everything then?'

'I suppose it is. Thank you for your time.' WPC Dixon stood and David led her to the front door.

'Just one more thing, sir. Those biscuits, where do you get them from?'

37

'This place looks so cool, Bridget,' Rachel declared.

David had to agree with his daughter – whether this was Scandinavian chic or not, the café looked fabulous. Bridget's colours dominated, the large beige wall filled with an exhibition of paintings by one of her friends, another wall two-tone grey, bare but for two recesses with scarlet glassware. Scarlet had been one of his colour preferences and there were bold splashes of it throughout the café – the cups and saucers, the wooden edging around the giant mirror above the bar, the doors, the aprons worn by the serving staff.

'Yes, a huge well done,' Joe added. David had seen a lot of Rachel's boyfriend in recent weeks and was rather fond of him, even though the knowledge that Joe was sleeping with his daughter wasn't easy to come to terms with.

The first night was turning out to be as big a success as they could possibly have hoped for. The café was packed and everyone was in good spirits, laughing and chatting away. Jabulani's band had been well-received and now customers were purchasing the full range of food and drink on offer.

'Dad, please can I have a glass of red wine?' Rachel asked, technically for the first time though she'd already had requests for white wine and beer turned down.

'Stop it, Rachel. You're not having any alcohol. I could lose my licence and get shut down on the first night.'

'I look old enough. Anyway if an inspector came in I'd hand my drink over to someone else,' she said looking across at Joe who had already turned eighteen.

'Absolutely not.'

'Fun killer. Never mind, we're off to a party now. Well done with this place, Dad. I'll see you later or maybe tomorrow morning, I'm not sure where I'm sleeping yet.' When Rachel kissed him he could smell alcohol and tobacco on her breath.

'Text to let me know,' he called out after her. He was unsure if she'd heard because the band had returned for an encore and the song, initially soft and melancholy, had picked up pace and volume. For the first time David felt that he could let all thoughts of what was needed wither away as he listened to the music.

There was a loud cheer as the song reached its climax. Jabulani spoke. 'Thank you, thank you very much. It's an honour to be here on the opening night of my friend's café. I must say a few words about David – he's been helpful and kind from the first day I met him. But hey, I'm not going to speak, we're going to perform a new song, *David and Bridget's Dream*

Café.'

There were no instruments for this one, just vocals, harmonies across several octaves. The lyrics brought laughter even though most listeners would be unaware of the significance of references to the local council, a lethal underground car park, Queensbury, tea at Harrods and a tight-arsed boss called Mary.

She wears ethnic chic
Thinks our work is bleak
Keen to criticise
Especially all the guys
It's scary Mary
Yes it's scary Mary

David roared with laughter until interrupted by a sharp poke in the ribs. He turned and faced his ex-tight-arsed boss. She was taking it in good spirits, all smiles as he would expect from the new Mary. The song ended with "*My God, it's scary scary ... scary Mary*" and there was wild applause.

Kanjani had finished their set and Jabulani's brother was thanking the audience, informing them that their first album was about to be released. One of the reasons for such a crowded opening night was the reputation that the band had acquired in the local area over recent months.

'Lucky you've resigned, David, otherwise it would be instant dismissal on a charge of gross misconduct.'

'It weren't me, your honour, it were Jabulani,' he exclaimed in mock defence. 'Thanks ever so much for coming along tonight.'

She moved closer and kissed him on each cheek. 'I

wouldn't dream of missing such an important event.'

David noticed Bridget looking across at them. She was behind the bar serving drinks; they were taking it in turns to support their staff there. 'Let me introduce you to Bridget.'

'Sure.'

As they headed across the room, Ross approached at considerable speed. He grabbed hold of David's hand and shook it furiously. 'Hello, mate. You've made it, I knew you would. Well done.' His attention turned to Mary. 'Are you going to introduce me to this beautiful lady?'

The beautiful lady didn't seem to be put off by the crass chat up line. 'I think I'm able to introduce myself. I'm Mary,' her sensuous new voice said.

'Hello Mary. I'm Ross, a close friend of this entrepreneurial wizard.' The entrepreneurial wizard needn't have been present because Ross's attention was now fully on Mary. He took hold of her hand and kissed it. She didn't seem to mind – she was beaming.

Red alert. *Keep away from him*, David wanted to warn her, but he was already relegated to bit-part player, in fact completely ignored as Ross invited Mary to join him at the bar for a drink. He watched as they waltzed off, his gaze drawn to the tight fitting purple skirt that Mary was wearing.

He caught Candy's eye and she waved. She had come with a group of friends, maybe students on her degree course. Presumably the relationship with Ross was over since she was sitting on the lap of a more appropriately-aged male. No doubt Ross would be on the lookout for a new woman and judging by what was going on by the bar, was already making good progress with Mary. They were sitting together on bar stools, his hand resting on her knee. David dismissed his gut reaction to intervene. Mary was tough enough to cope and who knows, it might end up as the perfect match. Bridget was serving them drinks – David hadn't got as far as introducing the two women.

And now another woman was on the scene. She came up to him with a man by her side, one rather formally dressed for the occasion in suit and tie.

'Hi.'

'Hello Jane.'

They'd had a heart to heart after the attempted arson attack, Jane full of remorse and grateful that he hadn't pressed charges.

'I thought I'd support your opening. I wish you lots of luck.' She looked across to Bridget, busy at the bar. 'Both of you.'

'That's kind, I appreciate you coming along.'

'This is Rupert, he's a friend from work.'

Rupert extended his arm and they shook hands. What with the tension of the opening night, Mary turning up, Ross chasing Mary, Candy with a new man, Rachel heading off to God knows where, and now Jane arriving, he was struggling to build up enthusiasm to speak to Rupert.

'Why not get some drinks? Now the band's finished I'm going to have to take over from Bridget at the bar. I'd better put on some music, too.'

'Don't worry about us, do what you need to do.'

Jane and Rupert followed David towards the bar, passing Ross and Mary who were laughing away. He felt a tinge of jealousy. He escaped into the small office and chose a Beach House album to play, appropriately gentle end-of-evening music. They had to close by eleven thirty. How to get the customers to leave on time was on his mind when Bridget joined him.

'It's beginning to quieten down,' she said. 'I know we want masses of sales but I'm dead beat. I wouldn't mind if everyone left now.'

They peeped out.

Candy and her friends were still partying, the youngest of the mixed age profile of customers that they had so hoped for.

'Wow, what a great night,' Bridget exclaimed.

'Yes, I think we're going to make a success of it. In fact, I know we are.'

'I believe so. When I first saw this idea on your list I thought it was a wild fantasy.'

'No, you were my wild fantasy! I've been thinking, partner. Now we're working together perhaps we should live together.'

'Let's not run before we can walk, David.'

'Do you think a run might ever be possible though?'

'We'll see, David.'

'No need to say "David" at the end of every statement!'

'What are you on about? Why are you laughing?'

'A private joke, it reminded me of someone I used

to know.'

'Sometimes your humour is utterly incomprehensible. I've got no idea why I'm fond of you.'

'It could be my money.'

'Ha ha.'

They watched as the band members packed up, leaving it to the more conscientious of their staff to collect glasses from the near deserted tables. Jane and Rupert, engaged in earnest conversation in the shadows of the far corner, were holding hands. David was happy to see that.

Candy and her gang were getting ready to leave. Drinks were being downed, coats put on, and the couples were having farewell hugs.

Propping up the bar ever closer to Mary, Ross was looking across at Candy. His loud false laugh was to indicate that he was having a whale of a time with a new woman. Candy didn't notice or didn't want Ross to see her notice. She waved at David and Bridget and blew them a kiss on her way out.

Ross had rested a hand on Mary's shoulder and was whispering something that was making her giggle. 'Who's that woman with Ross?' Bridget enquired.

'Why do you ask?'

'I saw you talking with her earlier. Who is she?'

David reddened. 'That's Mary.'

'Your ex-boss? God, she's not at all what I thought she'd be like. She's incredibly attractive. Don't you think so?'

'I suppose she is, I've never thought of her in that

way. She was just my boss.'

'Yeah, right. Come on, it's time we shut down,' Bridget said as she turned off the music. Stepping out of the office they observed the latecomer's arrival.

David was flabbergasted that she'd popped in to support their opening night, presumably having just got off duty as she was still in uniform. He rushed over to greet her.

'Hello, it's so nice to see you. I'd better not contravene licencing laws or you'll arrest me, but there is time to get you a quick drink before we close. What would you like?'

WPC Zara Dixon stood her ground near the entrance as the few remaining guests looked on.

'That's very kind of you, sir, but I'm still on duty. I need you to come with me to the station.'

Zara watched as the woman by Mr Willoughby's side took hold of his right arm. Next, Mrs Willoughby, assuming that was still her status, stepped up to Mr Willoughby and grabbed his left arm. The man who had been holding the maybe Mrs Willoughby's hand was chasing after her, grasping at thin air.

'The police station?' David asked, the woman on each side of him tightening their grip.

Diagonally from the right a third woman came hurtling towards him at great speed. She was pulling away from a man struggling to keep his arm around her shoulders. It was to no avail; he stumbled and fell to his knees. Ignoring the cries of the fallen one, this woman continued her dash towards Mr Willoughby, flinging her arms around him when she reached him.

Their noses collided.

'This place is fabulous,' she slurred. 'Fabulous. I'm going to miss you so much. Please promise you'll keep in touch.'

David was massaging his nose. 'Of course, Mary. I –'

Before he could finish the woman was kissing him, lip to lip, the embrace sustained, her arms around his neck. Mr Willoughby wasn't reciprocating, he couldn't even if he'd wanted to because his arms were still pinned down by the women each side of him. WPC Zara Dixon sensed that he wouldn't have minded reciprocating.

All eyes turned to the fallen man who was shuffling towards them on his knees.

'I know all about you two, you are a crafty bugger,' he said as the others looked down at him. During this distraction Mr Willoughby pulled away from the woman called Mary.

WPC Zara Dixon watched the man on his knees grab hold of Mary's calves, sending her tumbling.

'Get off me, you creep,' she cried out. Having pulled herself up she thwarted the man's attempt to do likewise by shoving him back onto the floor. At this point the other man, not Mr Willoughby nor the one on the floor, but the one who had been holding Mrs Willoughby's hand, (assuming she still was Mrs Willoughby), helped him up.

Unsure who to face, WPC Zara Dixon addressed a convenient gap to the left of David's ear. 'I'm afraid it's your daughter, sir. She's been apprehended for drunk and disorderly behaviour.'

And not surprising, she thought.

Also by R J Gould:

The Engagement Party
Eight parents, step-parents and partners; two young lovers;
one celebration destined to fail. Can Wayne and Clarissa's
relationship survive the trauma of the dysfunctional
families meeting for the first time?

Mid-life follies
Why has his wife abandoned him after twenty-three years
of blissful marriage? Is she having a midlife crisis? Should
he be having one, too? Their children discover that
immaturity isn't solely the preserve of the young.

The bench by Cromer beach
As the lives of five people living in a sleepy seaside town
intertwine, cracks emerge and restlessness grows in this
novel about aspirations & the realities of everyday life.

Nothing Man
Neville has such low self-esteem that the label 'Nothing
Man' is his own choice to define himself. Two women, a
mother and daughter, set out to show him that he's a
Something Man.

Jack and Jill went downhill
It's love at first sight when the pair meet at university.
They fail to recognise that their lives are replicating the
nursery rhyme plot as misdemeanours result in Jack falling
down and Jill tumbling after. Can their relationship
survive?